Jane's Melody

Jane's Melody
By Ryan Winfield

ISBN-13: 978-0-9883482-6-4
ISBN-10: 0988348268

Cover design by Sarah Hansen of Okaycreations.net
Cover image: Ilya Terentyev / Vetta / Getty Images
The Licensed Material is being used for illustrative purposes only; and any
person depicted in the Licensed Material, if any, is a model.
Author photo: Mike Chard

Summary:
A grieving mother must decide what boundaries she's willing to cross for
true love when she takes in her dead daughter's young boyfriend, a
struggling street musician, and finds herself falling for him.

Printed in the United States of America.

BIRCH PAPER PRESS
Post Office Box 4252
Seattle, Washington 98194

Also by **Ryan Winfield**

South of Bixby Bridge

The Park Service Trilogy
The Park Service
Isle of Man
State of Nature

For Mothers Everywhere

Part One

Chapter 1

THE DAY AFTER THE FUNERAL, Jane came back to the island cemetery and sat in her car, watching the rain fall on her daughter's grave. It had been raining seventeen days straight, according to the news. But Jane didn't care—the rain matched her mood.

She left the ignition on, with the wipers set on delay, and she watched as the water slid down the windshield, obscuring the dreary view beyond. She kept telling herself it wasn't true, that her Melody wasn't really gone. But then the wipers would sweep away the rain, and she'd be looking once again at her daughter's freshly covered grave.

Yesterday she had huddled beneath a tent, along with the small congregation of mourners, including her mother and her brother, neither of whom she could stand, and watched as the casket went down, wishing it were her inside instead of Melody. There were a few words spoken by the minister from the island church, and that was it. Her daughter was gone for good.

"A mother's not supposed to bury her daughter."

That's what her own mother had said to her as they walked back to the car. And she was right, although the way she said it left Jane feeling that her mother blamed her.

And maybe she was to blame, she thought.

A stab of guilt shot up Jane's spine, doubling her over in agony. She chanted her sponsor's slogan for relief:

"I didn't cause it, I couldn't control it. I didn't cause it, I couldn't control it. I didn't cause it, I couldn't control it."

When she was able to sit up again, she reached into the glove box and fished through the papers for the emergency pack of Virginia Slims she kept hidden there. She tapped a cigarette from the pack, fumbled the lighter lit with a shaking hand, and inhaled one long drag of calming smoke. Then she cracked the window and flicked the cigarette out into the rain.

The wipers swept the windshield clean again, and Jane nearly screamed when she saw a strange man standing over her daughter's grave. What was he doing here? His head was bent, either in mourning or to read the freshly engraved stone, and he wore a gray coat and rain-soaked blue jeans.

Jane felt suddenly guilty, as if she were spying on a private moment between her daughter and this stranger. That would have sounded silly to Jane had she said it out loud, but it made perfect sense somehow inside her own head.

The man bent and laid something on the grave.

Did he bring flowers, she wondered.

She reached for the wiper switch to clear the windshield again, but she hit the high beams and accidentally flashed her headlights. Just as the wipers were sweeping the window clear, the man turned and looked at Jane. Never before had she been so startled and so captivated at the same time. He was young— under 30 for sure—but the blank, almost numb, expression on his face, combined with the distance in his gaze, belied a hidden pain far beyond his age. He carried no umbrella, but he wore a baseball cap and rain poured off its brim, his eyes set in pools of shadow. As they looked at one another, her in the car, him straddling her daughter's grave, the rain streamed down the glass and slowly melted him from her view, until just a watery silhouette was left. Then that too was washed away. Several seconds later the wipers swept across the windshield again, but the stranger was gone.

Jane was soaked by the time she walked the twenty feet from her car to the grave. She stood where the stranger had stood and looked around, but he was nowhere to be seen. When she looked down, she thought how strange it was to see the strips of grass already laid back over the grave, the edges marked by muddy stains. She knew the coming spring would see the grass take root again, sealing Melody forever beneath it in a patient world belonging only to the dead. She wanted to roll the grass back and plant her hands in the dirt and dig until she reached her daughter. She wanted to climb inside the casket and hold her in her arms, like she had when she was still a little girl—before the drinking, before the drugs. And why not let them come and cover the grave back up and leave them down there together, she thought. She felt dead already anyway.

The glint of something on the grass caught Jane's eye.

She bent and picked up the coin that the stranger had left. Nothing special, just a silver dollar minted in 1973, the year Jane was born. She held the coin in her palm as if it were as fragile as a robin's egg, and she wondered what its significance was and why the stranger had left it. Jane knew so little about her daughter, hardly having spoken with her for an entire year before she died. She longed for a connection to Melody's life— some way to understand what had happened, a chance to make sense of the senseless, if that were even possible.

She stood a long time in the rain, looking at the coin in her hand, lost in her remembering, until she was drenched from head to toe and the coin rested beneath a pool of water in her palm. She had intended to return it to the grave where the stranger had left it, but, without knowing why, she slipped the coin into her pocket and walked back to her car.

Jane pulled into the small garage of her 1950s rambler and put the car in park, but she didn't turn it off right away. She closed her eyes and let the heater blow over her face—odors of her wet clothes mixed with pine air freshener and the lingering trace of her cigarette smoke. When she opened her eyes again, she angled the rearview mirror to see herself with the practiced motion of a woman who has checked her makeup a thousand times before a thousand boring coffee shop appointments to sell a thousand boring insurance policies. But for the first time she didn't recognize the face staring back from the rectangular glass. And it wasn't the lack of makeup that left her confused; it was the hopelessness in those eyes.

She reached up and pressed the garage door remote and watched as the shadow of its closing slid across the mirror, erasing her face until it retreated completely into darkness. The garage bulb had burned out long ago, and she'd been too busy to replace it—just as she'd been too busy to seek out her daughter and offer help. But she was glad for the lack of light now as she cracked the window and reclined her seat.

The car's illuminated dashboard cast dots of light onto the upholstered ceiling, and she pretended that they were really faraway stars. She remembered reading somewhere that carbon monoxide was odorless, but she smelled the gas fumes wafting in through the cracked window. She focused on her breathing;

maybe for the first time since that Lamaze class her friend had dragged her to when she was pregnant with Melody. Hard to believe that was twenty years ago now. Where does time slip away to when you're not looking, she wondered.

People had told her that life would go by fast.

But nobody said it would go by in a flash.

She began to drift off to a comfortable place between this world and the next, surrendering her thoughts to a state where time has no hold over events and where memories unfold and mesh together with lost hopes and forgotten dreams.

She remembered, she remembered, she remembered . . .

Holding her newborn daughter.

Purple cheeks, a button nose.

The hungry cry silenced by her breast, the joy of providing nourishment for someone so perfect.

Oh, to go back!

To be there forever in that warmth.

Stay, stay, stay.

Her mind flicked forward five years to their first night in this house. She saw again her daughter's smile when they woke to see snow outside the window. She remembered gripping the tiny, mitten-clad hand and leading Melody down the street to investigate their new neighborhood. Strange, she thought, but the little pink-rubber boots Melody had worn that day were in a box somewhere in this very garage where she sat remembering.

These memories were snatched away by a shrill sound.

A persistent ringing inside the house.

After a time Jane opened her eyes in the dark and tried to guess who might be calling. She'd only gotten a home phone because it had come bundled with her Internet service, and nobody even had the number except her sponsor. Let it ring, she thought. But then she knew that she couldn't. She knew that if she didn't answer, Grace would come looking for her. The thought of Grace being the one to discover her body, after all that she had done for Jane, was too much to add to the guilt already heaped onto her final thoughts.

She was dizzy getting out of the car, and by the time she reached the phone, it had stopped ringing. She stood beside it with her hand on the table, waiting for Grace to call again, as she knew she would. Ten seconds later it rang, and she lifted it off the cradle and forced herself to smile as she said:

"Hello."

"Hi, Jane. It's Grace."

"Oh, hi, Grace."

"I've been calling your cell all day. Are you okay?"

"I'm fine," Jane said. "Just fine."

"Come on, J. Don't tell me that."

"Don't tell you what?"

"You know what 'fine' stands for, don't you?" When Jane didn't respond, Grace answered for her. "It stands for Fucked up, Insecure, Neurotic, and Emotional."

Jane couldn't help but laugh, just a little.

"Well, in that case," she said, "I'm doing really, really fine."

"I'm coming over," Grace said.

Jane looked around at the mess—bedding still piled on the couch, dirty dishes stacked on the kitchen counter. She shook her head. You'd think her mother and brother could have at least cleaned up after themselves, since they had insisted on coming for the funeral but had been too cheap to stay at a motel. But no, they'd come and made it all about them and somehow managed to turn the most horrible day even worse.

"How about I come over there?" Jane suggested. "I was just heading off somewhere anyway, and I left the car running in the garage."

HER CLOTHES HAD MOSTLY DRIED by the time she pulled into the parking lot of Harbor Condominiums.

Grace buzzed her in, and she took the elevator to the third floor. She had barely raised her hand to knock when Grace flung the door open and hugged her.

"Oh, dear Lord, you're soaking wet. Come in here and sit down. I'll make us some coffee. I've got Peet's. Or would you rather have chocolate?"

"Coffee's good. Thanks."

Jane sat in an overstuffed chair and looked out the living room window at the marina below. The sailboat masts moved back and forth with a hypnotic rhythm, and the rain poured down, illuminated against the dusky sky by the orange-vapor dock lights, even though the clock on the fireplace mantle said it was only three in the afternoon.

Grace handed her a steaming mug.

"Two Splendas and a drop of cream," she said, sitting in the chair across from Jane. "Just the way you like it."

Jane held the mug in both hands, letting its warmth thaw her cold fingers. She took a sip and smiled at Grace to let her know that it was good. Grace sighed and leaned back in her chair and looked at Jane, but she didn't say a thing. A long time passed with the two women just sitting there together, the only sound the faint clanking of metal sailboat riggings through the insulated glass.

"Whatever happened to your sailboat?" Jane finally asked.

"Oh, God," Grace said. "That thing? Best day of our lives when we sold it. I thought I told you. Bob tried to pretend it was the real estate crash. But he wasn't any more a sailor than I am. Oh, I hated that thing. Cramped as the day is long. And the day is long when you're on the water with nothing to do."

There was another long silence between them.

"Did I tell you about that time we took it to the islands? I didn't? Bob made me promise, but oh, hell, it's too good not to tell. He anchored us for a romantic sunset dinner. Popped a bottle of sparkling cider and everything. Even had a red rose. Said he wanted to rekindle our sex life. Of course, he fell asleep before he even got a spark going. Anyway, the tide went out while we were down below and grounded us on a sand bar. Tilted it like a toy. We woke up when we fell off the bunk. Bob sprained his wrist. And, adding insult to his injury, we had to get towed off by the Coast Guard. Lord, it was embarrassing."

Jane smiled and sipped her coffee. She had forgotten how much better she always felt just being around Grace. But her relief was cut short when a stab of pain shot through her as she remembered that her daughter was dead. Grace must have seen it on her face because she let out a sigh and said:

"I'd ask you how you're doing, but I can't imagine you'd even know how to answer."

Jane fought back the tears and just shook her head.

"Is there anyone left at your house?" Grace asked.

"They left last night," Jane said.

"Were they drinking?"

"My brother was. And my mother should've been. Can you believe they fought so loud that my neighbor called me to make sure everything was all right? And she's half an acre away. The night before the funeral, too. I'd be embarrassed if I even cared about anything right now. God, I hate my family, Grace. I know it's not right to, but I hate them anyway."

"Have you tried praying for them?" Grace asked.

"I've prayed for them to get what they deserve."

"Good enough," Grace said, with just a hint of a grin.

A gust of wind drove rain against the window, and the masts crisscrossed faster against the darkening sky.

After a while, Grace stood and said:

"I'm going to fix the spare bed with fresh sheets for you. And don't even think to try and tell me no, because Bob's on an overnight to Dallas and I could use the company. I'm too old to be spending stormy nights alone. If you're up for it, I'll get the umbrellas and we can walk to the pub for some chowder."

Jane knew that any protest would be useless, so she just nodded and watched Grace walk off down the hall. When she was gone, Jane looked back out the window at the rain.

She knew it would stop someday. She knew spring would come and bring a fresh wind to blow the clouds away. And she knew the summer sun would rise again and paint the world once more with the colors she used to love. She knew it as well as she knew anything. She just didn't believe it.

Chapter 2

THE CAR BEHIND JANE'S HONKED ITS HORN.

She shifted into drive and drove onto the ferry. She was in the front of a vehicle lane, behind a group of dripping cyclists clad in yellow raingear and making their workday commute. They looked miserable but determined as they stowed their bikes and filed past her car on their way up to the onboard cafeteria, their clip-on bike shoes clacking loudly on the metal stairs. A ferry worker came around and blocked her tires, the corners of his bearded mouth half-attempting a smile, but giving it up when he saw the hopeless expression on her face.

For everyone else it was just another day.

With the ferry underway, Jane sat in her car and watched the dark rainclouds drift across Elliott Bay. The ferry vibrated under the thrust of its engines and her pine-tree air freshener bounced on its string from the mirror where it was hung. She watched as a seagull flew in front of the ferry, riding the wake of air thrown from its bow. Jane hadn't been to the city in a long time. Too long, she thought. If she'd only gone looking for her daughter, if she'd only offered her more help, maybe Melody would still be alive. She knew Grace would remind her that she'd done all she could, all anyone could—that she'd paid for five treatment centers and given Melody all the support possible, until it was time to release her with love.

She remembered what the counselor at the last treatment center had said: "You can throw her a rope, but you've got to make her climb up it herself." And she had thrown her a rope, hadn't she? She had offered to take Melody home, with only one ironclad rule: she had to stay clean and sober. But Melody turned the offer down and slipped away once more to be wasted with that junk she sought night in and night out, surfing the city from couch to couch.

The ferry blew its foghorn, startling Jane back from her thoughts. She hit her wipers to clear a spray of rain that had been driven by wind onto the ferry deck, and she watched as the Seattle skyline developed on the canvas of white fog ahead. She had lived in the city herself when she was young, attending the University of Washington, working toward a bachelor's degree in Woman's Studies. But then she had met Bruce and had fallen in love, or so she had thought. She was five months pregnant when Bruce took off, leaving her alone to prepare for her new baby, just another college dropout cliché. She had thought Bainbridge Island would be the perfect place to raise Melody—quiet and peaceful, a small-town island with great schools. And it was, for a while. But it seemed no place was immune from the influence of teenage drinking and drugs, especially when you were born predisposed to abuse them. Alcoholism surely ran in Jane's family. She suspected it ran in Melody's father's family too.

The ferry docked and the bikers mounted up and pedaled away into the rain. Jane followed them off and drove through town up toward Capitol Hill.

As she passed familiar places, she wondered if her

daughter had discovered them as well. Maybe Melody had even felt her ghost there in the old café, her head bent over school books. Or perhaps her daughter had seen her fingerprints on a shelf in the neighborhood bookstore that hadn't changed or likely even been dusted since she was born. Or had their eyes met across twenty-years-worth of wax on the bar in the Steampipe Lounge, where a cute girl could always hustle a Friday night drink or two if she had a fake ID? God, was I young and stupid, Jane thought. But she had to admit that it had been fun, too.

When she arrived at the apartment building, she double-checked the address, just to be sure. It was an old, run-down, three-story craftsman that had been converted long ago into walk-up apartments. But despite the peeling paint and sagging roofline, the address numbers on the curb were freshly painted and clear. So this was where her daughter had lived. This was where her daughter had died.

The rain had slowed to a drizzle, and Jane sat in her car and looked out the water-specked window at the red, third-floor door that her daughter had entered for the last time just ten days before. Had she known, Jane wondered. Had she stopped to drink in one last view of the city? Had the clouds cleared to present one final sunset to see her off? Had she had second thoughts? Or was she bent on getting inside for her fix, seeing nothing but the waiting oblivion she so craved? Jane only half wished she could understand.

They were the hardest steps Jane had ever climbed.

She knocked on the door and waited.

She knocked again.

"Keep your damn panties on," a female voice yelled from

inside. "I'm coming, already."

Soon a series of locks unlatched, and the door opened six inches on its chain, revealing a girl's pale face pressed to the narrow opening.

"I told the lady on the phone I wasn't agreeing to no damn inspection," the pale face said. "Besides, I haven't even had my kid since December, thanks to his asshole father."

"I'm sorry," Jane said. "I think you have me mixed up with someone else."

The girl leaned closer to the opening and looked her over.

"Oh, shit! You're Melody's mom. I'm sorry."

"I thought I'd finally come by for her things."

The girl's face disappeared as she turned to look into the apartment. When she looked back, Jane assumed she'd unchain the door and invite her in, but she didn't.

"Wait here," she said, instead. "I'll get it together for you. It'll just take a minute."

Then she shut the door and locked it again.

Jane stood on the step and waited. She looked down on the street below and wondered what path her daughter had walked home that day and from where. The neighborhood reminded her of places she had lived herself once she escaped her childhood home at seventeen and set out on her own. A tomcat pawed at the contents of an overturned garbage can; a kid kicked a soccer ball down an alley and back again, deftly dodging puddles; a lowered car cruised by with bass music pumping behind tinted glass; and a couple loudly argued in the open window of an apartment across the way.

Jane was about to head down to her car for a quick drag on a cigarette—just one to calm her nerves—when the door opened and the girl thrust a box into her arms.

"Is this all there is?" Jane asked, a little surprised.

The girl shrugged. She had run a comb through her hair and her breath smelled of cough drops when she spoke.

"There was some other stuff, but we shared it. I'm sure you know how it is."

Jane nodded, understanding what she meant.

"I was kinda surprised when you called," the girl said, "because Melody never mentioned nothing about having any family around here."

Jane felt tears well up in her eyes. She stood holding the box while one ran down her cheek.

"Shit," the girl said. "I didn't mean it like that. I'm sorry."

"Was it you who found her?" Jane asked.

The girl shook her head.

"Nah. I was at my boyfriend's all weekend. Candace was the one who came by that morning." She paused to look down, and then added in a quiet voice: "Sometimes I wonder if I'd only been home, you know?"

Jane knew the feeling all too well, but she didn't say so. Instead, she changed the subject.

"Is there anything you can tell me about her? I mean, what she was up to, or how she was doing?"

The girl sighed and tossed up a hand.

"I wish I could tell you something. But it's not like we were close or nothing. She only moved in a few months ago."

"Do you have any idea where she spent her time?"

"I dunno," the girl said. "You might try the Devil's Cup. They called and said they had a final check for her there."

"Melody had a job?"

"Oh, yeah," she replied. "She'd been at the Devil's Cup on Pike since maybe a week after moving in here. Said she was gonna enroll in beauty school too, now that I think about it. Even had the forms all printed out. It wasn't like you think. She just had a little setback, you know. Guess that's all it takes sometimes, though. One bad day, one bad rig. Anyway, enough from my ass about that. I gotta run and get ready."

Jane thanked her and turned to leave. She'd made it two steps down the stairs with her box when the girl called to her.

"Hey! I hate to mention it. You know. With everything. But Melody did owe me some rent."

Jane stopped and set the box down on the step and fished through her purse for her checkbook.

"How much did she owe you?"

"One fifty," the girl said.

"Who should I make the check out to?"

"You don't have any cash?"

Jane opened her wallet and counted her cash.

"I've only got eighty-five dollars."

"I'll just take that and call it even," the girl said.

Jane held the money out but stayed on the second step and made her come out into the light to get it. She saw the dark circles under her eyes, the red track marks on her arms, and she almost pulled the money back but didn't. The girl snatched the bills, thanked her, then quickly retreated into the apartment again and shut the door and locked it.

Jane drove to the Devil's Cup and circled the block three times until she found a parking spot near enough to walk. The coffee shop was small and tight, only a few stools surrounding a window counter, and filled with eclectic neighborhood kids with their faces buried in their iPhones. Jane got in line and listened as the people in front of her ordered their caffeine fixes to go—"Cafe breve," "Short drip," "Latte macchiato."

When it was her turn, the girl behind the register pulled a pink sucker from her mouth and asked:

"What'll it be, lady?"

She had red hair and a ring through her eyebrow. Face piercings must be in style, Jane thought, because her daughter had had a small diamond stud in her nose when she arrived at the mortuary. She still wondered sometimes if she had made the right decision to have them leave it in, despite her strong feelings otherwise. She guessed that she had.

"I'm Melody McKinney's mother," Jane said.

"I'm sure she's very proud," the girl replied, popping the sucker back into her mouth and talking with it in her cheek. "What can we craft you to drink today?"

"Did you know Melody?"

"Should I?" the girl asked.

"I was told she worked here."

"Oh," the girl said, looking suddenly mortified. "You're *that* Melody's mother. Sorry. I'm filling in from our Belltown location. Hold on a sec."

She disappeared into the backroom and came out a minute later with an envelope.

"This is her final check," she said. Then she looked down at the counter and quickly added: "Sorry. That sounded bad."

Jane tucked the envelope into her purse.

"I was actually hoping that I might be able to talk with someone who worked with Melody. Someone who knew her."

"You should come back during the week," the girl said.

"Lewis works then and he'd be the best person to talk to."

"Lewis?"

"Yeah. He's the manager. You can't miss him. Looks like a cross between a My Little Pony and the Statue of Liberty."

Jane stepped outside and took a deep breath of cool, damp air. She had felt the walls closing in on her in the small coffee shop, perhaps because she had kept picturing Melody standing behind the counter smiling at her instead of the rude redhead. If only she'd been here two weeks ago. It seemed a cruel lottery how some lives were cut short while others went on.

As she walked up the block toward her car, she heard a lonely guitar melody carried on the breeze, accompanied by an even lonelier voice. The song was nothing she had ever heard before, but it was beautiful, and it matched her mood.

She followed the music around the corner and found its source standing in a doorway. He was wearing a grungy ball cap and his head was bent over the guitar so that Jane couldn't see his face. His guitar case was open on the sidewalk in front of him, sprinkled with a few dollar bills and a few coins. Jane was so moved by the song he was playing that she stopped to dig in her purse for something to leave him, but she had given the last of her money to Melody's roommate. All she came up with was the silver dollar that the stranger had left on Melody's grave, and she didn't dare part with that.

She waited for the song to finish so she might ask the man how long he'd be there if she returned with a donation, but when he finally struck the last chord and raised his head, she was struck speechless by his eyes. It was him—the man from the cemetery, the stranger in the rain. The glimpse she had seen through her windshield had been seared into her mind. She would recognize those eyes anywhere, anytime.

Jane thought she saw a flash of recognition in his face too, but it quickly disappeared, replaced by a broad smile as he said:

"Got any requests?"

"That was really good," she said, deciding on the spot not to mention having seen him before. "I mean, really good."

He dipped his chin.

"Thank you, ma'am."

"Did you write it?"

"Well," he said, suddenly looking shy, "I haven't actually written it down anywhere yet, as I'm still working on it in my head, but the melody and the words are my own, if that's what you mean."

"That's really amazing," Jane said.

"I'm glad you like it. Usually folks prefer the old stuff that they know. Nostalgia, I guess. But as great a song as it is, I can only sing 'Hallelujah' so many times in a day."

She studied his face while he spoke.

"If you don't mind my asking, how old are you?"

He took off his ball cap and clawed his hand through his long dark hair. He sighed.

"Well, if they told me the truth about the day I was born, and if I don't die, I'll be twenty-five this July."

"You're not yet twenty-five and you wrote a song like that? Have you been writing music your whole life?"

"I couldn't say for sure," he shrugged. "I haven't lived my whole life yet." Then he smiled at her again and changed the subject. "Is there something you'd like to hear?"

Jane was so drawn by the fleck of green burning in his sad eyes that she leaned in to get a closer look.

"What's your name?"

"Not to be rude, lady, but this is how I make my living. Now, is there a song you'd like to hear? 'Cause if not, I've got to be moving on."

"But I want to talk with you."

"You've got the wrong guy."

He lifted his guitar over his head, squatted to scoop the change from its case, then closed the guitar up inside.

"I just want to ask you a few questions."

"There must be fifty guys down on First and Pine who'll talk your ear off for the price of a pint. I'm not one of them."

He pinched the brim of his cap as if to say goodbye and picked up his case and walked off with it.

"I saw you at the cemetery," Jane said to his back.

He stopped and slowly turned around.

"I was in the car watching you. Melody must have meant a lot to you, for you to show up in the rain like that."

Jane opened her purse.

"Here. You left this coin."

"Was she your sister?" he asked.

"No, I'm her mother."

A sad expression washed like a storm cloud across his face and his eyes flashed with grief. For a moment, Jane thought he might cry. But he dropped his gaze to the sidewalk and said:

"I'm sorry for your loss."

Then he turned and walked away.

No explanation, no goodbye.

Jane stood and watched him go.

No sooner had he disappeared around the corner when a raindrop splashed on the sidewalk in front of her where he had stood, as if his shadow were still there crying.

Alone on the sidewalk, Jane felt her own tears come.

Then a curtain of rain fell at once and Jane slumped down in the covered doorway where he had been playing, wrapped her arms around her knees, and watched the drops beat against the pavement—his melody replaced by the lonesome splash of water beneath the tires of anonymous cars rolling past.

Chapter 3

"You need to eat."

Grace pointed at the bowl of chowder in front of Jane, a look of motherly concern on her face.

"I know," Jane said, "but I just haven't been hungry."

"Here, dip some of this sourdough in there."

Grace pushed the plate of bread toward Jane and signaled the server, who was wiping down tables vacated by the last of the pub's lunch crowd.

"Can I get you two something else?" the server asked.

"Two Mac and Jacks please."

"Amber or the hefeweizen?"

"The amber's fine," Grace said.

She must have seen Jane's surprised expression because as soon as the server walked away, Grace turned to her and asked:

"What?"

"I've just never really seen you drink before," Jane said.

"Hey, just because my silly husband's in recovery, and just because your family should be, doesn't mean we can't enjoy a beer every now and again, does it? Besides, how else are we supposed to put up with them?"

"Good point," Jane said, laughing.

Not wanting to drink on an empty stomach, Jane managed a few bites of her chowder before the server came back and set the pint glasses in front of them. The beer was bold and bitter, but it tasted good going down, and after only a few sips Jane leaned back in her chair and actually began to feel a bit better. She looked at Grace and remembered the first time they had come to this pub, a week or so after they'd met when Jane sold her a life insurance policy. Hard to believe that that was fifteen years ago and that back then Grace had been her age now.

"Have you started back to work yet?" Grace asked.

Jane shook her head.

"I haven't taken a sales call in almost a month."

"Well, there's no rush, I guess," Grace offered. "I think it's okay to remind yourself that it's only been a few weeks since the funeral. How are you fixed for money?"

"I'm fine," Jane replied. "I've got savings."

She turned the beer glass in her hand and watched as the sunlight streaming through the pub's windows cast its amber reflection on the worn table.

"You know what I do now every night?"

"What?" Grace asked.

"I sit at my laptop and stalk Melody's Facebook page."

"Oh, Jane," Grace sighed. "It must be torture."

"It is and it isn't," she said. "Her wall's open, and I've been scrolling through her timeline and piecing together her life. It's like I didn't know anything about her. You know what her last post was? Two days before—well, before she died? She wrote: 'Love is life and life is good.' Can you believe that?"

"Have you talked to any of her friends?"

"No. I wouldn't know where to start. But almost every day someone writes another goodbye on her wall. A few of them even post pictures. Usually with a drink in her hand, of course."

"Well, what about this boyfriend? The musician?"

"He's not on there. But Melody wrote some posts about being in love. I wish he had been willing to talk with me when I bumped into him. I still have that coin he left on her grave."

"Maybe you should try again," Grace said. "Go find him and take another approach."

"You think so?"

"What do you have to lose? Lord knows, you can't spend all your time wondering, J."

"I don't know."

"You've got to find a way to carry on."

Jane picked up her spoon and idly stirred her chowder, an absent gesture since she had no intention of eating more of it.

"You think I should?" she asked. "Just go hunt him down like that?"

Grace nudged the plate of sourdough closer to Jane.

"Eat some bread, honey. You're too skinny."

"What would I say to him?"

"Maybe just try to get to know him first. Talk about his music or something. If there's one thing you can count on most folks wanting to talk about, it's themselves."

AS SHE DROVE HOME FROM THE PUB, Jane thought about what Grace had said. What did she have to lose, she wondered. The answer was nothing, because she'd lost everything already. She knew she wouldn't begin to even glimpse any sort of relief until she had a better picture of what her daughter had been up to in the months before her overdose. Plus, something in the young man's face had been haunting her—some look of hidden pain, as if he carried a burden he dared not share. Jane slowed her car and U-turned, heading toward the ferry.

The sun was casting golden shafts of light through a break in the clouds as the ferry pulled into the city pier and docked. Jane drove to the Devil's Cup and parked. She returned to the doorway where the young stranger had been playing his guitar, but nothing was there except an overflowing trashcan and some faded chalk drawings that warned of coming doom.

When she entered the Devil's Cup, she knew right away that it was Lewis behind the espresso machine, because he had giant spikes of pink hair encircling his otherwise shaved head, giving him the appearance of a cartoon Statue of Liberty, just as the redhead had said. Jane ordered a latte from a new girl at the register, and then she moved toward Lewis and caught his eye while he was grinding her espresso.

"Hi," she said, forcing a smile.

"Hi, there."

"My name is Jane. I'm Melody's mother."

Lewis nodded, as if he'd been expecting her.

"Becky told me you were in last week," he said. "Sorry

about what happened. Melody was a cool chick."

"Did you know her well?"

"No, I just met her when she hired on here," he answered. "But we hung out a couple of times."

"Hung out?"

His cheeks blushed a shade of pink that matched his hair.

"Not like that," he mumbled. Then he looked up at her again and added: "Although I wouldn't have minded. She was a pretty girl. She looked like you."

Jane didn't know what to say, so she just smiled.

"Anyway, we just met up with mutual friends after work for a couple beers at the Garage. You know, usual stuff."

"Do you know if she had a boyfriend?" Jane asked.

"I'm not sure," he replied, twisting the dials and dodging a spray of steam from the machine.

"What about the guitar player?" she asked. "The one who hangs out around the corner?"

He shrugged.

"Maybe. He came in here a lot when she was working. They seemed to always flirt a bit."

"Do you know where I can find him?"

He poured the steamed milk over her espresso and shaped the foam into a flower.

"You might try the Pike Place Market," he said, sliding the latte in front of her. "I see him playing there sometimes. Or maybe Pioneer Square."

By the time Jane found a downtown parking spot and paid

the meter, she had nearly half a mile to walk and she was glad she'd worn flats. The Public Market was bustling with tourists and locals taking advantage of the rare break in the rain, and Jane threaded her way through the crowds, listening to the timeless sounds of giggling children and their parents' calls to rein them in. Couples walked hand in hand, sharing pastries or fresh fruit purchased from the various outdoor stands, and everywhere were sprays of color from fresh cut flowers for sale.

She stopped to watch as the fish mongers lured a young boy to touch the head of an evil-looking monkfish, placed for just such occasions on a mound of shaved ice, only to pull the hidden rope tied to its tail and open the fish's fanged mouth beneath the boy's finger. He screamed and ran into his parents' arms. Then he laughed, and the crowd clapped.

Farther on, Jane walked red cobblestones with the sunlight on her face, and for a few delicious moments she forgot why she had come, and she soaked the city in with the smile of a carefree woman, which she had been once so long ago. Hadn't she? She could hardly remember anymore. Then the realization that her daughter was dead stabbed her heart, and she jerked painfully awake from her reverie and back to the task at hand.

She searched the faces on the sidewalks for the stranger, but she had no luck. She passed a group of soul singers in front of Starbucks, belting out gospel tunes in exchange for coins tossed into their upturned hats. On yet another market corner she encountered a lanky man, swimming in coveralls two sizes too big, playing a banjo and a harmonica at the same time while twirling several brightly-colored hula hoops around his slender waist. No wonder the stranger she looked for wasn't here, she thought. Who would want to compete with that?

She left the Market and continued down First Avenue to where the tourists gave way to a quieter crowd of city dwellers running errands or heading home from office-tower jobs. She walked for a long time, losing herself in the rhythm of her steps, until she reached the old red-brick buildings of Pioneer Square. There she strolled the quiet streets alone, past the art galleries, past the neon signs of missions and shelters, past the shadows of broken men slumped in doorways with brown bags propped between their legs. She saw last night's broken bottles in the street. She saw a pair of abandoned shoes turned upside down as if someone had vanished into the concrete.

The sun had dropped behind the buildings, leaving the sidewalk in shadow, and Jane shivered with a chill that made her wish she'd brought along a heavier coat. The air smelled of wet brick and coming rain. She was about to turn around for the long walk back to her car when she passed a man lying on a bench. He was charging his cell phone in the public power outlet at its base. He had a familiar ball cap pulled over his face.

"Hello, there," Jane said, looking down.

"This is bordering on stalking now," he said, without even bothering to remove the cap from his eyes.

Was her voice that identifiable, Jane wondered.

"Give a girl a break," she said, "I just want to talk with you for a while." When he didn't respond, she added: "It doesn't matter about what; just anything."

"Why?" he asked from beneath his hat.

"I don't know," she answered.

And she was telling the truth. She didn't know why she was here, why she had come to find him. Maybe just to have some connection to someone who knew her daughter.

He sighed loudly. Then he sat up, catching his hat in his hands as it fell away.

"Oh, my God!" Jane exclaimed, dropping to her knees to inspect his bruised and battered face. "What happened to you?"

"Life on the streets happened," he said.

"You've got to get this looked at," she insisted. "Your forehead needs stitches."

"I'll be fine," he said. "I've lived through worse."

"Is your nose broken?" she asked.

"I dunno," he replied. "I don't think so."

"Has it always been crooked?"

"A little, I guess."

"Are you hurt anywhere else?"

Jane noticed that one of his hands was badly bruised and she took it in hers and looked at it. It was lean and strong, his fingertips calloused from years of playing guitar. She saw the bruised and swollen knuckles.

"Did you at least get him good?" she asked.

"Yeah," he said, flashing a grin, even though it reopened his split lip. "But not before they got all my stuff."

Jane kept his hand in hers.

"I'll help you up," she said. "I'm taking you to the hospital right now."

"I'm not going to any hospital."

He pulled his hand away, but Jane maintained her grip.

"Come on, lady. It's just a few bruises and a black eye is all. I've been through worse. I'll survive."

"I'm not letting go," she said, tightening her hold on his hand. "Not until you agree to at least let me take you to your home and clean you up. Better not to add an infection to the list of injuries, wouldn't you agree?"

"Well, you're in luck then," he replied, sweeping his free hand out to take in the square, "because we're already here."

"Already where?" she asked.

"My home."

"You live on the streets?"

She looked around, as if suddenly realizing that danger might yet lurk in the growing shadows.

"Just temporarily," he said. "I'm on my way to Austin."

"What's in Austin?"

"What's it matter?"

She tugged his arm.

"Get up. You're coming with me."

"Coming where?" he asked, half-rising but still hesitating.

"What's it matter?" she asked, mimicking his tone. "You've got some place to be? Just come along. You look like you could use some food and a clean bed."

When she had helped him to his feet, she wasn't expecting

him to be as tall as he was. He bent down and unplugged his cell phone from the base of the bench and slipped it into his pocket along with the cord. Then he followed along beside her as she led him back toward her car.

"It seems odd that you don't have a bed, but you have a cell phone," she said, breaking the silence.

"It's the only thing I managed to hold onto," he replied. "It doesn't have any service, but there's free Wi-Fi downtown so you can at least check your email. It's a little trick you learn on the street. Of course," he added, flashing her a boyish smile, "I mostly use it to keep up with my stock portfolio."

Jane laughed, and then they walked again in silence.

She noticed that he was limping.

"I suppose I should know your name," she said. "Now that I'm taking you home."

He cast her a mischievous grin.

"Don't try and tell me you've never taken a man home before without knowing his name."

"Not without making him buy me a few drinks first. And certainly not one half my age."

After another minute walking, he said:

"My name's Caleb."

"Nice to meet you, Caleb. I'm Jane."

"How far did you say your car was again, Jane?"

"You want me to get it and come back and pick you up?"

"No," he said, "I can make it."

HALF AN HOUR LATER, he was sleeping beside her in the reclined passenger seat of her car as the ferry carried them into the setting sun toward the island and her home.

His face was turned away, but she could see his chest rising and falling as he breathed. She wondered if he dreamed, and if he dreamed, she wondered what he dreamed about. He wore a faded denim jacket and its collar was torn and stained with his blood. His jeans were riddled with holes, and his boots were unlaced. Only his hat seemed to remain from what he had been wearing when she spotted him playing his guitar in the doorway near the Devil's Cup last week. She wondered what it was like, life on the street. She couldn't imagine the vulnerability that must come with having no safe place to call home.

Eventually her thoughts turned to Grace and what she might say about her taking him home like this. She guessed she wouldn't say much, except maybe to caution Jane to check herself if she felt she was slipping into "fix it mode," which was Grace's code for a relapse into co-dependence. But what was wrong with fixing someone if they really needed fixing, Jane wondered. As long as it didn't harm you in the process.

The sun had fully set by the time the ferry docked, and Jane followed the other island commuters off, driving cautiously so as not to wake Caleb. When she pulled into her garage, she crossed around behind the car in the blue twilight and opened his door. He stirred and looked up at her and the expression of pain on his face nearly re-broke her already broken heart.

"Come on," she said, "let's get you inside."

She helped him into the house and down the hall to Melody's old room, the only other bedroom besides hers. She considered running him a bath, but he seemed far too tired to bother, so she sat him on the bed and helped him out of his jacket. Then she stripped off his boots, and laid him back on the bed. She tried to remove his hat, but he raised his hand to keep it in place and she let it be.

She went to her bathroom and searched the medicine cabinet, but she had disposed of anything stronger than Advil the last time Melody had been home—just visiting between rehabs, of course. She filled a glass, then ran hot water over a towel, and took them back into the room. She turned on the lamp. The swelling had gotten worse, or maybe it just looked like it in the shadows cast by the lamplight. But even so, his face was still attractive and there was a distance in his eyes that she couldn't account for, given his age.

"Here. Take these."

After making him swallow the Advil, she used the towel to gently wipe the dried blood from his face. When she finished, he leaned his head back on the pillow and closed his eyes.

She stood for a while, holding the towel and looking down at him. When she finally spoke to ask him if he was hungry, he didn't respond, and she realized that he was sleeping. She switched off the lamp and backed from the room, stopping at the door and listening for a moment to his quiet breathing before stepping into the hall and shutting the door.

Jane checked on him several times as she passed the evening watching the late shows on her bedroom TV. When she finally turned out her own light, she lay awake for a long time, just thinking. Her mind was an open file drawer which she could not shut. One after another, she pulled the memories out and inspected them before filing them away again.

Having someone in Melody's room brought up memories of other tortured nights lying awake, wondering if her daughter would still be there come morning. She remembered the night she was woken by police knocking on her door. They presented her with a drunken Melody when Melody was supposed to be in her room sleeping. That had been the beginning. From that day on, her little girl had been locked away somewhere behind a set of tortured eyes—eyes that Jane just hadn't been able to penetrate to find her daughter, no matter how she had tried. And she had tried. She'd tried counseling together. She'd tried bringing her to AA for teens. Outpatient treatment. Inpatient. She'd even tried scaring her straight by letting the police keep her for a weekend when she had wrecked Jane's car after stealing it to drive across the bridge to the reservation to buy booze with her friends. But nothing had worked. And as she had gotten older, she had gotten bolder, and all Jane had been able to do was watch. Watch and cry.

Then one night she hadn't come home at all. The local police had refused to file a missing person report until three days had passed, so she'd called everyone until the State Patrol had put out an alert. Two days after filing the report, she had received a message from Melody saying that she was staying at a friend's house in the city and wouldn't be coming home anytime soon. And she hadn't. Not until her first overdose when Jane had collected her from county detox and had brought her home to wait for a bed to open in one of many treatment centers to come.

Jane had been friends with Grace for a long time by then, but that had been when she had asked her to be her Al-Anon sponsor. She had needed to find some way to live with the pain, and she had found it in the company of men and women who had been through just what she had been going through. She remembered some of them talking in meetings about losing their loved ones to the disease, and although she thought at the time that she understood their grief, she had had no idea until she received that fateful call of her own from the coroner.

Enough, she thought. No more tonight.

But the thoughts kept coming so she stopped fighting and relaxed into them, letting the images wash over her and trying to direct her attention to the stranger in her daughter's bed.

She was back at the cemetery, and Caleb was standing in front of her car with rain dripping off his cap and that pained look in his eyes. Then she was on the sidewalk again, listening to his beautiful song. Now she was standing over Melody's bed, watching him sleep. She wasn't sure how yet, but he was the only connection to her daughter that she had. And she was determined not to let him slip away too soon.

Chapter 4

JANE WOKE IN THE MORNING to the screech of an alarm. She jumped out of bed, pulled on her robe, and raced from her room, running headlong into Caleb, who was standing in the hall waving a kitchen towel at the ceiling smoke alarm. They were briefly entangled in one another's arms. Jane looked up and saw a smile in Caleb's eyes as they embraced. The alarm stopped and Jane broke free and stepped back, taking a deep breath to collect her thoughts.

"Sorry about the alarm," he said. "I was trying to make you breakfast, but I guess I'm a little rusty in the kitchen."

"It's my stupid old toaster," she said. "It does that if you're not careful."

Caleb gestured to her robe.

"Looks like I woke you."

"I needed to get up anyway," she said, pulling it tighter. How about you? Did you sleep okay?"

He grinned, despite his split lip.

"Like a puppy."

"Well, you look great," she blurted out.

"Thanks," he said, shrugging. "So do you."

Jane blushed.

"I meant that you look rested. The swelling's gone down."

They stood there in the hallway, looking at one another for what seemed an eternity to Jane. Finally Caleb said:

"I think the eggs might be edible if you're hungry."

"I'm starving," Jane replied, happy to have the awkward moment behind them.

She followed him into the kitchen, wishing she'd had a few minutes to check her appearance in the mirror and maybe apply a little light makeup. It had been a long time since she'd had company in the house, other than her family, and forever since she'd had a man—even if he was just a kid compared to her.

Rays of sunlight slanted through the kitchen window and showed the lingering smoke, and Jane could smell the burnt toast as she looked at the spread on the table. Scrambled eggs, pancakes, her bottle of sugar-free syrup. Even the coffee was percolating. Very impressive.

She moved toward the drawer to get silverware, but Caleb blocked her and pulled a chair out for her. She sat. He retrieved forks and knives and brought them with napkins to the table.

"Do you always make breakfast for strangers in their own houses?" Jane asked, enjoying the rare chance to be served.

Caleb scooped eggs onto her plate.

"I've done my share of couch surfing," he said. "You learn to earn your keep."

Jane forked a pancake onto her plate and drizzled syrup on it. Then she waited for Caleb to take his seat before trying her eggs. They were good. Not too dry, not too wet. And the pancakes were golden brown, just the way she liked them. It had been a long time since Jane had eaten a solid meal, but this morning she cleaned her plate and then ate some more. The coffee pot beeped when it finished percolating, and Caleb got up before Jane could rise and poured them each a cup. They stole glances at one another across the table, but neither said a word as they drank their coffee and enjoyed the quiet.

"That was a pleasant surprise," Jane said, after several quiet minutes had passed. "Thank you."

"Least I could do, ma'am."

"Oh, please, for the love of God, don't call me ma'am. Makes me feel old enough to be your grandmother, when I'm only old enough to be your mother. Just call me Jane."

"Just Jane it is then," he said.

Jane sipped her coffee and eyed Caleb over the rim of her mug. She could certainly see why Melody might have found him attractive. Despite the swelling, his face was still handsome, but it was his mouth that kept drawing her eyes. His jaw was strong and slightly squared, touched with morning stubble. And his lips. There was a cut on the right side, but they were perfect otherwise, especially the way they stretched over his white teeth when he smiled. And then there were his eyes. Deep and green, pools of mystery that a woman could drown in if she weren't careful. Jane reminded herself to be careful. She also reminded herself that he had been Melody's love interest.

"Do you ever take off that old hat?" she asked, when he

caught her inspecting him. "You know it'll make you go bald?"

"Well," he said, "I'll really need it then, won't I?"

"You wouldn't let me take it off you last night."

He pulled the cap off and looked at it, running his other hand through his thick, unkempt hair.

"It was my dad's," he said. "Only thing he ever gave me besides my temper."

"Do you have a bad temper?" she asked.

"I keep it in check."

"And how do you do that?"

"Music."

Jane nodded. She understood what he meant. She kept her own emotions in check doing Sudoku number puzzles.

"What will you do now?" she asked.

"What will I do?"

"Yes, without your guitar?"

Caleb looked down at the table and sighed.

"I dunno. Borrow another guitar until I can earn enough to buy it back. You don't have one lying around here, do ya?"

Jane shook her head.

"Well, I'll find one anyway," he said. "Something always turns up if you need for it bad enough."

"Is that so?"

"It is for me."

"Then what?" she asked.

"Then I'll save up and get out of here."

"Head to Austin?"

"How'd you know I'm heading to Austin?"

"You told me yesterday."

"Oh," he said, nodding. "I was kind of out of it."

"Why Austin?" she asked.

"Running from the rain, for one thing," he said.

Jane smiled.

"That's reason enough for me."

"But it's more than that," he added, his eyes twinkling with excitement. "It's the best music scene going. Musicians. Labels. Industry scouts. Studios. And there's enough gigs for a guy to make a real living, even if he doesn't hit it big. At least that's what I hear. It's like Nashville but without all them silly award shows and shit."

"Why don't you just go then?" she asked.

"Just start walking?"

"Not right now. I meant before your stuff got stolen."

"Well, I was saving up to go. I missed the festival this year. But I'm hoping to get there before summer. I've got to have enough to get a place and make a real go of it. You get a bad rep pretty quick when you're hustling on the street corner. So my plan is to do my hustling here and then get a fresh start in Austin where nobody knows me."

Jane saw the hope in his eyes as he spoke about Austin. It was as if the pain that normally resided there was momentarily forced away, only to flicker back as soon as he finished talking.

"I could help you," she said.

"Help me how?"

"Help you get to Austin. Help you get set up."

Caleb held her stare, an intensity in his eyes that she wasn't used to seeing in people. Then he drained his coffee, pulled his hat back onto his head, and stood to clear the table.

"Thanks, but no thanks," he said. "You've already done more than enough for me."

Jane stood and followed him to the sink with her dishes.

"You're not even going to hear me out?" she asked.

"I'm not a charity case. Never have been, never will be."

"Help isn't charity."

He took the plate from her hand.

"Sure sounds like it to me."

"Well, for what it's worth, I wasn't even talking about a handout. I was selfishly planning to put you to work."

"Put me to work? Where?"

"Here."

"Doing what?"

"Leave the dishes for now and I'll show you."

She took him into the living room and pulled back the curtains covering the big window, revealing the tangled half-acre mess that was her backyard. A small creek ran across the property, and its banks were lined with blackberry brambles so thick that an observer wouldn't even know there was a creek there if the wooden bridge crossing it weren't partially visible beneath the thorns. Scotch Broom and other weeds consumed the rest of the yard, with one rosebush standing out as the only attractive plant.

"What a mess," Caleb said.

"I know it," she replied. "I've been neglecting it for years."

"You'll be able to make blackberry pies in a few months."

Jane shook her head.

"I hate blackberries."

"Nobody hates blackberries," he said.

"I do. They take over everything. I want them all pulled out. But you have to get them by the roots or they come back."

"Well, at least you've got a rosebush there."

"I want that pulled out too," she said.

"The roses?" he asked. "But why?"

"Haven't you seen their thorns? They're just blackberry bushes with flowers instead of fruit. I don't like any plant that can defend itself against me. Plus, it was a housewarming gift from my mother, which makes me hate it even more. You can't see it now, but there used to be a nice lawn and a vegetable garden buried beneath there. I'd like to pay you to clean it up."

Caleb shook his head.

"It's a long way out here from the city every day."

"That's why you'll stay here," she said. "Room and board are included."

"I dunno," he said, biting his swollen lip.

"You've got better offers?"

"It just seems like you could find a landscape company that could do it better than I could."

"I've tried," she said. "They all want to charge a fortune to even touch it. Really, you'd be doing me a favor."

Jane watched his eyes scan the yard, his mind calculating, working out a plan. Then he looked at her and asked:

"What would you pay me?"

"How much do you need to get set up in Austin?"

He cocked his head and wagged a finger at her.

"I told you I don't want any charity. Just tell me what the work is worth to you, and then subtract out something for my staying here. Take out for food too."

"Okay," she said. "How long do you think it will take?"

"That depends. Do you want a new lawn reseeded and everything once it's cleared?"

"Yes. And I'd like my garden back."

"Your garden too?"

"And a fountain."

He looked back out the window at the yard.

"I dunno," he said. "A month. Maybe two."

Jane paused to do the figures, mumbling them out loud.

"Let's see, eight weeks full time—that's three hundred and twenty hours. Figure twenty bucks an hour. I think that's fair, don't you? Let's say two hundred bucks a month for rent."

"Only two hundred?"

"I've got a low mortgage. You're messing up my math."

"Okay," he said, "go ahead."

"That makes six thousand dollars for two months' work."

"Six thousand dollars?"

"Is it not enough?"

"No. I mean, yes. It's fine. Too much, maybe."

"Well, it's hard work," she said. "Plus, you haven't seen how far back the yard goes yet. This is one of the last half acre lots on the street."

"I'm not afraid of hard work," he said.

"Good," she replied. "A handsome musician with a work ethic. I think that'll make a nice combination in Austin."

He looked into her eyes and she could see him studying her face, deciding if he could trust her. She felt suddenly self-conscious, standing there in her robe. She wondered what her face looked like in the natural light and if she looked as old to him as she did to herself in the morning mirror. Then she remembered that this man had been her daughter's boyfriend, and she scolded herself for even caring.

"You're sure this isn't charity?" he asked.

"I'm sure," she said. "You'd be doing me a big favor."

"And you won't interrogate me?"

"What do you mean?"

"I mean, this isn't just some ploy to make me a captive audience and grill me about your daughter."

"I won't ask you anything," she said.

"Okay. I'll do it. I'm going to give you the best backyard you've ever seen. Something right off the pages of one of those fancy magazines."

"Great," she said, clapping her hands together and smiling. "Why don't you go get showered and cleaned up. Then I'll take you to town, and we'll get you some clothes and some tools."

"Some clothes?"

"Yes," she said, "some clothes."

She reached out and grabbed his torn T-shirt, her fingers grazing his chest as she did, which sent a sudden jolt up her spine, although she wasn't quite sure why.

"I can't have you running around the yard wearing this ratty old get-up, now can I? What would the neighbors say?"

"THIS WASN'T PART OF THE DEAL."

Caleb shot an irritated glance at Jane.

"Oh, just relax and enjoy it," she said. "Haven't you ever had a manicure before?"

"No, I haven't, and I hope to never have one again. Don't you have any girlfriends you could do this stuff with?"

Jane just smiled at Caleb, watching him wince and scowl at the manicurist as she snipped his cuticles. She had to admit that he was cute in his new outfit—hiking boots, khakis, and a plaid button-up shirt. He might just fit in on the island after all, she thought. Now if she could just get him to ditch that hat.

She hadn't wanted to go back into the city, and the only clothing store on the island other than a boutique that catered to women, was the Outdoor Gear and Clothing Emporium. There they had filled up a small cart with enough clothes to last him at least several months, all of which Caleb insisted on repaying out of his earnings. The manicure, however, was on Jane. And he was fine with that, he'd told her, because he'd never pay for something as silly as having his nails clipped.

"You want pedicure too?" the manicurist asked, speaking with a heavy Vietnamese accent.

Caleb looked over at Jane.

"What's a pedicure?"

Jane couldn't help but laugh out loud.

"Yes," she said, addressing the manicurist, "he'll have a pedi also. And give him a paraffin dip too."

By the time they left the nail salon, they were both hungry again, but Caleb insisted that he wasn't up for what he called a "chatty girlfriend lunch," so Jane brought him instead to Island Barbeque House. They sat outside at the picnic table and ate ribs and cornbread. It was a bit chilly still, but the sunshine was a nice change after so many weeks of rain.

As Jane drizzled honey on a second piece of cornbread, she tried to remember the last time when she'd felt so hungry. It must have been almost a month ago, before the news about Melody. She didn't want thoughts of her daughter's death to dampen what was turning out to be a gorgeous day, so she pushed them away and turned her attention to Caleb.

"You have to admit you enjoyed it," she said.

"The nail thing?"

"Yeah. Come on. You liked it, didn't you? At least a little."

"I might have maybe enjoyed the massage chair. But don't tell anyone, or I'll lose all my street cred for sure."

"Well, who would I tell, anyway?" she asked. "I don't know anything about you."

Caleb squinted his eyes at her.

"Is this the part where you interrogate me, even though you promised not to?"

"No," she said innocently. "I'm just curious about you is all. Is that a crime?"

"There isn't much to know," he said.

"I don't believe that."

He took off his hat and set it on the table. He said:

"I was raised by my aunt after my dad died of liver disease, 'cause of his drinking. My mom had died in a car wreck when I was little. She was a drunk too. Killed herself and a pizza boy who was on his way back from a delivery. They tell me I was in the car, but I don't remember it. That's how I got this scar on my chin. Anyway, life sucks sometimes. My aunt brought me up in Spokane. Hot summers. Cold winters. Lots of nights alone in my room. School counselor discovered that I was synesthetic. Old man down the street introduced me to music. I worked paper routes and saved up and bought a guitar. Learned six chords. Wrote a thousand songs. Been in love with music ever since. My aunt passed when I was sixteen. They were trying to find me a foster home, but I took off. Hitch-hiked across the mountains for the city. I've been up and down ever since. Had some good jobs. Lost some better ones. But I never gave up on music. And now here I am. Dressed like a yuppie hillbilly and doing yard work for a lady who seems to want to help me for no apparent reason."

Jane sat listening, with a piece of cornbread suspended in her hand halfway to her mouth. Honey dripped onto the table.

"Wow," she said when he finished speaking. "I wasn't expecting all that."

He pulled his hat back on.

"I figure it's best to get it out of the way now," he said. "That way you can quit asking."

Jane set her cornbread down.

"I'm sorry about your family."

He looked away.

"You gotta play the notes you're given, you know?"

"So you don't have anyone?"

He shook his head. She didn't want to upset him just as he was opening up, so she changed the subject.

"You said you were synesthetic. What's that mean?"

"It just means I hear sound in color."

"You do?"

"Yeah. Not every sound. But some of them. And definitely music. And most voices."

"So what color is my voice?"

"Blue," he said. "A really pretty blue."

"Is that how you knew my voice when I found you?"

He nodded and bit into a rib.

Jane sipped her Diet Coke and eyed the beer sign in the Barbeque House window.

"It sounds like drinking runs in your family," she said. "It runs thick in mine too. Did you ever have any problems?"

"I dunno," he said. "I did a little, I guess. Early on. But I never touch it now because I never want to be like my dad."

"Never?"

"I swore it off."

"I don't drink very often either. My mom is a dry drunk, and my brother's straight up alcoholic. I was abstinent for a long time. Even joined the Mormon Church for a minute when I found out they don't let you drink."

Caleb smiled, a ring of rib sauce on his lips.

"I tried to join the Jehovah's Witnesses once, but my aunt wouldn't let me."

Jane laughed.

"I didn't know Jehovah's couldn't drink either."

"I don't know if they can or not," he said. "I wanted to

join because the guy came to our door and said that in their heaven animals could talk."

"Come on, you're pulling my leg. Talking animals?"

"That's what the man said. I had sort of adopted a stray cat, but she'd died a month or so before. I thought it would be the best thing in the world to be able to see her again. Maybe even have a conversation. Anyway, my aunt said they were heretics. But I'm not sure she even knew what she was talking about because when she got sick, she said God was punishing her for being an atheist."

"Punishing her for being an atheist?"

"Have you ever heard such a stupid thing?"

"No," she said, giggling. "If you don't believe in God, how could he be punishing you for not believing in him?"

"That's what I told her. But people believe strange shit."

Jane pushed her plate away.

"I don't know what I believe in anymore."

Caleb shrugged.

"Me either. Except music. I believe in music."

After finishing their lunch, Jane took Caleb to the island hardware store. They trolled the aisles, filling a cart with items he would need to start work—pruning shears, thick leather gloves, a shovel. When he asked her why she didn't already have all this stuff, she just shrugged and said she used to pay a neighbor kid to come and mow the lawn and pull the weeds but that he grew up and went off to college five years ago.

"So you just gave up and let it go wild?" he asked.

"I guess," she said. "I had my hands full with everything my daughter was going through. The yard took a back seat."

He nodded but didn't say anything more.

When they brought their cart to the front, the clerk behind the counter looked up from his *Guns & Ammo* magazine and his mustache crinkled up in a nervous smile.

"Oh, hi there, Jane," he said. "Becca's been meaning to ring you about that life insurance plan. We've just been a little spread out lately. But she knows she owes you a call."

Jane dismissed it with a wave of her hand.

"Anytime, Ralph."

Ralph glanced into their cart.

"Finally taking on that jungle behind the house, eh? And who's this young stud you've got here? Your backyard all-star? What happened to your face there, fella?"

"Nothing happened," Caleb said. "It's just a birthmark, and it hurts my feelings when people ask about it."

Jane saw the embarrassed look on Ralph's face, and it was all she could do to contain her chuckle.

Ralph shifted nervously on his stool.

"Well, let's get you rung up then," he said. "I'm sure you've got better things to do than jawing with silly old me."

He tallied the items and turned the register display toward Jane so she could see the total. She swiped her card and entered her pin. Ralph handed her the receipt.

"You must've decided to finally list the place," he said, obviously fishing for gossip.

Jane answered with a tight-lipped smile.

"I know them Peters Brothers have been dying to get their hands on that lot of yours. You want me to send 'em by?"

"No, thanks," she replied.

"You know, they paid a pretty penny for Mrs. Snyder's half acre. They put up three houses on it and sold 'em all in a month. Three. And one of the three even had a full mother-in-law above the garage. The island just ain't what it used to be."

"I agree with you there," Jane said, "but I'm not sure if that's a good or a bad thing."

"Hard to say," he nodded. "Hard to say."

Caleb gathered up their items, and they left the cart behind and headed for the exit. Ralph called Jane's name before they reached the door, and she stopped and turned back.

"We were real sorry to hear about Melody," he said, his voice filled with apology. "Real sorry."

Jane forced a smile and then followed Caleb out.

"Is everybody on the island like that?" Caleb asked when they were back in Jane's car and headed home.

"Ralph's all right," she said. "And the island's got a pretty good mix of people, I figure. Just like anywhere else."

"Sorry if I was hard on him," Caleb said. "I guess that *Guns & Ammo* magazine just reminded me of all the people I couldn't wait to leave behind in Spokane."

"You don't like guns?" she asked.

"It's not that I don't like them," he answered. "I just seem to be more comfortable when they're not around."

Jane laughed.

"And you want to move to Texas?"

"Austin," he corrected. "There's Austin and then there's the rest of Texas."

"You might want to keep that opinion under your hat when you get down there, cowboy," she joked. "I'm sure some of those country boys are pretty proud of their state."

"Maybe so," he said, looking out the window.

As they turned onto Jane's street a few minutes later, he

shook his head and said:

"Lying in the gutter looking down on folks again."

"What's that?" Jane asked.

"Oh, just a saying I heard somewhere. You know it takes a certain kind of person to cast judgment on people he hasn't even met yet, when that person himself is a homeless musician without a guitar. I can be a real asshole."

Jane smiled as she pulled into her driveway and parked.

"I wasn't going to say it," she said, "but I'm glad you did."

Chapter 5

THE MEETING WAS ALREADY IN PROGRESS as Jane entered and took her usual seat next to Grace.

Grace smiled at her and then returned her attention to the scarf she was knitting in her lap. Usually Jane was early, but she wasn't quite sure yet how Grace would respond to the news of her arrangement with Caleb, so she had intentionally left home late to avoid their customary catch-up session before the meeting. This Saturday morning Al-Anon meeting had been her and Grace's ritual for nearly six years—a respite in the weekly storm, they called it. Grace had encouraged Jane to come for several years because of her family, but it wasn't until Melody's problems with drinking that she had finally agreed.

Jane looked around the small room as the usual crowd sat patiently listening to a newcomer, a woman whom Jane had seen several weeks before but hadn't yet met, since she'd been so consumed with the grief of arranging her daughter's funeral. The woman was smiling as she spoke, but it was a nervous smile that threatened to flee from her face at any moment.

Jane focused in on what she was saying:

" . . . He's just so different when he drinks. It's like I don't even know him. And he does the funniest things sometimes, too. On Thursday he came to bed so drunk, he opened his own sock drawer and pissed in it. Then guess what he did? He went into the bathroom and flushed the toilet. Isn't that weird?"

She paused to let out a nervous laugh. The wiser women surrounding her nodded and smiled at her encouragingly. When she spoke again, her voice cracked and she got real.

"Truth is I don't know what to do. I feel like a prisoner in that house. And it's all lies. Everything. All we do is post these cute family photos on Facebook all the time to make everyone think everything's fine. But nothing's fine. And I can't ever say a word because his friends are on there, his boss. Sometimes, I just want to leave him for good. But our boy is only three now, and I have no idea where we'd go. And how would we survive? Anyway, I'm just glad I'm here and that I at least have this."

When she finished she wiped a tear away, and the woman next to her put her arm around her and hugged her close, but nobody said anything. It wasn't a place for critique.

"Jane. Would you like to share?"

"Who, me?"

The chairwoman who had spoken nodded.

"No," Jane said. "I wouldn't like to, but I will."

She paused to take a deep breath and collect her thoughts. She felt Grace's calming hand pat her knee.

"As most of you know, I buried my daughter Melody just a little over three weeks ago. I want to thank those of you who made the service. It meant a lot."

She choked up and paused.

Someone passed her a box of tissues, just in case.

"It still doesn't seem real," she continued. "I get these pains that shoot through me. Like I'm suddenly reminded that she's gone, as if I could ever really forget. It feels like I've lost a limb, but worse. The other day I stood in front of the freezer with the door open until the entire thing defrosted. I don't even know what I was after. I lose time like that. And I'm obsessed with how she died. What she was thinking, what she was doing? You know, it's strange, because the funeral home said the state certificate was filed as death by misadventure. But that's a lie. It was suicide. I don't mean to say that I know that she intended to overdose that very day. But Melody had been killing herself since she was fifteen." Jane paused to pull a tissue from the box and dab a tear away. "God, I hate this fucking disease. I hate everything about it. If I go the rest of my life and never set eyes on another alcoholic or addict, and I intend to try, my family included, I'll still have seen too many ruin too much."

She sighed, mildly relieved to have at least spoken about her daughter's death out loud. Then her relief quickly turned to nervousness because she knew she had to mention Caleb to the group. For some reason she giggled. But none of the women seemed to think that her giggling was strange.

"Now I've got a new project at home to obsess over. I've taken in my daughter's boyfriend. At least I think he was her boyfriend. He's a musician down on his luck."

Several of the women couldn't contain their grins.

"I know, right? Perfect for a hopeless co-dependent like me. And he's cute too. Really cute. But I promise to be good. I'm taking my inventory instead of his. And he's only staying for a few months, doing some work at the house for me until he can get on his feet. And he doesn't drink. So that's good."

When she finished, Jane looked over at Grace for any sign of disapproval about the news, but Grace just smiled and continued knitting the scarf in her lap.

After the meeting ended, and after the unofficial meeting after the meeting, where everyone caught up with one another, Grace followed Jane to her car in the clubhouse parking lot.

"It's shaping up to be a nice start to spring," she said.

Jane looked up. White puffs of cloud were passing in a blue sky.

"Yes, it is," she said. "I didn't think the rain would ever stop." Then she dropped her gaze to address Grace. "I hope you're not upset that I didn't mention Caleb before. He's only been at the house a couple of days now. And, well, I guess I just didn't know how to tell you."

"Oh, Jane, you don't ever need my permission. Not for anything. You know that."

"I know. But you've been such a rock for me, and I just don't know what I'd do without you. I felt like I should've said something to you."

Grace reached out and rubbed her arm.

"And you just did say something, honey."

"Did I do the wrong thing taking him in?"

"Well, only you can answer that, dear."

"Do you think I'm being smart?"

"I don't know if you're being smart or not, but I know that being smart doesn't always lead to being happy. And I'd rather be happy than anything else."

"Well, he's only working for me, Grace. That's all. This is strictly professional."

Grace lifted an eyebrow and Jane laughed.

"Okay, okay. I do think he's really attractive."

"Now you're talking straight," Grace said.

"But I'm not going to let anything happen."

"Nothing at all wrong with admiring the great architect's handiwork, sweetie."

"I shouldn't feel bad for looking?"

"You should feel human, dear."

"Thanks, Grace. You really are the best."

Jane opened her car door and got in. Before she shut the door, she turned back to Grace and said:

"Maybe I'll send him over to your place when he finishes with my yard. Since your mind's already in the gutter."

Grace didn't say anything, but as Jane pulled out, she could see her smiling all the way back to the club.

Jane stopped by the island grocery on her way home and bought enough food for her and her hungry houseguest for the week ahead. As she unloaded the groceries in the kitchen, she caught glimpses through the living room window of Caleb working outside. His shirt was off, and the sun was glistening off his sweat-covered back, highlighting the ripples of muscle as he hacked and pulled at the blackberry vines nearest the house. His pants hung low on his hips, and his tight lower back had two dimples that made her tremble with excitement. She found her gaze drifting back to watch him so often, her thoughts so preoccupied by his appearance, that she put milk in the cupboard and cereal in the refrigerator.

"You're acting like a silly little schoolgirl," she mumbled to herself, half laughing.

She felt guilty for looking, but she blamed Grace for even putting the idea in her head. She forced herself to look away and finish storing the groceries. Then she carried the toiletry supplies she'd gotten for Caleb into the guest bathroom— toothbrush, razor, soap. She'd even bought him a tube of men's styling cream, just in case he decided to ditch the hat.

On her way back to the living room, she stopped and looked into the bedroom. She smiled when she noticed that he had made the bed, even turning back Melody's pink sheets. She went to the closet and retrieved a spare set of white sheets and remade the bed, hoping he would feel a little more comfortable sleeping beneath something less feminine. She was about to put the pink sheets in the wash hamper when she thought better of it and carried them to the kitchen and threw them in the trash. Pink had always been Melody's favorite color, and Jane had left those sheets on her bed for years, washing them every month, just hoping that Melody would come home.

But Melody was never coming home.

It was high time that she admitted it.

Feeling a strange mix of liberation and guilt at having thrown the sheets away, she looked around at the rest of the house and the years of clutter that had accumulated around her life. Books she would never read again, board games that hadn't been played in years, completed Sudoku puzzles, and old photos of her mother and her brother that made her cringe every time she passed them. She kept them on display only because of some sick sense of family obligation. She felt suffocated in her own living room, suffocated in her own life.

She went to the garage and retrieved a box of black, plastic garbage bags and began filling them. She filled one bag, then another. She worked for hours, cleaning out cupboards and closets, until she had two piles of overflowing bags near the front door—one pile destined for the island dump, and the other for Goodwill.

"Looks like you've made more progress in here than I

have out there."

Jane looked up from where she knelt on the floor, sorting old CDs. Caleb was standing over her, thankfully with his shirt back on. She glanced at the pile of bags by the door.

"Doing a little spring cleaning is all. You want to help me take a load to the landfill?"

"You're in luck," he said. "My afternoon schedule just happened to free up."

"How very fortunate for me," she said, reaching to take his offered hand and pulling herself up. "We'd better hurry before they close. The island kind of goes to sleep around five."

By the time the car was loaded, they'd stuffed it so full that Caleb spent the ride to the dump pushing the wall of advancing plastic garbage bags back into the rear seat and away from Jane so that she could drive. They made it to the island dump fifteen minutes before closing and stopped at the scale and took their weight ticket. A flock of gulls scattered as Jane backed up to the unloading gate, only to settle again before she even had the car in park. She got out and stood, looking down on the piles of trash. The place smelled of rotten garbage and gull shit.

Caleb unloaded the car, backseat and trunk, stacking the plastic bags next to Jane, but leaving it to her to toss them in. When he finished, he stood beside her and asked:

"Sure you wanna throw all this stuff away?"

She sighed, closing her eyes and nodding.

"I think it's time that I uncluttered my life a bit. Besides, it would probably take another dozen trips to get rid of it all."

"That's one thing I really like about living the way I do."

"What's that?" she asked.

"No responsibility. No crap to tie me down. When you

have to fit everything you own into a backpack and a guitar case, you get pretty picky about the things you hang onto."

She turned to look at him. Some city kid nomad with his hands on his hips, his knowing eyes scanning the piles of useless trash stretching out beneath them.

"Don't you get lonely, though?" she asked. "Always being on the move like that?"

"Sometimes," he said. "But it seems to me lonely finds a person just as easy when they're settled down somewhere. And might be that it sticks better too."

"So you're both a musician and a philosopher, I see."

He turned to look at her and smiled.

"I wasn't aware that there was a difference."

"You know something, Caleb?"

"What's that?" he asked.

"I think I'm really starting to like you."

She reached over and heaved a bag off the ground and flung it down onto the pile of trash. When it landed it broke open, and a snow globe music box that she'd brought home for Melody from a trip to Victoria fell out and started playing. The fall must have jostled it to life. They stood and listened to its song until the globe stopped spinning and the music faded away forever, leaving only the distant calls of circling gulls. Then Jane threw the other bags in, one after another, until they were all heaped together on the pile below.

As soon as she'd finished, the closing horn blew, and a giant compactor blade crushed the pile of trash and pushed it to the edge where it fell down a slide into a waiting container attached to a semi, idling below. The semi pulled away, her cluttered memories destined for some mainland landfill, and another empty semi pulled into its place.

"How do you feel about Chinese?" she asked.

"I've never had any reason to feel one way or another about them," Caleb said.

Jane elbowed him, playfully.

"Not Chinese people, you dork. Chinese food. For dinner. Are you hungry?"

"I could eat, for sure."

"All right then. Let's get out of here."

Chapter 6

THE BELLS ON THE DOOR JINGLED when Jane stepped into Seattle Strings. She could smell the wood varnish and the wax as she walked the aisles, looking at the walls lined with guitars. The sound of someone tuning a guitar carried to her from a back room. Then it stopped, and a few moments later a kid was standing in front of her. He didn't look old enough even to be working, but his neck and arms were already covered in tattoos.

"Can I help you?"

"I'm looking for a guitar."

"Well, ma'am, you've sure landed in the right place then. We've got a few."

"Just Jane is fine."

"What's that?"

"Just call me Jane. I hate being called ma'am."

"Sorry," he said. "It's just that the owner likes us to say it. He says us Gen Y-ers gotta work on being more respectful and less narcissistic. But I'll call you Jane. Are you looking for acoustic or electric, Jane?"

"I'm not really sure. It's a gift."

"Well, maybe an acoustic with electronics then. Will it be

her first guitar?"

"It's for a man, if that makes a difference. And no. He plays, but he had his stolen."

"Do you know what kind of guitar he had before?"

"I'm not sure," she said, scanning the walls. "I'm not very familiar with guitars, but it kind of looked like that one there."

The kid reached up and pulled down the guitar and held it in front of Jane. The wood was lacquered with a beautiful burnt-orange color fading into black.

"This here's one of the best," he said. "A Gibson J-45 in Vintage Sunburst."

"It's pretty," she said.

Then she turned over the tag and read the price: $2,950.

"But maybe something in a lower price range?"

The kid rehung the Gibson and walked her down the aisle.

"Yamaha makes some good guitars that you can get into pretty cheap. But if you want the best quality without turning your purse inside out I'd go with the Dave Navarro. Funny thing is, it's got your name. This is The Jane."

He handed her a beautiful black guitar, a white tree branch and a bird emblazoned on its front.

"That baby's gonna do everything he needs, and it's on sale too for just under six."

"Six hundred dollars?"

"Plus tax, of course. Gotta feed the pig."

"And it's really called The Jane?"

"Yes, ma'am."

Jane was so absorbed with the beauty of the instrument that she hadn't even heard him call her ma'am.

"I'll take it," she said. "But I'll need a case for it too."

When Jane left the shop carrying the guitar, a wind was blowing clouds in from the west and the air smelled like rain. By the time the ferry was midway across the bay, the wind was driving whitecaps to crash against its side and sending spray onto the open portion of the car deck. The island seemed to be in the eye of the storm, and as Jane drove toward home she ran her wipers at full speed and fought with the wheel to keep gusts of wind from pushing her car off the road.

She pulled into the safety of her garage, shut the door, and sighed with relief. She reminded herself to replace the light bulb as she fumbled through the dark, carrying the guitar.

She was surprised to find Caleb still outside, working in the storm. She stood at the living room window with the guitar case in her hand and watched as he hauled a tangle of cut blackberry vines to the pile of them he had going. The creek was actually beginning to take shape from beneath the mess of brambles, and he'd already made good progress at removing the Scotch Broom, too. Caleb heaved the vines onto the pile, took off his cap, and leaned his head back and looked up at the stormy sky. He was soaked through. His shirt was clinging to his chest, and his long hair hung dripping from his head, which gave him the appearance of some Greek warrior challenging the gods above. Jane rapped her knuckles on the window.

He turned and saw her and a smile flashed on his face.

She waved for him to come in; then she retreated to her room to hide the guitar until she was ready to give it to him.

When she came into the living room again, he was standing just outside the open slider under the eve of the roof.

"Would you mind grabbing me a towel?" he asked. "I'd hate to drip water all over your house."

Jane went and came back with a towel.

Caleb kicked off his boots and set them aside, tossing his soggy hat on top of them. Then he peeled his wet shirt over his head and tossed it down too. Jane held the towel out for him, but he ignored it and unbuttoned his pants. She saw the cut of his hips and the band of his boxers before she instinctively looked away. He laughed.

"Haven't you seen a man in his shorts before?"

Jane thrust the towel toward him.

"Not in a long time, I haven't."

"Well, I'd hate to be uncharitable," he said, taking the towel and wrapping it around his waist.

Then he stepped inside and closed the door.

Jane could feel him standing in front of her, and she could smell the rain on his skin. He stood there for a long time and when she looked up into his eyes, he was smiling at her. The swelling was gone; only the hint of a black eye remained. From the bruised and battered face of the kid she'd taken home, a gorgeous man had emerged. His lashes were thick and long, causing his green eyes to flash when he blinked. His face was rugged and handsome. A man's features: the perfect arch of his eyebrows; the slight slant to his nose. But it was his mouth and the almost feminine beauty of his lips that fascinated Jane more than anything else. She forced herself to look down from his face. When she did, she noticed the cuts on his hands.

"Why aren't you wearing the gloves I bought you?" she asked, taking his hands in hers and inspecting them.

He lifted her arm and twirled her.

"If you wanna dance, just say so."

When Jane had spun full around and was facing him again, she pulled her hand free and hooked it on her hip.

"It isn't funny, Caleb. Those thorns are nasty, you know. You have to wear the gloves from now on."

"Okay, okay. I'll wear the gloves."

"Good. Now go take a shower and get dressed. I've got a surprise for you."

"What's the surprise?"

"If I told you, it wouldn't be a surprise now, would it?"

"Just give me a clue then."

She pushed him toward the shower.

"Get in the shower. I'll put your clothes in the dryer."

"Don't dry my hat," he called back to her from his way to the bathroom.

After Jane had set his clothes to dry, she opened the flue in the living room fireplace and lit a Duraflame. It was one of the colored ones meant to crackle, and it hissed and popped and burned in a rainbow of shades. It was casting a nice light into the storm-shadowed room by the time Caleb rejoined her. He was wearing a clean pair of kakis and a T-shirt, and he smelled like soap as he sank into the chair across from Jane.

"Fire's nice," he said.

"Thanks. I hope you're hungry, because I ordered a pizza."

"Pizza's great," he said. "But I'm wondering how it is you keep your awesome figure. I mean the way you packed away the Chinese the other day. And now pizza."

Jane smirked at him.

"I'll take that as a compliment."

"Good. 'Cause I meant it as one."

"Well, you've got a funny way of flattering a woman then."

He leaned back into his chair and grinned.

"Was the pizza my surprise?"

She shook her head.

"No. It wasn't. Wait here."

She rose and went to her room. The second she walked back into the living room carrying it, he leapt to his feet.

"You didn't!"

She held the case out to him.

"I did."

He put up his hands and shook his head.

"I can't accept this."

"You haven't even opened it yet. What if there's a pair of garden shears or maybe a lawn edger in there?"

He laughed, taking the case from her and sitting with it on his lap. He unclasped the latches and lifted the lid.

"Oh, my God, it's gorgeous."

"It happens to be called The Jane."

"Well, then," he said, lifting the guitar from its case, "no wonder it's so beautiful."

He set the case on the floor beside his chair and caressed the new guitar in the firelight.

"I'm not sure if it's as nice as you're used to," she said, "but the guy at the shop said it was a good one. And he had music notes tattooed on his neck, so I assumed he knew what he was talking about."

"It's a great guitar. Even better than the one I had before. But there's no way I can accept this, Jane. It's too much."

"You don't have a choice. It's a gift."

"A gift for what?"

"For what? You can't earn a gift, silly. It's just for fun."

"Well, I'd like to pay for it out of my earnings."

"Absolutely not," she said. "Don't you dare try and take away my joy. It's a gift, and that's that. If you want to give me anything in return, you can play me a song."

Caleb looked at her, and his smile could have chased the storm away for the way it warmed her heart. When he spoke, his voice was low and sincere.

"Thank you, Jane. This is the kindest thing anyone's ever done for me."

Jane felt herself blush.

"Go on and play something," she said.

He bent over the guitar and began to play a melody that she hadn't heard before, but it reminded her somehow of a sad

November afternoon. He played for a long time, becoming familiar with the guitar. He looked up occasionally, and his eyes seemed far away, staring into some distant past well beyond the walls of Jane's living room. Then he began to sing:

Dun' know how to fix us
Dun' know where to start
And even if you hear this
I ain't so sure it's smart
'Cause hurtin' you was killin' me
And together couldn't ever be
Like we dream when we're apart

Look'n in a drink
I wanna be consoled
Tryin' not to think
But our story still unfolds

That night you took me in
I'd nowhere else to go
Fighting my father's gin
It seems so long ago

Our pasts on trial
Our futures on the run
You woke me with a smile
And rose the morning sun

But fear's silent yell
Crept in like a thief
And August's trust fell
Murdered with the leaves

All we did was fight
And threaten each other with the end
This hurts like hell to write
But I'd do it all again

Dun' know how to fix us
Dun' know where to start
And even if you hear this
I ain't so sure it's smart
'Cause hurtin' you was killin' me
And together couldn't ever be
Like we dream when we're apart

Together it just couldn't ever be
Like we dream when we're apart

He finished and sat still with his head hung over the guitar. When he finally looked up, his eyes were wet.

"That was beautiful," Jane said, genuinely moved.

"Thanks. I'm glad you think so."

"Who wrote it?"

He set the guitar in its case.

"I did."

She was momentarily speechless, both impressed that he had written the song and somewhat jealous over the emotion in its lyrics. She wondered who he had written it for.

"Whoever she was, she must have broken your heart."

"I was young. Hearts break easy when you're young."

Jane sat watching the firelight play shadows on his face. She wanted to ask him more about the song and about his early love, but then the doorbell rang.

"There's the pizza," she said, rising to answer it. "I hope you like pepperoni and mushrooms."

Jane tipped the delivery driver a ten for having braved the storm and carried the pizza back into the living room. They sat beside the fire and ate. Gusts of wind threw rain against the window, and an occasional flash of lightning was followed by the distant peal of thunder. The fire log crackled.

Jane laughed as Caleb picked the mushrooms off his pizza.

"You're only doing that because I said I hoped you liked them, aren't you?"

He shook his head.

"I hate mushrooms. Always have."

"How can anyone hate mushrooms?"

"Easy. They're slimy things that belong on a log in a forest. A much better question is how can anyone hate blackberries?"

"Well, I've never seen a mushroom cut up someone's hands the way those blackberry vines got yours. And you're just lucky they're not in bloom or your hands would be bee stung and stained with blackberry juice on top of it. I wasn't kidding about the gloves. I want you to wear them."

"Yes, Mother."

"Hey, that's not funny."

"I was only kidding. Hand me another piece, will you?"

"Here, this one's got extra mushrooms."

When they'd finished eating, Jane boiled water and stirred them each a cup of cocoa while Caleb added a fresh log to the fire. When she came back into the living room, he had taken a seat on the couch instead of his chair. She handed him his mug of cocoa and turned for her chair, but he patted the couch.

"Sit here, next to me."

She sat down beside him.

Several minutes passed, the cocoa too hot yet to drink, the fire log hissing and popping as it caught flame.

"You want to watch TV?" Jane asked.

"Not really," Caleb said. "I'd rather talk."

"Okay, what do you want to talk about?"

"You."

"Oh, God. Let's just watch TV."

He laughed.

"Really. I'm curious about you. I mean, I laid my life story out for you over ribs the other day, and you haven't told me anything about yourself yet."

"There isn't much to tell."

"That's what I tried to say too, but you didn't believe me either. Don't be shy."

"Okay, what do you want to know?"

"I dunno," he said. "Like how long have you lived here? And why aren't you married, or at least out in the city breaking hearts like every other woman who looks like you do? And how come you always smile so cute like that and look down when someone pays you a compliment?"

Jane kept smiling, but she looked up at Caleb. She blew on her chocolate to buy herself a moment.

"How about I answer your first question? I've been here a little over fifteen years."

"So you must own it then?"

"Yes," she said. "We'd been in an apartment since Melody was born, but my job had been going pretty well, and they had a first-time-buyer program where you didn't need much down, so I bought it. She was five when we moved in."

She felt the familiar stab of pain, and the memories flooded in. She paused to collect herself, determined not to cry.

"Our first night here we slept on an air mattress, expecting the moving truck the next morning. But it snowed almost a foot overnight, and we had to camp out here on just that air mattress for three days. But you know what? Those are some of the best memories of my life."

"What about her father?" he asked, quickly adding, "if you don't mind my asking?"

She shook her head.

"It's fine. There isn't much to tell. He abandoned us while I was pregnant. He never even met Melody, if you can believe it. His own daughter. Never paid a dime of support, either."

"I'm sorry to hear that."

"Anyway, for all I know he's dead too."

As soon as she said it, her heart ached with grief, the pain so unbearable that she almost spilled her cocoa.

"Oh, God, Look at me, sitting here and crying. I'm sorry, Caleb. I just miss her so much sometimes."

Caleb took the mug from her hand and set it on the end table with his. Then he wrapped his arm around her and pulled her close. It felt good to be held, and Jane gave up on trying to hold back her emotions. She let herself weep. In a way she was crying more for that little five-year-old girl who had died long ago than she was for her twenty-year-old daughter who had died just recently.

When she could collect herself enough to speak again, she turned her head on Caleb's chest and looked up at his face.

"Can you tell me anything about her?"

A look of pain flashed in Caleb's eyes.

"I'd rather not talk about it."

"That's not fair, Caleb."

"Come on, Jane. You said you wouldn't interrogate me."

Jane pulled away and turned on the couch to face him.

"I'm not interrogating you, Caleb. But is it too much for me to ask you to tell me anything about my daughter, whom you obviously knew? I mean anything."

"I didn't want charity," he said. "And I didn't want to be here just because you want to pump me for information about your daughter."

"Are you that callous?" she asked. "You won't even tell me anything? Not one thing."

"I think it'd be better if we talked about something else."

"No, dammit! I don't want to talk about something else. I want to talk about Melody."

Jane hadn't realized that she was yelling until she finished. The room was again consumed by silence, broken only by the crackling fire log. Caleb sat staring at her for a long time, a look of anguish on his face, but she couldn't tell what he was thinking. Then, just when it looked like he might actually say something, he stood and walked from the room.

She heard the bedroom door close behind him, and she sat alone on the couch and watched the firelight reflecting off the glossy surface of his new guitar, sitting where he had left it in its open case next to the fire.

Chapter 7

"Don't you just love spring?"

Grace bent over to pick a daffodil, and then she looked at Jane over the flower and added:

"So how's the yard coming?"

After their usual Saturday meeting, they had decided to go for a walk on their favorite island trail. Grace had yet to bring up Caleb, so Jane knew this was her way of asking about him.

"It's coming along pretty well," Jane said as they began walking again. "Caleb's got most of the creek uncovered. But there's a lot left to go. I think maybe there was more yard than he'd expected."

"And how's everything else?"

"Everything else?"

"Yeah."

"Well, that kind of leaves it wide open, doesn't it?"

Grace smiled.

"That's the idea."

"I don't know," Jane sighed. "I feel like it's time for me to get back to work. Don't you think so? There's a conference in Portland next week, and I'm considering going. Just to get away for the week."

"Get away from what?" Grace asked.

"The island. The house. Caleb."

"Ah-ha. There it is. Are you two not getting along?"

"It isn't that. We get along great, really. Maybe too well. And he's a perfect houseguest."

"How so?"

"Well, he makes us breakfast almost every morning. Even does the dishes after. And he insists on doing his own laundry when I'll let him. Some nights I get treated with live music in my living room. And he's smart and fun to talk to."

"Sounds pretty well near perfect to me," Grace said. "Plus, he's easy to look at."

"Yes," Jane said, blushing slightly. "That's the problem. I think I'm attracted to him, Grace."

"Well, who could blame you?" Grace asked. "A young, handsome man working around your house."

"But I feel guilty every time I look at him."

Grace twirled the flower in her fingers and nodded

"Besides," Jane said "it would be wrong, wouldn't it?"

"You have to decide that, dear."

"Some people are just off limits."

"That's true if you believe it."

"How come you always speak in riddles?" Jane asked.

"Because I'm old enough to know that life is nothing but one big riddle with a question for an answer."

"I guess you're right," Jane said. "Then again, you always are. But he still won't tell me anything about Melody. If I bring it up, he shuts down. Don't you think that's strange?"

"Everything in its own time," Grace said. "It's like these daffodils. They're the first ones up with spring, but they'll be long gone by the time the roses bloom."

"I don't know," Jane said. "I just feel like this conference might be a good getaway for me."

"Maybe it will. Sometimes a change is as good as a rest."

"I hope so, because I'm not sleeping well at all. I'm either up tormenting myself with memories of Melody, or I'm tossing and turning and thinking about Caleb sleeping just down the hall. It's torture, really. I don't think I've had a good night's sleep since . . . well, in years, to be honest."

"I've got some Ambien at home I can give you, if you want it," Grace said. "It really helps me when I can't sleep."

"I didn't know you had trouble sleeping."

"I usually don't. But lately I've been having these terrible headaches that keep me up. The Ambien seems to work."

"Maybe I'll try one," Jane said.

After several minutes walking, Grace stopped abruptly on the trail. Jane followed her gaze to the top of a tall cedar. A bald eagle sat perched above its enormous nest in the crook of a high branch, staring off somewhere above the treetops.

Grace spoke, almost to herself:

"We only get so many springs."

"What's that?" Jane asked.

Grace looked away from the eagle and into Jane's eyes.

"It just seems so fragile, doesn't it? The whole thing. Life.

The world. You know, I remember being a little girl just like it was yesterday. I never thought there was any limit on anything then. No expiration date on living. But with each passing year, everything gets a little more precious. I just wish I knew how to cherish it all back then. I really do."

"Are you feeling okay?" Jane asked.

"I think I'm just feeling," Grace answered. "Life is short, J. You only get one chance to get it right."

"Sounds kind of depressing, doesn't it?"

"I don't know, honey. I don't know."

They started walking again.

Grace was quiet. After a while she looked up and said:

"Don't you let fear have a place in your life, J. Not even a tiny place. Get rid of it from every hidden corner. Chase it away with the truth, and do what you want to do while you can."

"Is that a piece of advice?" Jane asked. "I don't think I've ever heard you give me specific advice in all these years."

"Maybe I've never been so sure of anything until now."

IT WAS LATE AFTERNOON when Jane got home, and she found the sliding door open and Caleb working outside in the yard. He was making good use of the portable stereo Jane had dug from a box in the garage for him, and rock music from the local station was carrying into the house. She stood for a while at the door and watched him work.

His shirt was soaked with sweat, and it clung to the shape of his back, showing the width of his shoulders and the narrow cut of his waist. His movements were smooth and sure, almost automatic. He hacked the blackberry vines down, pulled them free, and tossed them aside onto a blue tarp. Next he grabbed their severed stems with his gloved hands and ripped them from the ground, roots and all. Then he picked up the curved sickle and cut again. He had cleared a good deal beyond the creek this last week. Jane could almost make out the shape of her former garden.

She realized that the work in her yard would someday be done, and that when it was, Caleb would leave for Austin, as he should. The thought filled her with a melancholy that she could not explain. After all, she hardly knew him.

Deciding maybe she just needed some rest, she retreated to the privacy of her bedroom, turned on the TV, and took the Ambien that Grace had given her. The History Channel was running a series on the Bible that held her interest for a while, but as the Ambien kicked in, the desert scenes of ancient warfare began to bleed together in her mind, making the show difficult to follow. She flicked through the channels until she found an all-day rerun of the latest season of The Bachelor. She paused the DVR and went to get something to eat.

As Jane neared the kitchen, she heard the dryer buzzing over the sound of Caleb's music. A man who could do laundry and yard work at the same time would make a nice partner for some lucky woman, she thought, detouring to turn it off. As she folded the laundry, her head began to feel light and her eyelids heavy. She put the clothes away in Caleb's room, but as she started for the door, she stopped and turned back and grabbed one of his T-shirts. Then she went to the kitchen and retrieved a Costco-size bag of Doritos.

In the privacy of her room again, Jane undressed and pulled on Caleb's T-shirt. The cotton was still warm from the dryer, and it felt good. Then she climbed into bed with the bag of Doritos and started her show again. The Ambien seemed to be working on her appetite and her emotions more than it was on her ability to sleep, and she ate the chips one after another as she watched the rose ceremony on TV, the tears streaming down her face and running her mascara.

Several times she wiped her hands, without thinking, on the front of Caleb's shirt. Before long it was covered in orange finger stains. Still she couldn't stop eating the chips. She sat in an Ambien-induced trance, mindlessly eating and crying as the handsome blond bachelor selected the lucky ladies who got to stay, and the unlucky one who had to leave. Jane saw her own fate tangled up in the disappointment on the rejected woman's face. She thought about Caleb playing that sad song beside the fire, his head bent over his new guitar. She thought about him standing shirtless in front of her, rain-soaked and smiling, his eyes on hers as he unbuttoned his pants.

She reached for another Dorito, but the bag was empty. Hadn't she just opened it? She seized the bag by the bottom and held it over her head and tipped an avalanche of orange crumbs into her mouth and onto the front of Caleb's already stained T-shirt. She was so configured when there was a tap at the bedroom door, and it opened. She sat, frozen, with the bag suspended above her open mouth and locked eyes with Caleb, who was now standing in her open doorway. He looked more amused than shocked, but Jane was overwhelmed with embarrassment. Before she could say anything or even lower the Dorito bag, he flashed a grin, retreated into the hall, and pulled the door closed behind him. Jane would have been even more mortified had the Ambien not completely kicked in shortly after and blurred the image from her mind as it knocked her out for the night.

SUNLIGHT FROM HER WINDOW slid down the bedroom wall and landed on Jane's face, waking her. She yawned and stretched, sitting up in bed. She felt more rested than she had in a long time. But as she looked at the closed bedroom door, she had a sudden image of Caleb opening it last night and seeing her in his shirt covered in crumbs. She looked down and saw her orange fingers and the Dorito stains plastered on her chest.

"Oh, God," she said, aloud.

The empty Dorito bag crinkled beneath her bare feet as she stepped out of bed and rushed to the bathroom to check her appearance in the mirror. The front of his white T-shirt was streaked with orange handprints and dotted with black tears. Mascara tear-tracks dripped from her eyes. Her hair was a wild mess. And worst of all, orange powder ringed her entire mouth. She looked like a circus clown gone mad.

"Ugh. I can't believe he saw me like this," she mumbled to

herself, stripping out of his shirt and starting the shower.

When she had showered and dressed and fixed her face in the mirror, she took a deep breath, pulled her shoulders back, and entered the kitchen. Thankfully, Caleb wasn't there. She found a note from him next to the coffee pot, saying that her breakfast was in the microwave. She could hear his music playing outside through the cracked sliding door. She poured herself a cup of coffee and sat at the table and thought.

You're acting crazy, she told herself. Here you are walking around your own house on eggshells because you're attracted to your dead daughter's boyfriend. It's wrong. Some people are just off limits. Aren't they? She knew it was wrong, but she still thought about him all the time. Wasn't that why she had put his T-shirt on last night? To feel him close to her?

She finished her coffee and retrieved his T-shirt from her bathroom and treated the stains and loaded it in the washer and ran it by itself. As she passed the open door to his room, she noticed Melody's baby book lying on the dresser. She entered the room and picked the book up and sat down on the bed with it. She ran her fingers across the puffy, pink-silk cover, the lace ribbon stitched to its spine. She remembered picking the book out—the day the doctor told her that she was having a girl. She remembered looking through it in the maternity store, the blank pages, an unwritten story of her and her daughter's lives ahead. Melody was already her best friend, turning and kicking in her swollen belly. She remembered the hope and joy she had felt at the thought of filling the book's pages.

She opened the cover and looked at the birth certificate glued to the front page. Melody's footprints were stamped there like the impressions of a tiny angel walking briefly across the world of the living. Her vision blurred, and she blinked the tears away.

She turned the pages and read the notations she'd written there, so long ago now—

Melody's first ten days.

Her first tooth, her first word, her first step.

As she flipped through the pages, the entries thinned until they faded away completely by year five. Why had she stopped filling it in? Because being a single mother was tough, and life had gotten busy. But too busy for this? Jane's stomach seemed to sink into a pit, dragging the rest of her with it into an unholy abyss of depression. Her very soul moaned for the chance to go back—for God to turn back the clock and let her start over again, let her try something different this time.

A single tear dropped onto the page and swelled the paper, blurring the ink on the last entry Jane had made—

We're excited to move into our new home tomorrow. Especially Melody, who makes me drive by it every time we're in the car. She loves Destiny's Child for some reason, and she has me turn up "No, No, No," so she can sing along every time it comes on the radio, which seems to be every third song. She'll start school soon, and I can't imagine how I'll get by without her during the days. She's become quite the little helper at my appointments. Where does the time go?

When Jane had finished reading, she looked up and saw Caleb standing in the doorway, watching her. His hat was off and he held it to his chest, as if in respect for her grief.

"I hope you don't mind," he said. "I was looking for a drawer to put my things in, and I found it."

Jane closed the baby book and wiped her eyes.

"No," she said, "it's fine."

Caleb pulled his hat back on, stepped into the room, and sat down on the bed next to her. She felt the mattress give beneath his weight, and she tilted slightly into him.

He nodded to the book in her lap.

"You wrote some nice memories in there."

"Thanks. I'm not sure why I stopped."

"Well, I feel like I know her now after having read it."

"You mean know her better?"

Caleb sighed.

"There's something I need to get off my chest with you, Jane. Something I feel just awful about."

She set the book on the bed and scooted herself up against the headboard so she could see him. His head was hung, and he was looking at the floor.

"I never knew Melody," he said.

"What do you mean you never knew her?" she asked. "That's ridiculous."

He shook his head.

"I never knew her. Never even knew her name until . . . well, until after she was gone."

"But I saw you at the cemetery. You left that silver dollar on her grave. I still have it in my purse."

He turned to her, and his eyes were filled with sadness.

"I wish I'd gotten to know her. I really do."

"I don't understand."

"Let me explain. You see, I used to play around the corner from the Devil's Cup and she came by one day and stopped to listen. She was so beautiful, but so tortured at the same time. I felt like we were kindred spirits in a way. I played her a song, and she tossed that silver dollar in my case. The next morning I went in and ordered a coffee from her. I put the same silver dollar in her tip jar. But she came by my corner and tossed it back in my guitar case that same afternoon. It became this little game we'd play every day. I don't know. Kind of flirting, I guess, but never talking."

Jane felt very fragile and very confused.

"You never spoke with her?"

Caleb shook his head solemnly.

"But I started looking forward to her coming by. You know, it was the highlight of my day. But then one morning I went into the coffee house, and she wasn't there. She wasn't there the next day either. After a week or so went by, I finally asked about her, and the girl there told me what had happened. She told me her name. I went to the library and looked her up and found the funeral announcement in the paper. I was late, but I showed up anyway. I wanted to say goodbye. To just pay my respects, I guess. And to give back her coin."

There was a long silence when he finished. Jane could hear the washer spinning across the hall. She didn't know what to feel. She felt numb and a little confused.

"Why didn't you tell me?"

"Honestly? Because I was selfish. When you offered me work and a place to stay, I really needed both. I was afraid that if I told you the truth, you wouldn't want me here. And I feel terrible about it, Jane. I see the way it's tearing you up inside, too, not knowing. I just had to tell you. I'm sorry. I really am."

Jane sat for a long time, looking at his face, his sad eyes. She could see that he was uncomfortable with her silence, but then she wasn't sure what to say to him either.

"Did you like her?"

"I liked her."

"We're you attracted to her?"

"I'm attracted to you."

"What?"

"Everything I liked about her, I love in you."

Jane felt a funny kind of confused, an excitement wrestling with disappointment and grief.

"What are you saying?"

"I'm saying ever since I saw you I've been attracted to you, Jane. I think about you all the time. Every night. I lay here in this bed at night, and I wonder if you're awake down the hall. I can't get you out of my head, and I don't even want to."

"I don't under—"

He leaned over and cut her off with a kiss.

She sat stunned, her hands frozen in her lap. She felt his strong, calloused fingers on the tender flesh of her neck, and she felt his soft lips on hers. She smelled the soap from his morning shower mixed with the sweat on his shirt. A warmth she hadn't felt in a long time flashed alive deep inside her and traveled up to her lips and parted her mouth to let him in. He tasted as sweet as any forbidden fruit could. Her hand left her lap, and she pulled his cap off and tossed it on the floor and buried her fingers in his thick hair and pulled him closer and kissed him harder. She was overwhelmed by her need. She needed to taste him, to feel him. She needed to let herself be possessed by him. Right here, right now.

But then the sun peeked through the window curtains and shone on her eyelids, sparking a tiny ember of guilt that grew until all she could think about was the fact that she was kissing the man her daughter had had a crush on, in Melody's own bed. And worse, she was worried she couldn't stop.

She pulled away from him and stood.

He looked up at her from the bed with pleading eyes.

She turned away and raced from the room without a word. She stopped in the kitchen and poured a glass of cold water and drank it down. Then she went to her bathroom and flicked on the light and looked at herself in the mirror. Her lips were red and swollen with lust. She ran the tap with hot water, splashed it on her face, and scrubbed to rid herself of the guilt. She brushed her teeth, spit, and rinsed with mouthwash—not because he had tasted badly, but because he had tasted so good.

When she was finished, she sat on the edge of her bed with her face in her hands and cried. She cried because she missed her daughter. She cried because she was alive and her daughter was dead. She cried because her entire life was a failure, and the proof of it was buried along with her hopes in that little cemetery plot and capped off with a marble stone that she had paid extra for.

It was nearly a full hour later by the time she left her room. She found Caleb sitting on the bed where she had left him, staring at the floor. She sat down beside him again and sighed. Several moments passed. Neither of them said a word.

"Have you been sitting here this whole time?"

Caleb nodded.

"I'm sorry," he said. "I'm an idiot and I'm sorry and that's about all I can say."

"It's not you," Jane said. "I liked it. I liked it a lot."

"Then what is it?"

Jane's throat swelled with emotion so as she could hardly speak. She just shook her head and softly said:

"My daughter."

"God, I'm so sorry, Jane. I really am stupid. I just felt . . . well, I guess I felt really vulnerable and really attracted to you, and I acted on it. I really am a fool. I don't mind heading back on foot if you don't want to drop me at the ferry."

"Don't be silly," she said. "You're not going anywhere."

"I'm not?"

"No."

She turned to look at him, and she felt the hint of a smile returning to her face, despite her grief.

"Who's going to get rid of these damn blackberries for me if you leave?"

His eyes flashed with relief. He leaned toward her, and she thought for a moment that he was going to hug her, but he appeared to think better of it and patted her knee instead.

"Thanks, Jane."

"Let's not be all awkward now," she said, pulling him to her and wrapping her arms around him. "We're both adults, and we've both been through a lot."

It felt good to be in his arms. She reached up and wiped a tear away from her cheek so he wouldn't see it when she pulled away. Then she took a deep breath and let him go.

"And tomorrow morning, try not to burn the toast."

"Oh, I'm making you breakfast again, am I?"

"Of course," she said, smiling. "It's part of the deal."

JANE LAY AWAKE in bed that night, thinking.

She thought about her daughter silently flirting with Caleb. Walking by him every day and passing the silver dollar back and forth like a game. She wondered if it was Caleb her daughter's post had referred to when she wrote on Facebook about being in love, or maybe it was someone else altogether. She wondered what might have changed if they'd actually spoken. Maybe Melody would have found a reason to live—some hope to lift her up above the fog of depression. She doubted it. But she wished it just the same.

When she thought about her daughter rotting away in that box, she felt like screaming. She felt like screaming and hurting herself. But after so many years of worry, she had no voice left for grief. And she couldn't imagine feeling a worse sort of pain.

At what moment had everything gone wrong?

At what crossroads had she taken the wrong turn?

Were there warning signs she had ignored?

She lay in bed, looking up at the dark ceiling, wishing she could change the past. But the past was locked in the cruel grip of time. The world kept spinning; the clocks kept turning.

She knew Melody had been born with a certain kind of melancholy in her heart, not unlike other babies might be born with a simple birthmark. She knew also that this propensity for sadness must hide somewhere inside herself as well. It was a kind of genetic curse that had torn daughter and mother apart, a curse that made Jane lie here and remember in the dark.

In the swirling chaos of these nighttime musings, her mind drifted to Caleb. She couldn't stop thinking about his kiss—the way he'd just taken charge and gone for it. The strength of his hands, the softness of his lips was an intoxicating mixture, and the thought of it now made her burn to feel him again. She tried to remember what he had said to her. Had he said he loved her? No. He had said the things he liked in Melody he loved in her. And that was different. But she also remembered him saying he spent nights lying awake and thinking about her. She wondered if he was down the hall thinking about her now.

If he had never even spoken to her daughter, was he still off limits to her? Would she be a bad person for finding a bit of relief in a man's touch? Who could judge her?

Jane threw the covers back and got out of bed. Before she knew what she was doing, she was standing in front of Caleb's door with her hand on the knob. Just do it, she told herself. You're both adults. Why not? Because Melody had liked him. And that makes it wrong, doesn't it? Yes. No. Maybe.

She twisted the knob halfway, hesitated, then gently turned it back and pulled her hand away.

THE NEXT MORNING, she dressed in her best business suit and packed her suitcase for the week. She found Caleb in the kitchen, drinking coffee and reading yesterday's Sunday paper. When he saw her he set the paper down on the table.

"What?" Jane asked, pouring herself a mug of coffee.

"I've just never seen you dressed like that."

"You don't like it?"

"No," he said. "I love it."

"You do?"

"You look like an executive or something."

"Well," she chuckled, "I am your boss, so I guess it's time I started acting like it."

She sat down across from him. He didn't have his hat on, and his hair was hanging partially in his face. He looked a little tired, and she wondered if he had been up thinking about her, just as she had been up thinking about him.

"Do you have a meeting today?" he asked.

She shook her head.

"No, I'm leaving."

"You are?"

"Yes. I'm going down to Portland for a health insurance convention. I'll be gone all week."

She had never seen a man's face look so sad so suddenly. He looked down at the paper on the table.

"Oh," he said. "Okay."

Jane reached into her purse and slid an envelope across the table to him.

"What's this?" he asked, picking it up.

"It's half your pay. I got it from the bank last week."

Caleb slid the envelope back.

"You don't have to do that."

"But I am doing it," she said. "You should only stay on if you really want to. Not because you need to. It isn't fair for either of us to hold the other hostage."

He swallowed and looked away.

"Do you want me to stay?" he asked.

"Of course." She thought she saw him smile slightly, but it disappeared when she added: "I want my yard finished."

"Sure," he said. "Okay then."

"You shouldn't feel stranded here either. There's a house key in the envelope and some extra money for groceries and cab fare, too. There's a bicycle in the garage if it's nice and you'd rather ride to town. I had new tubes put on it last year."

"How long will you be gone?"

"The conference goes until Friday. But I might stay the weekend; I'm not sure. I'll be back by Sunday at least."

Jane saw the pained look in his eyes, and she wished she could make it disappear. She wished she could reach across the table and take his hand and tell him that everything was okay, that she just needed a little time by herself to think. But there was something between them now, something that wouldn't allow her the intimacy of even such a small gesture. It was as if they were strangers all over again.

"I'll miss having you around here," he said.

She forced a smile and nodded.

She knew she would miss him too, but she wouldn't allow herself to say it. Instead she looked at her watch and rose.

"Well, I better get going if I'm going to make the eight o'clock ferry."

Caleb rose from the table.

"I'll get your suitcase for you."

Despite her protests, he carried her suitcase out to the car. He lifted it into the trunk and then turned to say goodbye. She knew he wanted to hug her, so she climbed into the driver's seat and shut the door before he could. Then she started the car and rolled the window down. He leaned his arm on the roof and looked at her. His eyes were sadder than ever.

"I'm not going to Mars," she said.

"I know it," he replied, sighing. "I just don't like the way things got all screwed up between us, is all. It doesn't feel right to leave it like this."

"Things are fine," she said.

"Well, they don't feel fine for me."

"Maybe we can talk when I get back."

Jane reached up and touched his cheek.

Caleb grabbed her hand and pressed it to his lips. When he let it go, his smile melted her heart. She wanted to kiss him. She wanted to turn off the car and take him back inside and make love to him. She wanted to know what it would feel like to lie naked in his arms, to wake up and look into his green eyes.

Instead she shifted the car into reverse and backed from the garage. He followed her out to the drive. She sat with her foot on the brake and locked eyes with him through her open window. She felt like she might cry, and she wanted to say something to lighten the mood.

"If you do make it to town, maybe you could get me some more Doritos. I seem to be out."

A momentary smile flashed on his face. She committed it to memory, put the car in drive, and pulled away.

She looked in the rearview mirror once, and she could see him standing in the driveway, watching her go. He lifted a hand as if to say farewell, then let it drop at his side as he faded away and blurred into the houses and trees in the distance. Jane wiped away a tear and wondered if she'd ever see him again.

Part Two

Ryan Winfield

Chapter 8

CALEB HACKED AT THE BLACKBERRIES as if they were somehow responsible for every misfortune that had befallen him in this life. He stood among the thorny vines and yanked them from the ground with his bare hands until his fingers and forearms were sliced and bleeding. The stinging pain came in waves—a welcome distraction, chasing away his sadness over Jane's leaving. He couldn't explain why exactly, but his heart had broken the instant she drove away.

He hated himself for having lied to her, for having let her believe that he knew her daughter when he really didn't.

He remembered the first time he saw Jane, sitting in her car in the cemetery. He'd been spooked because she looked so much like her daughter—as if Melody's ghost were watching him stand over her grave. Wishing to avoid an uncomfortable situation, he'd taken off and hitch-hiked back to the ferry. Then she'd appeared in front of him on the sidewalk near the Devil's Cup, and it was déjà vu all over again. At first he'd thought she was Melody's sister. But then when she told him that she was her mother, he was racked with guilt, because although he had had passing feelings for Melody, he felt even more attracted to

Jane. It was as if the things he saw and liked in Melody were present in Jane in even higher concentration.

But he had taken off again. Why? It was the only way he'd ever learned to deal with uncomfortable situations. But when Jane found him in the square and took him home, he thought her offer was too good to be true. He was afraid that if he told her the truth about not really knowing her daughter, she wouldn't want him to stay on. But now he'd screwed it all up with that little lie. That and his stupid kiss. What had he been thinking, he wondered. And on her daughter's own bed, too. What an idiot. He knew that any chance he might have had with Jane had disappeared this morning when she pulled away.

He stood among the blackberries, breathless and bleeding, enclosed in a thorny prison of his own making.

His chest heaved; his eyes stung with sweat.

Or were they tears?

He turned and tore his way through the piles of vines and stormed across the yard to the house. He went to his room and snatched up his guitar and sat down on the bed and played. He played songs he knew well—songs of heartbreak and loss. But then, as his emotions began to settle, he plucked a new tune, something even sadder, the chords laced with remorse. Still he couldn't help but weave a hint of hope beneath the melody, a wish for a new beginning. Not just for him, but for Jane. He saw too often the torture in her eyes, and he wished he could somehow ease it away. He was afraid he only added to it.

THE NEXT MORNING his hands were swollen and raw.

He sat for an hour at the table in front of an uneaten plate of eggs, staring at the envelope of money Jane had left there for him. When he finally lifted his mug, the coffee had gone cold. He rose and dumped it out in the sink. Then he stood looking out the window at the empty drive.

He went outside to work, but even wearing the gloves the pain in his hands was almost unbearable. He worked for an hour before stopping to survey his progress so far. There was a lot more yard than he'd originally thought, and he just couldn't imagine getting it all cleared without help. Worse, he could see new blackberry vines sprouting up in places he had cleared. He stripped off his gloves and tossed them on the ground.

In the house he grabbed two plastic garbage bags, doubled them up, and stuffed his worn clothes inside, along with his few possessions. The clothes he'd yet to wear he laid out on the bed with the tags still on so that Jane could return them. Then he closed the guitar up in its case and laid it on the bed next to the clothes. Maybe she could return it, too.

In the kitchen, he counted the money in the envelope—$3,200 in crisp, new bills. He thumbed out five $100-dollar bills, folded them, and stuffed them in his pocket. Then he slipped the remaining $2,700 back into the envelope and left the envelope on the table. He slung the bag with his belongings over his shoulder, stepped outside, and locked the door. He turned over a rock in the flowerbed and stashed the key. When he stood, he raised one hand and laid his open palm on the closed door, as if blessing the house. He wished her happiness. Then he turned and walked off down the street.

The road lay gray before him, surrounded by trees, and the late morning sun was drawing a mist off the damp concrete. He heard a car coming, and he stepped aside and jerked out his thumb, but the driver sped past and disappeared over a hill.

He passed deep ditches rimmed with blackberry vines, as if they were following from Jane's yard just to taunt him with the unfinished job he was leaving behind. He thought about Jane. He thought about her thick hair and how it stuck up a little on the left side every morning as they drank their coffee together. He thought about the sparkle of humor always burning in her eyes, the touch of sarcasm curled on the edges of her lips. He thought about how she had tasted when he had kissed her, and what he wouldn't give to have met her some other way.

A woman's cry for help jerked him from his thoughts, and he froze on the side of the road and turned his ear to listen.

The scream came again. But where?

There. Beyond those trees.

He was already running across the street by the time his sack of clothes hit the pavement. He scrambled down into the ditch and up the other side, tangling himself in a rusty, barbed-wire fence hidden beneath the brush. He opened a gash in his thigh while freeing himself from the fence, and he felt warm blood running down his leg as he parted the barbed wires and slipped beneath, running in the direction of the scream.

Soon the trees thinned, and he came upon a small, fenced

enclosure in the middle of which stood a solitary goat. Inside the enclosure the ground was barren and muddy, and the goat was collared to a chain that was staked into the dirt. It tossed its head and focused its strange goat eye on Caleb and bawled an almost human scream. It sounded like it was calling, "Help."

"Are you kidding me?" Caleb asked, breathing heavily, with his hands resting on his thighs.

He took in the pathetic scene.

The goat walked to the end of its chain and nibbled at the useless dirt, as if to plead its case against starvation in the only language it knew. Everything inside the fence was stripped to dirt, but there was a circle of absolute desert that marked the limits of the goat's leash.

Caleb stepped closer to the fence.

"You must be starving in there, fella. How about I move you out here where there's some grass?"

The fence was made of old chicken wire stapled to wooden posts that leaned loosely in their holes. Caleb lifted a post out where the fence ends met, parted the wire, and stepped inside. He had taken several steps toward the stake that held the goat pinned when a flash of black caught his eye, and he looked up just in time to see the goat charging him with its head down. He jogged backwards until he ran into the fence and could retreat no further, and he stood there with his back pressed against the wire, watching the goat rush him with its nubby horns. The goat hit the end of its chain, came clear off the ground, and then fell back on its haunches, bellowing in the dirt just a few feet from where Caleb stood.

"Ornery old bastard, aren't you," Caleb said.

The goat rose and sifted the dirt at its feet with its nose, as if its falling there might have somehow stirred up something for it to eat. Caleb could see its ribs beneath its patchy coat. He inched along the fencing to the opening and stepped out of the enclosure. Then he walked the perimeter and tore branches and leaves free from shrubs and trees until he had an armful. When he carried his harvest back to the fence, the goat was standing erect at the end of its chain, watching him with a strange mix of wisdom and mischief peculiar to its kind. Caleb made sure to stay out of reach as he hurled the offering into the worn circle. The goat rushed upon it and began eating.

Caleb could hear the crackle and crunch of branches in its teeth almost all the way back to the road.

Several miles later, when Caleb reached the terminal at the end of the island road, he heard the blast of a departing horn, and he saw the ferry pulling away. Cars were already lining up for the next boat, which he knew would be along soon. He turned south and walked into the small town. When he entered the hardware store, he found Ralph sitting behind the register, as if he'd never left. The only thing to mark the passage of time was a more recent issue of *Guns & Ammo* lying on the counter.

Ralph recognized Caleb immediately and nodded hello.

"How come every time you come in here you look like you've been dancing with a bear?" he asked.

Caleb looked down at the bloody tear in his pants and the

110

blackberry cuts on his forearms.

"Good question," he said. "How come every time I come in here, you're reading the same magazine?"

Ralph looked down at the magazine and smiled.

"Just keeping up with the Joneses. Getting my son a new Sig Sauer before those bastards in Washington ban them."

"Well, I don't think you have to worry," Caleb said, staying neutral. "I'd be more than a little shocked if those bastards in Washington get anything done."

Ralph nodded his agreement.

"How's that yard coming along?"

"Slow," Caleb replied. "Seems like those blackberries grow back faster than I can hack them down."

"Them things is hell on a yard," he said. "They come on like an alien slime. You know, I seen a vine cut down in three pieces and left on the ground. Two days later there was three new blackberry bushes growing. They're like worms. You cut one in half and you get two. You got to get the roots and all. We've got a poison'll keep the new ones down, if they're still green. Won't do nothing for the grown ones, I'm afraid. But you should be wearing gloves anyway, you know. We sell some that go clear to the elbow and cover those arms."

Ralph walked Caleb through the store and loaded a basket with several jugs of Roundup spray and a pair of yellow, elbow-length leather gloves. As he rang the sale into his register, Caleb looked around and asked him:

"You got any goat food?"

"Goat food?"

"Yeah."

"The whole point of having a goat is they'll eat anything."

"Ever seen one eat dirt?" Caleb asked.

"Shit. I seen one eat a tire right off a tractor once."

"Do they eat blackberries?"

"I'm sure they would."

Ralph finished ringing up the supplies, and Caleb paid with two of the hundred dollar bills he'd taken from the envelope. Then he stuffed the change in his pocket, tossed the gloves in the sack with his clothes, and slung it over his shoulder again. He picked the jugs of Roundup up off the counter.

"Is there any place I could catch a cab around here?" he asked. "Or do I need to call one?"

"There's always a line of them waiting at the ferry. Just back up the road there. It ain't too far."

"Thanks."

He turned for the door.

"You tell Jane to let me know if she's planning on selling that place," Ralph called. "I got my ear to the ground for her."

Caleb stopped and looked back.

"I'll be sure to let her know."

The cab dropped Caleb off at the house, and he paid the fare and thanked the driver. Then he set his items down on the stoop and retrieved the key from where he'd hidden it and opened the door. He picked his things back up and went inside.

He emptied his clothes onto the bed in the room and

placed them with the others in the dresser drawers. Then he went into the kitchen and put what remained of the $500 back in the envelope, along with the receipts for his purchases and the cab fare. He grabbed two apples from the kitchen fruit bowl and stuffed them in his pockets. Then he found Jane's bicycle in the garage and wheeled it out to the drive.

After checking to make sure he had the front door key in his pocket, he closed the garage door and ran out beneath it. Then he mounted up and rode off down the street.

Once the houses gave way to trees, the roadside all looked the same, and it took him some figuring to try and find the spot again. When he did he dismounted and laid the bike in the ditch where it couldn't easily be seen, and ducked beneath the barbed-wire fence. There was no crying now as he approached the enclosure, and he wondered if someone hadn't come down from somewhere higher on the hill to finally free the tethered goat, or at least to move its stake to new ground. Yet he found the goat right where he had left it, lying in the dirt with no trace left of the branches he had thrown in.

Caleb paused to look around.

There was an overgrown path leading up the hill, but no house or other structure was visible from where he stood. He stepped inside the wire fence and held an apple out in his hand. The goat rose and walked toward him, stopping every few paces to eye him suspiciously. When it reached him, it sniffed the apple loudly before nudging it from his hand with its nose. The apple fell to the dirt with a thud, and the goat bent and ate it in three bites. It looked up, expecting more. Caleb reached out and patted its head.

"Easy now, fella," he said.

He stepped into the circle and made his way calmly to the center. He seized the stake with both hands and braced and pulled it free from the dirt. Then he carried the stake through the fence. The goat followed. Once outside the barren pen, Caleb had to drag the goat along by the chain because it kept stopping to graze on the vegetation they passed. When he finally got it to the fence and had coaxed it safely through the barbed-wire with the remaining apple, he retrieved his bicycle from the ditch. He wrapped the chain around its frame, wedged the stake in its water bottle holder, and mounted up and pedaled off down the street, leading the goat with the apple in his hand. The goat trotted along beside him, its hooves clacking loudly on the asphalt, the extra length of chain rattling along behind them. It was a sturdy mountain bike, and Caleb pedaled slowly in a low gear. Even so the goat grew tired and began to lag behind, drawing out the slack in the chain. Finally Caleb stuffed the apple back in his pocket and rode with both hands on the bars, and they settled into a comfortable routine.

A minivan passed them by, and Caleb could see three pale faces pressed to the back glass. They must have been a strange sight on that island lane: a man on a bike, leading a goat on a chain. The sky darkened, a misty rain began to fall, and Caleb's thoughts drifted to Jane. He laughed, remembering the look on her face when he had opened her door and seen her with that

Dorito bag suspended above her mouth. He'd knocked first, and he could've sworn she had said to come in. He wasn't sure who had been more embarrassed—her or him. She had looked so cute, though, sitting there crying and covered in crumbs with that silly dating show on the TV. And hadn't she been wearing his shirt, too? Wasn't that a sign of her liking him?

The bike came to a sudden and unexpected stop, and Caleb plunged headlong over the handlebars and onto the pavement. He picked himself up and brushed the bits of asphalt off his skinned forearms, grateful that he had gotten them in front of his face. When he looked back, he saw the bike lying on its side and the goat standing with its feet planted in the street at the end of the chain. He marched toward it.

"You little son-of-a-bitch!"

The goat lowered its head and made as if it might charge. Caleb stopped and checked himself.

"All right. Easy now. I might be a little pissed myself if I didn't know where I was going. But that's no reason to try and kill me. We're almost there, and I promise it's a whole lot better than that pen you were starving in. Here. Have another apple."

The goat softened its stance at the sight of the apple in Caleb's outstretched hand. It scarfed it down, and they made their peace and set out again toward the house.

This time Caleb walked beside the bike.

Chapter 9

JANE SAT AT HER COMPANY'S TABLE in the Red Lion Hotel banquet room, listening to an economist drone on about the effects of the Affordable Care Act on the supplemental health insurance business. The room was a dimly lit sea of pale faces gazing toward the podium where the economist was silhouetted against the blue glow of his PowerPoint slides. Jane wondered why he didn't just sum up his forecast as optimistic gloom. Yet then there would be no reason to sit through his boring lecture, she guessed.

Her thoughts drifted to Caleb, as they had almost every spare minute of the four days she'd been in Portland. She had a sinking feeling in her gut that he had taken his money and left. She knew it was a risk leaving him his earnings, but then she couldn't bear the thought of holding him hostage with it. Besides, maybe it would be best if he was gone when she got back. Maybe it was time for her to move on, to stop replaying the end of her daughter's life.

But part of her hoped he had stayed. She already missed his constant presence in the yard. She missed waking up excited because she knew she would see him over her morning coffee.

She even missed his melancholy eyes, recalling the moments of joy they had shared that erased the sadness from his stare and gave a sense of purpose to her life. She began to feel regret. What was it Grace had said? "Don't let fear have any place in your life. Not even a corner." Why hadn't she just opened his door that night? Why hadn't she crawled into his bed?

She imagined feeling his strong arms around her, feeling his mouth on hers. Her lips began to tingle at the thought. He had kissed her, hadn't he? He had made the first move. What was it that had caused her to stop him? Guilt, she reminded herself. But perhaps she had overreacted. Now that she knew that Caleb and her daughter were never intimate, that he hadn't even known her beyond a few flirtatious encounters on the corner, she wondered why she was still afraid.

Jane felt something brush her leg beneath the table. She looked over, and the man sitting next to her smiled. He was handsome in a plucked and groomed sort of way, but his suit bulged at the waist, and his collar was tight at the neck, giving him the appearance of a man who had spent too many afternoons over steak and martini lunches.

He leaned in and whispered to her.

"Exciting stuff, isn't it?" he asked, rolling his eyes.

"Like watching paint dry," Jane replied.

"Are you staying here at the hotel?" he asked.

"Yes. I'm down from Seattle."

"I'm all the way from Phoenix. My name's Tony."

"I'm Jane."

"Nice to meet you, Jane. I saw you in the CRM workshop yesterday. Maybe we could grab dinner together tonight?"

The way he said it led Jane to believe that he was after much more than dinner. He was handsome, but not in a way that attracted Jane. She'd always had a hard time with men. The ladies at her Al-Anon meeting called her a serial first-dater. Men just never seemed interesting to her. There was always a sense of sad desperation hidden beneath their façades, as if they had no purpose to drive them. No fire. No life.

"Not tonight," she said.

He leaned in closer.

"Come on. You said yourself this was boring. So why not spice it up a little bit?"

"I have a boyfriend," she said, half wishing it were true.

The man grinned and held up his hand to show her the wedding band on his finger. Then he winked.

"What happens in Portland stays in Portland."

Jane looked at him. He raised his eyebrows, waiting for her to respond. Suddenly, she longed to be home with Caleb, to be sitting in the living room by the fire, listening to him play his guitar. To smell his sweat when he came in from working in the yard. To hear his voice. To see his eyes.

"Sure," Jane said. "Meet me in the restaurant at eight."

The man smiled as if he'd won a prize.

Jane closed her day planner and slipped it inside her purse. Then she winked at the man, politely excused herself from the table, and left the banquet room.

HER WATCH READ 8:30 P.M., and Jane was standing on the upper deck of a ferry, midway across Elliott Bay. She chuckled to think of the creep in Portland, anxiously waiting for her to show in the restaurant bar. She felt sorry for his wife.

It was a clear night, and the sky was sprayed with stars, visible even through the wash of orange light thrown by the city behind her. She breathed in the cool night and shook her head to let the breeze tickle her hair. The ferry couldn't carry her home fast enough. Not tonight.

The call came on the speakers that they were approaching Bainbridge Island, and Jane returned to her car and waited for the ferry to dock. She began to feel nervous. What if Caleb wasn't there? What if she'd come back early only to find her house empty and dark? A car honked, and she pulled forward, debarked the ferry, and headed for home.

As she pulled into the garage, Jane noticed in the wash of her headlights that her bicycle had been moved from where she kept it. It kindled a small hope in her chest. She shut off her car and went to the door. She stopped and considered knocking. What if she startled him? Or worse, what if he had company? She shuddered at the thought. Ultimately she decided to just go inside and announce that she was home early. As soon as she opened the door, she heard the guitar music in the living room, and her face broke into a smile.

She found him sitting beside the fire, lost in a song. Not only had he not heard her pull into the garage, but apparently he hadn't even noticed her enter the room. She stood watching him as he hummed along to a haunting melody, seeming to search for words to match the music.

She cleared her throat and he looked up.

His eyes glinted in the firelight, as if he'd been crying.

Were they tears for her, Jane wondered.

He set the guitar in its case, calmly stood, crossed the room, and took her in his arms. She felt the longing in his tense body; she smelled the outside in his hair. When he pulled away to look at her, she saw a question in his eyes. She smiled, as if silently communicating that she had come back for him.

He leaned in and brushed his lips against hers.

A shiver ran down her spine; her knees went wobbly.

She tilted her head back and rose into his kiss. She placed one hand behind his neck and pulled him hard against her open mouth; she reached around with her other hand and gripped his ass. He tasted sweet, like coffee and caramel, and she felt an overwhelming need to feel his naked skin against hers, and to explore every inch of his body with her tongue.

She was about to pull him toward her bedroom when the knock came at the door.

"You've got to be kidding me," she said, looking into his eyes and shaking her head. "What terrible timing. I hope you weren't expecting company."

"Just my girlfriend," he said, smiling.

"Well, I hope she's into watching," Jane said, pushing him away playfully. "Because I'm not into sharing."

The knock came again, only louder this time.

"You had better not be selling something this late," she called out as she turned the deadbolt and pulled the door open.

She found herself looking at a police officer. His partner stood behind him on the step below, and Jane could see their cruiser parked in the driveway. The officer looked over Jane's shoulder, peering into the house as he spoke.

"Good evening, ma'am. We're responding to a domestic disturbance call."

"A domestic disturbance?"

"Yes, ma'am. Who else is in the house with you?"

"Just me and my . . . well, my boyfriend, I guess."

"Would you mind if we came inside for a moment?"

Jane looked at the officer. He was young, with a wispy blond mustache above his thin lip. He looked like a high school kid in a cadet program. She wondered when she had gotten old enough to be older than the police. Then she looked at his partner behind him, and he was even younger.

"Hey," she said, "aren't you Alice McKnight's son?"

He looked embarrassed.

"Yes, ma'am."

"How can you possibly be old enough to be a cop already? I remember you in diapers."

"Ma'am," the lead officer interrupted her, "we'd like to come inside for a moment, if it's all right with you."

"Sure," she said, stepping aside. "I think you've got the wrong house, but come on in and see for yourselves."

The officers came inside, their new leather belts squeaking

loudly. The younger one's radio squawked, and he fumbled the volume control and turned it down. Caleb appeared from the living room and looked at the officers.

"Is everything okay?"

Jane opened her mouth to speak but the lead officer cut her off—

"We're investigating a disturbance call."

Caleb looked confused.

"I was playing my guitar, but there's no way that was too loud. You sure you have the right house?"

"Do you both live here?" the officer asked.

Jane and Caleb answered at the same time:

"Yes—"

"No—"

The officer eyed them suspiciously.

"We got a call about a woman screaming."

"Who called?" Jane asked.

"Just a concerned neighbor," the officer replied.

"If it was Mrs. Parker next door she's always dredging up drama where there isn't any."

"You wouldn't mind if we had a quick look around then?" the officer asked.

"I know what it was," Caleb said, laughing to himself. "It's that damn goat."

Jane looked even more confused than the officers.

"What goat?" she asked him.

He jerked his thumb toward the sliding door.

"Out in the backyard. I brought it home to help with the blackberries. I thought it was screaming because it was hungry, but I guess it doesn't like being chained up either."

The officer looked from Caleb to Jane and back again.

"Sir, would you mind stepping outside with my partner?"

"Why?" Caleb asked.

"Just so he can ask you a few questions."

"You want to question us separately to see if our stories line up, is that it?"

"It won't take a moment, sir," the younger one said. "Right this way."

Jane briefly locked eyes with Caleb as the younger officer led him outside. The lead officer came around to Jane's other side and turned her attention from the door.

"Is everything okay, ma'am?" he asked.

"It's fine," she said. "This is a misunderstanding. I just got home from Portland. Literally ten minutes ago."

"Is there anyone else in the house?"

"No."

"What about this goat he's talking about?"

"You'll need to ask Caleb."

"My partner will ask him. I'm asking you."

"Well, we didn't have a goat when I left four days ago."

Just then a shrill cry broke out, coming from the back of the house. The officer's hand instinctively moved to the grip of his holstered gun. He told Jane to stay put and went urgently to the door and instructed his partner to stay with Caleb. Then he passed through the house to the sliding door, opened it, and went outside into the dark.

"This is crazy," Jane mumbled.

The scream came again, louder this time with both doors open. Jane caught Caleb's eyes, but he only shrugged.

A minute later, the officer came back inside and pulled the sliding door closed. He approached Jane with an embarrassed-look on his face and attempted an awkward smile.

"Sorry to have bothered you, ma'am."

He stepped past her and went outside. He apologized to Caleb and led his partner away toward their patrol car.

"What was it?" Jane heard his partner ask.

"He wasn't lying. There's a darn goat back there."

When Jane and Caleb were alone again, inside the foyer with the door shut, they both broke out laughing.

"You should have seen him grab for his gun," Jane said.

"You should have seen the other one's eyes. They got big as dinner plates."

"Where did you get this goat again?"

"I found it."

Jane raised an eyebrow.

"You found it?"

"Well, I kind of borrowed it."

"How do you borrow a goat?"

"I just found it and brought it home."

"So you stole it?"

"No, I borrowed it."

"Does the owner know you have it?"

"No, but it was starving."

"Then you stole it."

"Yeah, I guess I stole it. But wait until you see how many of those blackberries I've cleared with its help. It just eats and eats. You won't believe it. We're almost done and ready to start tilling for some grass seed."

"Well, tomorrow it's going back where you got it."

Caleb took a step toward her.

"Let's talk about tomorrow, tomorrow."

"What do you want to talk about tonight then?" she asked.

The corners of Caleb's mouth rose ever so slightly.

"I don't want to talk at all."

"You don't?"

He shook his head.

"Then what do you want to do?"

"Everything," he said.

"Really?"

"Really."

"Like what?"

The question had hardly crossed her lips when his mouth pressed against hers. He kissed her, and she forgot everything else. She was no longer standing in her foyer; she was no longer on planet Earth. She felt his hands rise to her breasts. She felt his thighs press against hers, and she felt the hardness between them through his jeans. She walked him backwards down the hall, breaking away just long enough to take a few steps, then stopping to kiss him again. He stripped his shirt over his head and tossed it aside, his lean chest flexing, then grabbed her and kissed her again. She pulled away and took a few more steps, frantically unbuttoning her blouse. Suddenly they were in the doorway to her room. Did she really want to go through with this? Was she sure she wouldn't regret it?

He flicked on the light.

She shook her head and turned it off.

He reached around and unclasped her bra, and her breasts fell free. He bent his head and took her nipple into his mouth.

Jane couldn't believe that this was really happening. She was excited and nervous at the same time. She wondered if he'd still like her as much afterwards. She wondered if she'd be any good. After all, it had been a long time. Way too long.

She buried her fingers in his thick hair. Light leaked in from the hallway and she could see the muscles of his bare back. She felt him reach down and unbutton her slacks. Then he slid them over her thighs and pulled them off. She stepped out of them and stood before him in the shadows, naked except for her panties.

He's fifteen years younger than you, she reminded herself. What if he's disappointed with your body? What if he's used to twenty-year-old nymphos who know how to get it on? What if he likes it freaky? What if. What if. What if.

As she stood thinking, he stripped off his jeans and stood before her in his bulging boxers. The sight made her shiver with excitement. He walked her backwards toward the bed, and she hit the mattress, sat down, and was eye level with his waist. She reached her fingers beneath the band of his boxers and brushed her nails against him. It moved slightly with hard anticipation, his thigh muscles flexing. Then she pulled the boxers down, and he sprang free. Her nervousness fled, quickly overwhelmed by the excitement of seeing his naked perfection standing in the shadows in front of her.

She cupped him in her hand and took him in her mouth. She felt him shudder and moan. He reached down and took her breast in his hand. Then he placed his other hand behind her head and guided her. She reached around and buried her fingers in his muscular ass, and she felt him harden even more. Then, when he could stand it no longer, he pulled away and pushed her back onto the bed. He crawled on top of her, and they kissed for a long time. He kissed her tenderly and slowly at first, his desire gradually working into frenzy. He gently bit her lip, and she felt herself go tense with anticipation. He left her mouth and kissed her neck, then traveled down her bare chest and made his way to her thighs.

Oh, God, yes. Right there.

A last flicker of nervous fear crossed her mind, but it was quickly chased away when she felt his warm breath through the thin fabric of her panties. Her long neglected juices began to flow, soaking the thin fabric through. He gently slid her panties off and tossed them aside. She lay naked now beneath him, nothing between them but the shadows. She gripped his hair and pulled him up to her, and their lips met again.

He lowered himself between her legs.

She gasped when he entered her.

It had been so long that it was almost like the first time all over again. He moved inside her with gentle thrusts of his hips, and she dug her nails into his back, watching over his shoulder as his body rose and fell. He was long and lean—his body a picture of perfection. He smelled like sweat and grass and sex.

The bliss that she felt was almost too much, as if she might burst into tears because it felt so good. The pleasure, the relief.

When he kissed her again, his lips were gentle, and his eyes were open. She could just make out the whites in the dark and she knew he was looking right into her soul. This wasn't just sex; this was making love. She began to relax, letting him have her completely, and she fell into his rhythm and rolled her hips along with his as he drove her higher into a place where all thought was replaced by only need. Here there was no corner of fear left. Here there was no doubt.

Her breasts bounced, her nipples brushed against his chest. Sweat rose on his skin, and still he moved as if he were dancing her to the moon. She felt herself rising, lifting off the bed. The darkness was chased away by a warm red glow, and all sound disappeared from her ears. His head dropped, and he teased her nipples with his tongue—first one, then the other.

She gripped his hair.

She felt him going deeper.

She tightened herself against him.

Then he seemed to lose control and thrust faster, and she

threw her head back and rose to meet him. She was almost there. Wait, she told herself. Wait for him. She felt his muscles tense, his entire body rigid and slick with sweat.

"Jane," he called out. "Oh, God, Jane!"

Then he moaned, and she knew he was cumming, and she let herself go. It came in vast waves of pleasure that surged up to her head and down to her toes, and she released his hair and reached down and grabbed his ass and pulled him deep inside her and held him there. He arched his back and she could feel him throbbing inside her, a small moan escaping her lips, and she turned her head and let the ecstasy wash over her.

When the flood had subsided to tiny waves of pleasure, he pulled free, rolled over onto his back, and pulled her into his arms. She heard him sigh. She was smiling, and although it was dark in the room, she could tell that he was smiling, too. This silent after moment was almost as good as the climax.

Several quiet minutes passed with just the sound of their heavy breathing, together, side by side, fatigued. Jane sank into the mattress, and she couldn't remember a time when she'd felt so good, or so relaxed. After a while he leaned over and kissed her—a long, gentle kiss that said more than any words could. Then he rested his head back on his pillow and closed his eyes, as if to relive the entire experience in his mind.

She lay there, watching his naked chest rise and fall in the shadows. She had no idea where they went from here, but she was sure that this moment had been more than right—it had been exactly what she had needed. She also knew that she was completely and hopelessly in love with him.

She only hoped that he loved her, too.

At last she snuggled in beside him and closed her eyes. She thought of running to the bathroom, but she felt too good to even move. The last thing she heard before she drifted off was a shrill and distant call from the backyard. Somehow it set her to dreaming about Sirens calling to a passing ship.

The song had been heard; the crash was imminent.

Chapter 10

SHE WAS ALONE IN THE BED WHEN SHE WOKE—

For a brief moment she thought that the events of the night before had been only her fantasy. That she had somehow dreamed that Caleb was making love to her.

But she felt too good for it to have been imagined.

Plus, she could still smell him on her skin.

She got up and went to the bathroom and freshened up. Then she checked herself out in the mirror. From certain angles she could still see the youthful figure that everyone had always complimented her on. But from other angles she could see the effects of forty years on her body. The slight sag of flesh here; the subtle wrinkle of skin there. She was almost certain that Caleb was used to co-ed hard bodies, and she was nervous over how he felt about her this morning when he woke.

But then she remembered him calling her name the night before—"Jane. Oh, God, Jane." He had said it as if he meant it, as if it were a cry of surrender ripped from his lips.

She brushed her teeth and gargled with mouthwash. Then she pulled on her cutest Victoria Secret sweats and T-shirt. She walked to the bedroom door, hesitated, then went back to her bathroom and put on mascara, blush, and some pink lip gloss. Then she smiled at herself in the mirror.

"You're beautiful," she said to her reflection. "And you're smart too. Any man would be lucky to have spent the night with you." She laughed at herself. "Oh, shit. Not even my own reflection would believe that. Just get out there already."

She found the kitchen table set for breakfast, but Caleb wasn't there. She poured herself a mug of coffee and walked to the living room and stood looking out the slider at the yard. The sun was up and glistening on the dewy lawn where there was still grass. The blackberries were completely cleared on this side of the creek. The bridge was fully exposed, and on its other side, near the fence that marked the edge of her lot, stood the goat with its head bent into the remaining blackberry thickets. She could see a chain around its neck leading to a stake in the ground.

"So you're the culprit, eh?"

"Guilty as charged."

Caleb hugged her from behind, and her heart skipped. When she leaned her head back to look up at him, he smiled at her, his hair wet from a shower. He kissed her, and it was all she could do to hold the coffee mug steady in her trembling hands. He pulled away and looked at her. There was none of the usual sadness left in his eyes, and his smile relieved any insecurity that she had been harboring

"Good morning," he said.

"Yes," she smiled back, "it is."

"How'd you sleep?"

"Better than ever."

He grinned to hear it, as if he were somehow responsible. Which, of course, he was. Jane felt herself blush, so she looked out the window again and nodded toward the goat.

"Is that your new friend out there?"

"That's him. He's an incorrigible little bastard, but he must eat twice his weight a day."

"Well, he's got a head start on us this morning. What did you make for breakfast? I'm starving."

"Oh, you still expect me to cook, do you?"

"Of course," she replied. "And then I'd like a bubble bath and a foot rub too."

"As tempting as that sounds," he said, "It's a work day for me, and I've got a yard to finish and a tyrant for a boss."

Jane laughed and followed him into the kitchen.

"Today your boss might make an exception for bed rest."

"Is that right?" he asked, pulling out a chair for her to sit.

"If he's particularly good," she said, "then yes."

"Don't you mean if he's particularly bad?"

The way his grin curled his lips as he said "bad" brought up images of last night, and she felt her face flush. She considered skipping breakfast and dragging him back into her room that instant, but he had already turned his back and was cracking eggs in a bowl and whipping them. She sipped her coffee and enjoyed watching him work. Whatever he did, whether playing his guitar, cooking eggs, or making love to her, he gave it his full and undivided attention. Now he stood over the stove with the tip of his tongue between his teeth and chopped ingredients. Jane could smell butter in the pan. When he finished cooking, he presented her with a spinach and mushroom omelet and a side of wheat toast.

"I thought you hated mushrooms," she said.

"Still do," he replied, "but I bought you some at the store because I know how much you like them. And look what else I picked up for you?"

He stepped over and opened the pantry door and showed her an entire shelf lined with bags of Doritos. She felt her face blush with embarrassment, but she couldn't help but laugh.

"That's just mean."

"Oh, come on," he said, "You've never looked cuter than you did that night. And, I did knock, by the way."

"You really think I looked cute?"

"Yes. But that doesn't mean I'm letting you off the hook for the orange stains in my T-shirt."

Jane laughed. She waited for him to sit, and then she tried her omelet. It was good. They talked comfortably as they ate, him telling about his adventures with the goat, her telling about her adventures with the insurance salesman in Portland. When they had finished eating, a silence fell over the small kitchen, and they sat looking at one another across the table. Jane began to feel a little self-conscious again, and she wondered what she looked like to him in the natural light coming in through the kitchen windows. She wondered if it showed her age.

"Why are you looking at me like that?" she finally asked.

Caleb cocked his head to the side and smiled.

"Because you're gorgeous."

"Oh, come on. I can't be that great to look at."

"Best thing I've ever seen," he said. "You know, all those others mornings I was sneaking glances at you, too. The only difference now is I don't care if you catch me staring."

"But don't you think I'm too old for you?"

"I think you're perfect."

"But I'm—"

"Perfect," he cut her off. "You're perfect. Listen, there's nothing more attractive than a mature woman."

"Oh, is that what I am now? *Mature.*"

"Maybe that wasn't the right word. I'm just saying that there's something very sexy about the fact that you've lived a little. Seen and experienced some things, you know. Like, you have some substance to back up your looks. That and you're just incredibly gorgeous. And I'm not even going to mention how . . . um, well, how skilled you are in the sack."

Jane felt her heart beating and an ache rising.

"You're just trying to get me back into bed," she said.

"Definitely so. But I mean it, too. Truth is I was a little nervous last night."

"You were?"

"Yes."

"Nervous why?"

"Because I wasn't sure I was experienced enough."

Jane smiled and looked down, batting her eyelashes as she ran her finger along the edge of her coffee mug.

"Well, you maybe could use a little more practice."

"Are you offering your services for that?"

She looked up and smiled flirtatiously.

"Offering? I've been sitting here for ten minutes, making small talk and wondering when you're going to drag me back to my bed and ravish me."

He was up in a flash.

Her heart hammered in her chest as he led her down the hall by her hand. Her entire body was tingling with excitement, and she felt like she was doing something naughty. But this time he took things slow. He laid her on the bed and kissed her, eventually moving around to nibble on her ear.

"You're beautiful," he whispered.

"Tell me again."

"You're beautiful, you're beautiful, you're beautiful."

Then he lifted her arms over her head and peeled off her shirt, exposing her naked breasts. The bedroom curtains were only partially drawn, and sunlight filtered in and landed like liquid gold on her skin. It felt good. Caleb kissed her breasts and smiled up at her. He flicked his tongue across her nipple. Then he moved down and kissed her belly, inching lower and slowly peeling back her sweats, kissing his way down her legs until he stripped the sweats entirely off and tossed them aside. He took her foot in his hands and massaged it.

"Is this what you had in mind?" he asked.

"That feels really good," she moaned, "but I was thinking maybe something a little higher up."

He moved his hands past her ankle and massaged her calf.

"Here?"

"A little higher."

He moved up her leg, leaning down and gently kissing the inside of her thigh.

"How about now?"

"You're almost there."

His smile disappeared, and all she could see was his thick hair. She felt her panties pull aside, and she felt his warm tongue on her. A shiver ran down her legs; her toes curled over.

"That's the spot," she whispered.

She rested her head on her pillow and tried to quiet her racing thoughts. He had said she was beautiful, she reminded herself. Multiple times. He had even said she was perfect.

The attention he paid to her was tender and complete, and soon she could think of nothing else but somehow getting him inside her. As if reading her thoughts, he moved up her belly, paused briefly at her breasts, then rose to her mouth and kissed her. The taste of him mixed with her drove her wild with need.

"I want you inside me now," she said.

"Is that an order from the boss?" he asked, grinning.

"Yes. Dammit. Yes."

He peeled off his shirt and shimmied out of his pants. The sight of his naked body in the golden light nearly brought her to climax. When he moved on top of her, she turned her head to the side, but he reached up and turned it back, looking deeply into her eyes. She could see endless pools of thought swirling in the depths of his green irises, and she suddenly felt as if she'd known him in another life—as if she'd been here waiting in this world for him to arrive, to find her purpose in his gaze.

A moan escaped her lips as he entered her.

Last night had been wild, hot, and exciting, but this was different. This morning, he was making love to her like no man ever had before. She could see the longing in his eyes, and he never once took them away from her. They rose together with perfect timing, and she saw his pupils dilate when he came; still he held her stare as she bucked and shivered beneath him. When the overwhelming release had faded, he leaned down and kissed her, then whispered in her ear.

"I love you."

She couldn't believe what she had heard. Had he just said he loved her? She studied his face, trying to read his intentions there. He just smiled and looked down on her and said it again.

"I love you, Jane."

"You do?"

"Yes, I do."

"You're just infatuated with me because this is exciting. Because I'm an older woman. What did you call it? Mature."

He sighed, rolled off of her, and flopped down on the bed beside her, his head propped on his hand.

"I wish you could see yourself through my eyes," he said.

"And if I could, what would I see?"

"You'd see the most amazing, kind, smart, and beautiful woman you'd ever been lucky enough to lay eyes on."

"Doesn't it seem a little soon to know if you love me?"

"Not for me," he said. "And I wasn't aware there was a required grace period before a person could acknowledge their feelings. I think I knew it the first time I saw you, and I think it scared the hell out of me. But I'm not going to live in fear."

Jane remembered what Grace had said about not letting fear have a place in her life. But she wasn't sure if she was ready to expose her whole heart to him yet. He was young. He could afford to be careless in love. Jane couldn't. She knew she loved him already, and she knew there was no way to change that. But somehow saying it exposed her to a kind of heartbreak just the thought of which was more than she could bear.

"It's okay," he said. "You don't have to say it back right now. I'm patient. You'll say it when you're ready."

"Is that right?" she asked, reaching out and brushing her nails across his bare chest. "Well, it seems like you have a good dose of confidence to go along with your patience."

He laughed.

"Confidence is important when it's all you've got."

"Well, let's just take it slow and see what happens."

He leaned over and kissed her, saying:

"If last night and this morning are your idea of taking it slow, then I'm all in."

Then he pulled away and looked at her.

"But there is one little thing I'm kind of worried about."

"What's that?"

"Well, we didn't use any protection."

"It's okay," she said, "I'm on the pill."

"You are?"

"Yes. I take it religiously, every morning."

He looked both relieved and a little sad.

"So, you're pretty active then?"

"You mean sexually?"

"Yeah."

Jane laughed. If he only knew, she thought.

"Are you active?" she asked.

"No," he said. "It's been a long time for me."

"How long's a long time?"

"I dunno. Maybe six months. And she was a steady girl."

Jane shook her head.

"If six months is a long time, then it's been ever for me."

"You mean: forever?"

"No. I mean ever. It's been so long I can't even put the *for* in front of it."

Caleb laughed.

"Then why do you take the pill?"

"I don't know. Wishful thinking, I guess. Or maybe habit. Plus, it's good for my skin."

He leaned down and brushed his lips against hers.

"Well, in that case, I see no reason why we shouldn't get some more practice in before I go back to work."

Chapter 11

JANE SLOWED THE CAR and pulled to the side of the road.

"You sure this is it?"

"Yeah. That's the fence that caught my leg."

"So you just went in there and walked it out?"

"It was starving, Jane. Plus, the guy at the hardware store said they'd eat blackberries. What would you have done?"

She just shrugged.

"I think this is part of Mrs. Hawthorne's property. We'll have to circle around on Agate Drive to get to the house."

After driving in circles for several minutes, they located the driveway at the far end of a wooded street. A rusty mailbox painted with the name HAWTHORNE hung from an iron post.

The drive was long. Gravel crunched beneath their tires and spit up inside the wheel wells, pinging loudly. As the trees thinned the drive widened, and they came upon an old yellow house from some bygone era. It was leaning pitifully to one side, with brown moss covering its cedar roof. The elaborate porch had once been painted white, but the paint had mostly peeled away, revealing the gray, weathered wood beneath.

"Nice place," Caleb said as they got out of the car.

Jane looked around.

"Believe it or not, I came out here ten or eleven years ago to speak with Mrs. Hawthorne about long term care insurance, and it looked just the same back then."

"Does she live here alone?"

"She did then. Her husband had died a few years before."

"Maybe she's gone and joined him then."

"Why would you say that?"

"I dunno. She sure wasn't feeding her goat."

The porch steps bowed and creaked as they climbed them, and paint chips fell from the door when Jane knocked.

A long time passed and nothing happened.

Caleb reached past Jane and knocked again, only louder. There was a great clattering from inside the house, followed by a shout and then the sound of shuffling. The door creaked open, and an old woman stood before them with cats circling betwixt her slippered feet.

"Hi, Mrs. Hawthorne. I'm one of your neighbors—"

"I know who you are," the old lady spat out, shrugging her shawl higher on her thin shoulders. "And the answer's no. I still don't want to buy any of that damn insurance you're peddling. Money down the drain is all it is."

Jane was a bit taken aback that she remembered her. Now she herself was beginning to remember just how difficult Mrs. Hawthorne had been to deal with.

"We're actually here about something else."

"The answer's the same—No!"

Jane ignored her.

"May we at least come in?"

"I guess it would be rude to leave you standing on the porch, wouldn't it?"

The house was piled with hoards of old possessions, and they had to weave their way into the living room. Dust billowed from the couch when Jane and Caleb sat, setting them both to coughing. The old woman lowered herself slowly into a thread-bare chair, propped her elbows on her knobby knees, rested her chin on her clasped hands, and stared at them. She had a long hooked nose and bright, beady eyes, giving Jane the impression of an old and wizened bird sizing them up from its perch.

"We're here about your goat," Jane said.

The old lady stirred.

"If it's about his crazy hollering, there isn't anything to be done about it."

"It isn't that," Jane said. "It's more like we'd like to rent him from you."

"Rent him? What would you want with old Bill?"

"His name's Bill?" Caleb asked, speaking for the first time.

"Bill Clinton, actually," the old lady said.

"Okay, I'll bite," he said. "Why is he named Bill Clinton?"

"Because he tries to hump everything he sees. Crazy thing even mounted the neighbor's Newfoundland once. And if you wanting to rent him has anything to do with those bestiality ranches I've seen talked about in the news, well, you can leave now. I don't go in for all that, no matter what you're offering."

"No," Jane said, containing a chuckle, "nothing like that. It's just that we've got some blackberries to get rid of."

"Well, I don't get around to doing much yard work myself since my last hip replacement, so you can imagine it would be tough for me to part with old Bill without a pretty enticing offer. And, of course, you'd need to transport him yourselves."

"Actually, he's already at my place now."

"Well, if he's run off and done any damage to anything, I can't be held responsible."

"That's the other thing," Jane said, "Caleb here thought he was abandoned, so he took him home."

"Because he was starving," Caleb interjected.

The old lady's eyes darted back and forth between them, calculating how this new piece of information might be useful.

"Now, that changes things. How long's he been stolen?"

"Four days. And I didn't steal him; I borrowed him is all."

"That's what Bernie Madoff tried to pull when he ran off with a third of my life savings. Stealing's stealing, young fella. No matter how you dress it up."

"That's why we're here," Jane said. "We'd like to rent the goat from you and make it right."

The old lady leaned back in her chair and absently reached a claw over its arm to pet a passing cat.

"Fifty bucks a day sounds fair to me."

Caleb laughed.

"Fifty bucks a day? For that busted old goat? You've got to be kidding. I can get a goat that faints for that much and charge admission for the kids to see it. Besides, we ought to be charging you for feeding him.

"And I ought to turn you in to the sheriff for thieving him," the old lady replied.

"Maybe we should turn you in for animal cruelty."

Jane held up her hands.

"Whoa now, let's not get all worked up here."

"Forty dollars a day then," the old lady said.

Caleb shook his head.

"You know what? I don't trust you won't leave him staked down there in the dirt to starve to death anyway. How about forty bucks to buy the goat?"

The old lady eyed him with interest.

"I might not be college-educated, young man, but I know how to hold the money. You see that lamp there on the table. Pick it up. Go ahead. Pick it up and tell me what's written there beneath it?"

Caleb looked at Jane and shrugged. Then he reached and lifted the lamp and looked.

"There's an old yellow piece of tape that reads 1976."

"What else does it say?"

"It says two dollars and fifty-five cents."

"That's right. Now lift that clock there next to it. What's that one say?"

"Says: 1982, five dollars."

The old lady nodded.

"And if you'd like you can get up off that couch you're

sitting on and turn it over too."

Caleb set the clock back down.

"I get the point."

"Good. I know the price of everything I've ever bought. And I know the price of everything I've ever sold, too."

"There's a big difference between knowing the price of a thing and knowing its value," Caleb replied.

Jane thought she saw the old lady smile.

"Maybe. But I know that goat is worth a lot more than forty lousy dollars."

"Fine," Caleb said. "Seventy-five."

"I'll take three hundred dollars for him."

"Yeah, right. Maybe if it was five years younger and didn't scream like it was being murdered all the time."

"Well, what will you give?"

"We'll pay one hundred."

"Two-fifty."

"One-twenty-five."

"One seventy-five and it's sold."

"Done."

Jane sat watching, riveted by Caleb's negotiating. She was observing a side of him she hadn't seen yet. She liked it.

After Caleb had paid the old woman from his envelope of money, and after she had made him change with rolls of old quarters and dimes that she kept in a coffee can, he had her sign a bill of sale. He wrote it on the back of an envelope that she fished from her recycling bin. Then they shook hands all around, and the old woman followed them to the door. As they descended the steps, she called to Caleb:

"Would you do an old lady a favor, young man?"

Caleb stopped and turned back. She lifted her bony finger and pointed to a huge pile of cut firewood lying in the grass.

"Would you mind bringing in an armload of that wood? It gets cold at night, and I like a fire."

Jane followed Caleb to the woodpile and helped stack his arms with as much wood as he could hold. As he toted it up the steps past the old woman, he said:

"That firewood should be stacked up next to that shed and covered with a tarp. Otherwise it'll go to rot before you get a chance to burn it."

Mrs. Hawthorne shrugged, as if it couldn't be helped.

When Caleb came out again, he was alone.

"That was sexy," Jane said when they were in the car.

"It was just a little wood. I could've carried more."

"Not that," she said. "Watching you negotiate. Where were you when I was here trying to sell her insurance ten years ago?"

"I was fifteen is where I was."

Jane laughed and shook her head.

"I keep forgetting how young you are."

IT WAS LATE AFTERNOON by the time they got home, and Jane joined Caleb in the backyard to inspect his work. He had made remarkable progress while she was away in Portland.

There was an enormous pile of dead blackberry vines,

dried and browned on the tarp, and Caleb dragged them to a clear spot in the yard and stacked them up to burn. Jane found an old tin of lighter fluid in the garage, and Caleb doused the vines and lit them. Then they set out lawn chairs and sat looking at the flames as the sun went down. Their newly purchased goat stood at the end of its leash, just beyond the fire, twisting its head left and right as if to hear them better.

"It's looking good back here," Jane said.

"Thanks. I'll need to rent a tiller maybe next week, buy some topsoil, and get it ready for seed."

Jane was happy that he was making such fast progress, but part of her was worried about what would happen when he finished. She pushed the thought aside. She saw the rosebush her mother had given her, standing alone where Caleb had cleared the weeds around it, its branches thick with buds.

"I thought you were going to pull out that rosebush?"

"I can't bring myself to do it," he said. "Are you sure you want it gone?"

Jane sighed.

"I don't know. The roses are pink, and that was Melody's favorite color. At least my mother got that right, I guess."

"Is she really all that bad?"

"Just hope you never have to meet her and find out."

"Well, I'd like to meet her anyway."

Jane changed the subject, pointing beyond the rosebush.

"I think I'd like a little garden over there," she said.

"That's no problem. I found some railroad ties along the

fence that I can border it with."

"And I want a fountain."

Caleb laughed.

"A fountain? Why not have me put in a swimming pool while you're at it?"

"Sure. As long as you promise to swim in it naked."

Caleb grinned at her, his face glowing in the soft light. He sure could turn her on with just a look.

"We could go practice in the bathtub right now."

"Who will watch the fire?" she asked.

"Good point. Maybe we should practice right here."

He leaned over and kissed her. Jane felt her own fire start, the need rising deep in her abdomen. She planted her hands on his chest and pushed him away.

"Not here with Bill Clinton over there watching," she said. "You heard what Mrs. Hawthorne said. He might break free of his chain and try to join in."

"Good point," he said. "'Cause I don't like sharing either."

She stood and stretched.

"I'll go make us some dinner. You watch the fire. When it burns down, we'll see about lighting another one inside."

THEY MADE LOVE TWICE THAT NIGHT—

When Caleb had finally kissed her one last time, and had rolled over exhausted and gone to sleep, Jane lay awake, propped up on her elbow, looking at him in the low light of her bedroom lamp—the sweet face that she already loved.

It was strange, but when he was awake something in his eyes made him appear older than he really was, but when he was sleeping, the years seemed to fade from his expression, and he looked like a kid dreaming of endless summers somewhere. His lips were curled into the hint of a smile, and strands of his dark hair lay across his relaxed brow. What did age matter, she wondered. Wasn't love timeless? If it wasn't, it should be.

She thought ahead ten years to when she would be fifty, and he would be only thirty-five. What would people say? Would he listen to them? Would she? She heard Grace's voice in her head, telling her that being anxious over something that hadn't even happened yet was sure to make the thing you were worried about happen soon enough.

"Live for today," she always said. "Just be right here, right now, because the present is always enough."

Jane leaned down and touched her lips to his forehead. He stirred slightly and smiled in his sleep. Then she switched off the lamp and rested her head on her pillow, letting herself be lulled to sleep by the soft sound of his breathing.

Chapter 12

DESPITE HOW HER BODY ACHED from two days of almost non-stop sex, Jane had never felt better as she pulled into her Saturday morning Al-Anon meeting.

The women inside greeted her with the same expressions of condolence she'd become accustomed to from them since her daughter had passed away. But when they saw the smile on her face, they couldn't help but smile back and make guesses.

"You look better than ever."

"You must have been to the spa."

Grace, on the other hand, just looked at her with a knowing grin.

When it was Jane's turn to share, the women were all on the edges of their seats, excited to hear what turn of events was responsible for her sudden change in mood.

"It's official," she said, deciding to just throw it out there. "I'm sleeping with my gardener." She paused to watch several of the women nod to their neighbors as if to say 'I told you so,' and then she added: "Plus, as I'm sure some of you know from me sharing last week, he's fifteen years younger than I am."

Several women gasped.

"But he really is an old soul, and I feel more comfortable with him than I have with any other man, maybe ever. But something's eating at me, too. I'm happier than I can remember being, but I don't feel entitled to it. Sometimes I get this stab of grief about my daughter, and it almost seems like I'm a terrible person for being happy. I mean, it hasn't been that long since Melody passed. Shouldn't I still be racked with grief? Shouldn't I be tortured every day like I was just a few weeks ago? Am I being selfish? These questions keep popping up in my mind. Anyway, I'm just putting it out there to hear myself say it—to take the power out of it—because as my wise sponsor here Grace always says, 'You're only as sick as your secrets.'"

After the meeting some of the ladies went to the local diner for coffee and pie. Jane tagged along and snagged a seat next to Grace and waited for a private moment to talk.

"So you think it's all right?"

"Do I think what's all right, sweetie?"

"Me and Caleb?"

"Oh, I don't know. Do you?"

"You think it isn't?"

"I'm just happy that you're moving forward, J. Wherever that leads you. Just trust your gut and don't be secretive. That's the only advice this old lady has for anyone anymore."

"Come on, you're not that old."

Grace reached to her bag and held up the half-knitted scarf she'd been working on during the meeting.

"Not that old? Really? I'm knitting, Jane. When did you all let me start this up anyway? And you're not the only one who wants a personal midlife crisis musician lying around her house, either. My old strings could use a little plucking too, if you know what I mean? Sex is a rumor for me."

Jane just shook her head and laughed.

WHEN SHE GOT HOME Caleb was gone and so was her bicycle. For a brief moment her heart sank, thinking maybe he had left for good. But she found his clothes and his guitar right where they always were in his room, so she figured he must have just gone out for a ride.

She sat for a while on the small bed and looked at the pink walls. She could see the brush strokes where the light hit, and she recalled with perfect clarity the day she had painted them, singing to entertain Melody, who painted beside her with her own tiny brush. It had been a big step moving her into her own room, and she remembered coming back here to check on her every half hour for the first several nights. Melody had always been a difficult child, often crying for hours for no apparent reason. Colic, the doctors had said. But Jane couldn't help but wonder if there wasn't something wrong with her even then, something that the drugs and alcohol had finally relieved when she found them—until they conspired to kill her, of course.

Jane had heard addicts share about never having felt quite right until they first discovered their drug of choice. The idea filled her with an immense guilt, not just for being unable to arrest the progress of her daughter's disease but for possibly having passed it on to her in the first place.

As she looked around the room, she decided it was time to let go of the past, at least symbolically. She got up and went to her car and drove to the hardware store.

Ralph wasn't working, but an energetic young man she hadn't met before helped her pick out several gallons of latte-colored paint with primer, along with the rollers and brushes she'd need to do the job. She was driving back home when she came upon Caleb riding her bicycle on the side of the road, the back of his shirt drenched with sweat. She slowed beside him and rolled down the passenger window.

"You must be training for the Tour de France," she joked.

Caleb laughed.

"How'd you guess?"

"I figure if that Armstrong guy can win it while he's on drugs, imagine how well you could do clean and sober."

"I think my outfit is a little wrong, though," he said. "I'd need to get one of those costumes. You know, the ones with the flags of the world and all that."

"Maybe I'll sponsor you," she said.

"Maybe I'd like that," he replied.

"Where'd you go?"

"Just for a ride."

"A ride where?"

A car pulled up behind Jane's and honked. She looked in her rearview mirror and realized that they were taking up nearly both lanes, so she smiled at Caleb, sped off and continued home. She parked in the garage and got out and leaned against the back of her car, waiting. Before long Caleb came pedaling onto her street and turned into the driveway.

"You look exhausted," she said. "How far did you go?"

Caleb stowed the bike, came around the car, and kissed her. The combination of coffee on his breath and the smell of his sweat turned her on. When she pulled away and looked him over, she noticed that he had wood chips caught in his hair.

"What on Earth have you been up to?" she asked. "And why won't you answer me? You're being sneaky."

"I'm not being sneaky."

"Then where were you?"

"I went over to Mrs. Hawthorne's place."

"You little sentimental sap. You rode all the way over there and stacked that wood for her, didn't you?"

"I was bored is all," he said. "Besides, it was sure to rot where she had it."

"Did the old nag at least thank you?"

"She's not that bad."

"Oh, come on."

Caleb laughed.

"She said she couldn't afford to pay me, but she wanted to give me a little reward. So she gave me this."

He dug in his pocket and pulled out a small, worn, pewter figurine of a man playing a trumpet. Jane noticed a weathered piece of tape on its base that read: 1963, 55 CENTS.

"Generous of her," Jane said.

Caleb took it back and laughed again.

"I told her I was a musician, and she dug through twenty boxes to find it. I thought it was nice. You'd be surprised at all the stuff she's got saved up."

"Nothing would surprise me about her."

She opened the trunk, taking out her cans of paint.

"Well," she said, "it looks like your poor hands could use a break from yard work. You want to help me paint?"

"What are we painting?"

"Melody's room."

Caleb looked at her for a moment.

"You sure you want to do that?"

"I'm sure."

"Then I'd love to help," he said.

They moved the bed and dresser into the hall and spent the afternoon taping off the walls and painting over the pink. It was a strange feeling for Jane to see the past disappear beneath the sweep of her paint roller, the pink being covered up one pass at a time. When there was only a small corner of pink left on the final wall, she hesitated with her roller in her hand. She stood there for a long time and paint began to collect beneath the roller and drip down the wall.

Then she felt Caleb's arms wrap around her from behind, and she felt his gentle kiss on her neck.

"I love you," he said.

"I love you, too."

Jane hadn't planned to say it; the words just slipped out.

And the moment that they did, she knew she could never call them back again—that with those three simple words she had committed her heart into Caleb's care, to nurture or ruin at his will. She felt vulnerable, but she also felt good—as if she had given up control and was finally willing to trust.

Trust the universe.

Trust destiny.

Trust Caleb.

He reached up and wrapped his strong hand around hers on the handle of the paint roller, and together they pushed it up the wall and erased the final stretch of pink. Then he took it from her hand, set it down in its tray, and rose to take her in his arms and kiss her. They stood kissing for a long time. Jane felt an unbearable need to consummate her declaration of love, to fully surrender to him there and then.

She pulled him to the ground, kissing him. She struggled to remove her pants, got them half off, and then undid his belt and his zipper. They lay intertwined on the floor amidst the old sheets she'd used to protect the carpet and the nearly empty buckets of paint, each of them half-clothed and lost in the absolute worship of the other.

He entered her and she felt complete, as if they had been made to fit together, as if they had always been one and had only been separated by the illusion of space and time until this surrender brought them together again. Jane looked up into his eyes and silently promised never to add to the pain she saw there, and she swore by his expression that he had understood.

Before long, she felt it coming on, and she let it happen—allowing her body to completely surrender to the moment as she lay beneath him seized in the glorious grip of an orgasm for nearly a minute, and then he came too. She felt the warm flood of his relief enter her, and she heard the whimper of ecstasy that parted his perfect lips.

They embraced on the floor, peaceful and drained.

Jane smelled the drying paint mixed with the sweet scent of their sex, and she wrapped her arms around him tighter and buried her head in his neck and breathed him in. She kissed his sweaty skin, tasting his salt and a hint of the outdoors.

If she could just lie like this forever, she thought. Forever wouldn't be nearly long enough.

Chapter 13

HAPPINESS SPED THE CLOCK—at least that's what Grace always said, and Jane guessed she must be right because the next several weeks passed like a dream.

With her savings running low, and not wanting to dip into her small retirement plan, Jane began taking sales calls from her company again. It turned out to be a good thing, because it got her thinking about other people and their needs rather than obsessing about her own misfortune about the death of her daughter. Whenever someone she knew brought it up, she felt a little guilty because she wasn't as sad as she thought she should be. But Grace had told her there was no wrong way to grieve, and Jane supposed that she was right about that, too.

Caleb spent his days working in the backyard, making fast progress. The blackberries and Scotch Broom were soon gone, and he had started to have hay bales delivered so that the goat could eat. Some evenings, if she was home early, or he was working late, Jane would join him to help, and she found the physical labor refreshing. The weather was unseasonably nice for Washington, broken only by an occasional spring shower. Even then the rain seemed only to wash everything clean.

They rented a gas-powered tiller, and she sat in a lawn chair with a cup of coffee and watched as Caleb guided it across the yard, his strong back moving away from her, his sexy smile coming back. She never thought she could love a man so much. There seemed to be nothing he couldn't do, and it made her feel safe to have him around. It wasn't just his work ethic that she loved; he was sweet and kind also. She caught him on several occasions sneaking over to Mrs. Hawthorne's place on her bicycle, and she guessed he was doing work for her there, too, or perhaps just keeping her company.

"I'm getting a little jealous," she had joked with him one night when he came back from there. "I know how much you like mature women, and Mrs. Hawthorne is much more mature than I am."

He had just smiled and kissed her.

On another afternoon, she called him in from the yard and sat him down with her laptop open and asked him questions as she filled out a health insurance quote form.

"What do you need all this information for?" he asked.

"I'm getting you a health insurance policy."

"What? Why? I'm healthy as can be."

"I know, but what if something happens?"

"To me? Nothing's going to happen."

"You never know," she said. "I meet with people all the time who've lost everything because they got sick or injured and were underinsured."

"But I don't have anything to lose."

"Well," she said. "You've got me. And I've got you. And if you get sick, I want you taken care of."

"Fine," he said, relenting. "But you have to promise you'll take the premium out of my pay."

"With all these deductions you've got me making, you'll be lucky to have anything left," she joked. "You might have to keep working for me forever."

He leaned forward and kissed her.

"You'd like that, wouldn't you?"

"Maybe," she said, smiling.

On a particularly hot and sunny day, she came home from an afternoon appointment and found him working on a strange project. He had staked overlapping black, plastic garbage sacks into the ground, making a sort of long runway down a natural slope in the backyard, leading to the creek.

"What's this?" she asked, handing him an iced tea.

He drained the tea, crunched the ice between his teeth, and handed her back the glass. Then he hooked his hands on his hips and looked down on his project with pride.

"My original plan was to make a foot path down to the bridge there. Maybe with garden stones and some ground cover between them. Anyway, the bags are to keep the seed I'm about to spread from taking hold where I want the path. But while I was doing it, I had an idea."

"An idea for what?"

"Go put a bathing suit on, and I'll show you."

"A bathing suit? Why?"

He leaned over and kissed her.

"Don't you trust me, baby?"

The way he said "baby" would have made her do just about anything, so she smiled and went to change.

When she came out again, wearing her favorite bikini, she stood near the house in the shadow of the roof, feeling shy. He looked her up and down and whistled. The goat raised its head and bleated out from the corner of the yard, either responding to Caleb or adding its own approval to her swimwear.

Caleb walked a circle around her.

"If I didn't know better," he said, "I might just think you were trying to seduce your gardener."

"Maybe I am, but it isn't fair that I'm standing here nearly naked and exposed, and you're still dressed."

He immediately peeled off his shirt and tossed it aside.

Jane looked at his strong chest and his shredded abs and she felt a familiar ache that she knew he could relieve. Then he stepped out of his pants and stood before her wearing nothing but his boxers. She wanted to take him inside that second.

"Better?" he asked.

She looked him up, then down, and nodded. But when she reached for him, he stepped away and held up his finger.

"No, you don't. I'm not going to let you distract me from my project, you sexy siren you."

He turned on the hose and dragged it over to his runway of plastic bags and sprayed them wet. Then he locked the hose head on spray, laid it down, and let the water run the length of bags until it spilled into the shallow creek.

"I still don't understand what you're doing," Jane said.

"Didn't you have a Slip 'n Slide when you were a kid?"

Jane threw her head back and laughed.

"Are you telling me you've spent your whole day back here making a Slip 'n Slide?"

"Don't knock it until you've tried it," he said.

"I'm not going down that thing."

"Yes, you are."

"No, I'm not."

"Suit yourself."

He lunged forward and dove onto the plastic bags and slid down them, landing in the creek with a splash. Then he stood up, laughing, and shook water from his hair.

"Come on," he called, "I'll catch you."

Jane stepped up to the slide and hesitated. She felt silly even thinking about it. She looked around to see if any of her neighbors could see them, but the trees were flush with leaves, providing complete privacy in her yard.

"Don't be a chicken," Caleb called.

She crouched down and jumped onto the slide, surprised by how slick it was and how fast she slid. She plunged off the end and into Caleb's waiting arms—he cut her laughter off with a passionate kiss. She felt carefree, standing waist-deep in the creek and wrapped in her lover's arms. She felt young again.

They climbed out and scampered up the hill and slid down again, splashing one another and then wrestling in the creek.

The goat stood watching them from above, chewing its hay, as if they were little more than a curious distraction from its meal. They played for nearly an hour, until the slide was covered with mud, and their skin was rubbed raw from the plastic. Then they hosed each other off, went inside, and made love on her bed.

They lay in each other's arms afterwards, completely naked and completely happy. This was living. Jane ran her fingers up and down Caleb's chest, tickling his nipples with her nails.

"Have you had many lovers?" she asked.

It seemed like a long time passed before he answered.

"Not really. I mean, I've had a few steady girlfriends over the years. But I wouldn't say they were many."

"Like the one you wrote that song about?"

"Yes, she was one."

"Tell me about her."

"I met her when I first came to Seattle. I was young and renting a little room on the hill. I think I was working for the moving company at the time. Playing music at night, of course. She came to one of my gigs and wanted to meet me after."

"Did you love her?"

"I thought I did."

"But you didn't?"

"I'm not sure I even knew what love was back then, to be honest. I think we were infatuated with each other, maybe."

"What happened?"

"We fought all the time. About stupid shit, too. We just weren't compatible. Plus, she was edgy. You know?"

"I don't know. What do you mean by edgy?"

"Like she was in love with depression or something. Or at least in love with the idea of it. She used to carry around three or four suicide notes everywhere she went, and she was always working on them. Whenever we'd fight, she'd pull one out and start writing away. I can't tell you how many bathroom doors I broke down over the years to make sure she was okay."

"Did she ever end up doing it?"

"Killing herself?"

"Yeah."

"No. She ran off and married some software engineer at Microsoft. Cleaned herself up into a trophy wife, I guess. Last time I saw her, they passed me in the street, and she was pushing a kid in an REI stroller. She saw me, but we didn't say anything to each other. She looked happy. What about you?"

"I thought about suicide once. After Melody died."

"Well, I'm sure glad you didn't do it. But I meant what about other lovers."

"Oh. Well, I've dated, of course, although it's been a long time. When Melody was young she was my priority. I always told myself I'd need to be really sure about a man before I'd introduce him to her. But I was never sure, so she never met any of them. Lots of first dates. Then, when she got older and started having her trouble, I was just too wrapped up with her problems to even think about dating. Not that guys didn't hit on me, and sometimes it was flattering. Of course, my friends were always trying to set me up, annoying as that is."

"Have you ever been in love?"

Jane sighed.

"I thought I was in love with Melody's father. But, like you, I don't think I even knew what love was back then."

"But you do now?"

"I think so."

"And what is it?" he asked.

Jane looked up into his green eyes. His long lashes caught the light falling in through the window.

"You tell me," she said.

He paused for a moment, as if considering his answer.

"Okay. I don't know if I have the right words, but love is this feeling I get when I look at you. A feeling that as long as you're near me, or in the world even, then everything will be okay. That everything has meaning. It's as if the world was all shades of sepia—like an old movie reel—and that everywhere I looked I saw suffering and pain. Then I heard your voice, I saw your face, and somehow the color came into everything."

Jane smiled.

"I like that."

"What does it feel like for you?" he asked.

She sighed.

"Hmm . . . let's see. Do I have to answer that?"

"I told you."

"All right, fair is fair, I guess. I know I love you because it feels like I'm finally whole now. Like I've gone my entire life missing something, and now I've found it."

"Like a puzzle piece or something?"

"Does that make sense?"

"Yes," he said, "it kind of does."

"Maybe I can put it like this: there was always this ache in my guts, an aloneness, but whenever I'm with you it seems to disappear. I remember reading somewhere that you have to learn to love yourself before you can love someone else. But I don't think it's true. I think you have to learn to forget yourself before you can love someone else. At least I seem to forget about myself when I'm with you. I feel light. I feel happy. You know, I never told a man that I loved him before. At least not since Melody was born. But I love you, Caleb. I really do."

He kissed her forehead.

"When I hear you say those words, all I see is blue. The most beautiful blue you could imagine."

"I love you, I love you, I love you."

"I just hope you never stop loving me, Jane."

"I won't," she said, laying her head back on his chest.

A short time later she heard her cell phone ringing in the kitchen, where it was charging. She let it go to voicemail, but it immediately rang again.

"I had better go get that."

"Okay," he said, sliding out from beneath her. "I'm gonna jump in your shower."

He was already in the shower when she returned from her short call. She stripped off her clothes and stepped in with him and wrapped her arms around him.

"What's wrong?" he asked, looking down at her face.

"My brother's in the Seattle jail for a DUI."

"Shit. I'm sorry."

"Maybe this time it'll do him some good."

"Are you okay?"

"I learned to let go of his consequences years ago. This is par for the course with him. But that's not the worst part."

"What is then?"

"My mother's coming down to go to his hearing, and she wants to stay here for a few days."

Caleb nodded.

"I understand. I'll get lost for a while if you need me to."

Jane hugged her arms around him tighter.

"No way," she said. "You're not going anywhere. I need you here with me. But if you wouldn't mind maybe sleeping on the couch, it might make things easier with her."

Caleb placed two fingers under her chin and lifted her face to his, looking deep into her eyes.

"I just want to support you any way I can, baby. And I'll sleep anywhere you ask me to."

Jane rose to her tiptoes and kissed him.

"Thank you."

"When's she coming?"

"Tomorrow."

"Well, we better make use of today then while we can."

He pressed her against the shower wall and kissed her. She felt his naked body melded together with hers, and she felt the warm stream of water running between them. When he pulled his mouth from hers, the look on his face was wild with need.

She reached down and he was hard.

It felt risky and exciting and Jane could hardly believe that she was standing naked in her shower with the proof of Caleb's attraction for her pulsing in her hand.

She guided him to her. He crouched down slightly and picked her up and pushed himself inside her. She'd never felt him harder. She wrapped her arms around his wet shoulders and held on while he thrust himself deep, again and again, like a starved and hungry lover, slapping her bare ass against the tile shower wall, the steam rising between them, her moans echoing in the acoustics of the confined space, and she heard him calling out to her between her moans—

"Oh-God-Jane. I'm-Going-to-Cum-Jane. I-Love-You!"

She let go of his shoulders and reached down and dug her nails hard into his ass, and she felt him burst inside her with the most amazing mixture of pleasure and pain written on his face.

Chapter 14

SHE SHOWED UP EARLY, pounding on the door and waking them. Jane jumped out of bed and pulled on her sweats. Caleb yawned and stretched, smiling at her from the bed.

"Come on," she said, "you've got to get out of here."

"Where should I go?"

"Well, Mother will expect to have Melody's old room, so maybe just pretend you were sleeping on the sofa."

He laughed, got out of bed, and dragged a blanket with him into the living room. Jane followed him, collecting the trail of discarded clothes they'd left lying everywhere these last few days. Caleb flopped down on the sofa and either pretended to go back to sleep or actually did. Jane couldn't tell as she rushed past him to stuff their dirty clothes into the hamper.

Her mother pounded on the door again, and when Jane finally opened it, she stood on the step with an impatient scowl on her face and two large suitcases at her feet.

"You'll be lucky if I don't come down with pneumonia the way you've left me standing out here in the cold."

She stepped past Jane into the house, then looked over her shoulder and nodded to her luggage.

"Aren't you going to get that?"

Jane grabbed the bags and followed her inside.

She brought the bags to Melody's old room and set them against the dresser. When she turned back, her mother was standing in the doorway, surveying the room.

"I see you've erased any trace of her already. I would have left it as it was myself, but then I guess we all have our own way about things. Whose guitar is that in the corner? I hope you're not wasting your time trying to learn. You never did have an ear for music, you know. Now, your brother, he had the gift. Do you remember when he played the saxophone?"

"I remember when he pawned the saxophone that you bought him so he could buy drugs, but I don't remember him playing much. The guitar belongs to my houseguest. He's here doing some work for me in the backyard."

Her mother looked down her nose at Jane.

"Humph," she said, a sour expression on her face. "If I'd known you had a houseguest, I would have stayed at the hotel."

"Gee, Mother. If I'd known that, I would have been sure to have mentioned it. So I guess we both lost out."

"Well, I'm here now. I'd like some coffee, if it isn't too much trouble. The service on the train was just awful, and then I had to wait for the ferry, of course. I guess it would be too much to ask for you to drive down and pick me up."

Jane ignored her mother's last statement and stepped past her out the door.

"I'll put some coffee on."

They sat across the table from one another with nothing at all to say. Her mother was even grumpier than usual, but Jane tried to allow for the fact that she'd been traveling since early this morning and that her favorite child was once again in jail. The house was quiet, and Jane heard the guest shower turn on.

She knew that Caleb was up.

Her mother must have heard it also, because she asked:

"Will I be sharing a bathroom with your houseguest?"

"Yes, Mother."

"Well, I hope he's not one of these filthy illegals I see working around our old neighborhood. The whole block really has gone to hell, you know."

"I believe it," Jane said, adding under her breath: "I know the devil already lives there."

"What's that you say?"

"Nothing, Mother."

A short time later, but not soon enough for Jane, Caleb walked into the kitchen and poured himself a cup of coffee. When he turned around, he smiled at Jane and said:

"Good morning, Miss McKinney."

"Good morning, Mr. . . ." Jane realized that she couldn't remember Caleb's last name, and she stumbled embarrassingly over her recovery when she saw her mother eyeing her. "Oh, hell, you don't mind if I just call you Caleb, do you?"

"No, Caleb's fine," he said, smiling at her slyly.

"Caleb, I'd like you to meet my mother, Mrs. McKinney."

"Nice to meet you, ma'am."

Caleb reached out his hand to her mother, and she leaned forward in her seat to inspect it before she accepted his offer. When Caleb had released her hand, she picked up her napkin and wiped it clean. Then she tossed the napkin on the table and sighed, looking right past Caleb to address Jane.

"Well, I think I'll retire for a little rest, if you don't mind. And if you plan on having your helper work in the yard this morning, please have him keep the noise down."

With that, she stood and walked from the kitchen.

When Jane heard the bedroom door close, she turned to Caleb with an apology in her eyes.

"Thank you."

"It's funny," Caleb said, keeping his voice low, "but the first thing I thought when I saw her was how much she looked like you. She really is beautiful. But the second she spoke, you two looked nothing alike. She's all red and you're all blue."

"Well, let's just try to put up with her until she goes home. Which hopefully happens soon."

Caleb leaned in conspiratorially, keeping his eyes on the kitchen entrance as he stole a quick kiss.

"By the way," he whispered, before pulling away, "my last name is Cummings. And as my insurance agent, I would expect you to know that."

"Such a lovely name you have, Mr. Caleb Cummings." She brushed her lips against his, extending their kiss. "I might just have to try it on myself and see how it sounds."

"I'd like that," he whispered back.

Then he pulled away and smiled, speaking in a loud voice for her mother's benefit:

"I'm off to work in your yard now, Miss McKinney. I'll try my best to keep the noise down."

HER MOTHER APPEARED briefly again at dinner, once again refusing to acknowledge Caleb directly. She only mentioned him once when she asked Jane how old her "little helper" was, as if he hadn't been sitting at the table right next to her.

After an uncomfortable meal where everyone picked at their food, she finally brought up Jane's brother and their plan for the following morning.

"I'd like to get an early start," she said, dabbing her mouth with her napkin. "We should really try to see him before the arraignment at ten."

"I'm happy to drive you into the city," Jane said, "and I'll wait to take you back, but I won't be going inside to see him."

Her mother's face pinched up in sour indignation.

"That's just ridiculous. He needs your support."

"No, he doesn't," Jane said. "He needs help. And he can't get it from me. This is what, Mother, his fourth DUI? He's lucky he hasn't killed someone by now. And how many of your cars has he wrecked without a license? And still you let him live with you. I'm not responsible for his choices, and I won't suffer the consequences for them. And you shouldn't either."

Her mother cast a glance at Caleb.

"This is no way to speak about your own brother in front of strangers."

"Maybe I'm sick of secrets, Mother."

"It has nothing to do with secrets," she said. "McKinney's don't air their dirty laundry in public."

Jane laughed.

"Dirty laundry? Like all those early years when Dad got drunk and beat us all the time, and you just drank your wine and pretended everything was fine? Don't let the neighbors hear. Is that what you mean, Mother?"

Her mother sat with her mouth agape, apparently shocked by Jane's accusations. Then she said:

"I haven't had a drink in nearly twenty years now, and you know that. Not one."

Jane crossed her arms and looked away.

"Sometimes I think you'd be better off if you had one."

"What's that supposed to mean?"

"It means you're a dry drunk, Mother."

There was a long and uncomfortable silence.

Jane watched as Caleb moved the uneaten food around his plate with his fork. Then she heard her mother's chair slide on the linoleum as she stood from the table. Jane could feel her standing there and staring at her, waiting for her to apologize as she always had in the past. But Jane refused to apologize this time; she refused even to look at her.

After standing for nearly a minute, her mother stormed from the kitchen and slammed the bedroom door.

Jane rose from the table with her plate and dropped it in the sink with a clatter. Then she stood with her hands on the counter, staring out the kitchen window at the shadows of bats flitting across the blue evening sky. She felt Caleb's arms wrap around her, and she felt his lips touch her neck.

"I love you," he whispered.

Jane closed her eyes and sighed, taking comfort in his words. Somehow he knew just what to say, and maybe more importantly, what not to.

SHE WAS ASLEEP, and dreaming about him, when he crept into her room that night and woke her with a kiss. She pulled him onto the bed and rolled on top of him, reaching down to free him from his boxers. She had only been wearing a long night shirt, and she hiked it up and guided herself down to him, placing her hands on his bare chest and riding him in the dark.

It turned her on more than a little knowing that there was a risk of being discovered by her mother, and it was all she could do to keep herself from moaning as she rode herself to a climax. She sat atop him quivering with pleasure until he slowly pulled her down beside him, kissing her, and shifting his hips to keep himself inside of her.

Apparently, he wasn't finished.

Another half turn, and he was on top, gently coaxing her back. She spread her legs wide and raised her hips to take him as deep as she could, and he worked himself there with hard and steady thrusts, until she felt him grip her shoulders and shake like a man possessed, filling her with his warmth.

CALEB WAS OUT WORKING in the yard by the time she rose the following morning, and she stopped for a moment at the window to watch him. The goat stood across the yard from her, chewing on hay and watching him too. He was using a shovel to spread topsoil from a wheelbarrow in preparation to lay down seed. She noticed the smooth movement of his lean arms and strong back, working together in perfect rhythm, and she thought there must be no place he looked more at home than he did when he was working—except maybe when he had a guitar in his hands. She could almost picture what the yard would look like when the new grass had taken hold, and she wondered again what would happen to him when he was finished. She knew music was in his blood, and she knew Austin was calling.

Her mother appeared from her room, dressed in a white suit and wearing a big summer hat, as if she were heading to church rather than to court. They said good morning to one another, but neither of them meant it.

When they got to the ferry, Jane left her mother in the car

and went up onto the deck to get some air. It was a gray and windless morning and a misty drizzle hovered above the water, making the city ahead appear to shimmer against the dark sky. She stopped by the onboard cafeteria on her way back to the car and purchased two coffees and two blueberry muffins.

Her mother took the coffee, but waved the muffin away.

"You need to eat, Mother."

"I'm fine. I had my Ensure this morning."

"That's not enough."

Her mother said no more as she sat staring ahead, holding her coffee in both hands as if she were strangling it.

The ferry docked, and Jane waited for the cars ahead to debark, their brake lights flashing brightly and reflecting off the wet pavement. She followed them off and headed up toward the courthouse, driving by memory. She passed the parking garage and pulled up to the entrance and stopped the car. Her mother sat still beside her, not moving to get out.

Finally, she unclasped her seatbelt and said:

"You're really not coming in?"

Jane shook her head.

"I'm going over to the library. Just call my cell when you're done, and I'll pick you up."

"Don't you have any feelings for your brother?"

"I'm releasing him with love, Mother."

"And what's that supposed to mean?"

"It means I don't have any energy left for alcoholics and addicts. If he gets help and straightens himself out, I'd love to see him. Until then he's on his own to pay for his decisions."

"So you won't help with bail?"

"No."

"That seems awfully harsh."

"It might be the best thing anyone can do for him."

"Just letting him rot in there with all those criminals?"

"Letting him hit bottom, Mother."

"But he's not like them, Jane."

"He's no different."

"He's my son."

Jane looked over and noticed that her mother's eyes were wet. For a moment she saw herself sitting there, remembering her own pain over watching Melody destroy her life. She knew that her brother had always been her mother's favorite, and she knew that somewhere beyond the denial there must be genuine concern for what he had become—maybe even the same guilt over having caused it that Jane had sometimes felt.

She reached over and touched her mother's shoulder, a small gesture of compassion, but one that carried the weight of a thousand words unsaid. Her mother reached up and placed her hand over Jane's, forced a sad smile, and nodded. It was the only act of intimacy between them as adults that Jane could remember. Then her mother opened the door, stepped out onto the curb, and closed it without a word. Jane watched her walk away, her big white hat receding up the steps toward the courthouse, her posture proud, despite the frailty of her thin and wasted figure. Her image blurred away to just a blotch of white as the tears welled in Jane's eyes.

As she pulled from the curb and drove away, she wasn't sure if she was crying because she knew that she would lose her mother someday, or if she was crying because she knew that she'd never really had a mother to lose.

Chapter 15

AS HE PEDALED UP THE DRIVE, he saw her standing at the sitting room window, looking out through the fogged glass as if she'd had news of his coming and was waiting for him.

By the time he dismounted the bike and climbed the stairs to the porch, she was gone from the window and the door was standing open. He took off his jacket and shook the rain from it, then put it back on, stepped inside, and closed the door. He stood in the dark and crowded foyer and listened to the creaking from above as she plied her rooms, filled with untold ancient treasures. When she finally descended the stairs again, stepping carefully and using the handrail, she couldn't hide the smile on her face.

"You found it?" he asked

"I did," she said.

She alighted from the last step, bustled past him, and led the way down the dim hall to her living room.

The coal remnants of last night's fire were still glowing in the firebox, and he stirred them with the poker and added fresh wood while she retreated into the kitchen to fetch them tea. When she came out again, he had the fire going, and they sat in front of it in matching chairs—the fabric of hers worn to threads from years of sitting alone, and his with upholstery that was nearly new. They sipped their tea in silence.

"So aren't you going to show it to me?" he finally asked.

"Oh, all right," she said, setting her teacup down loudly on the end table. "Lord, help us when your impatient generation is actually running this country."

She dug a claw deep into the pocket of her sweater and hauled out a small box covered in blue felt. He reached to take it from her, but she pulled it away, wagging her long and bony finger at him. She held the box out in her palm and lifted the lid. Inside was a beautiful yellow-diamond engagement ring, set in platinum and surrounded by smaller white diamonds. The square-cut canary stone shone like a miniature sun in its bed of blue silk. Caleb reached out and plucked the ring gently from the case. He held it up and turned it to catch the light coming in through the window. It was obviously an antique, the quality of its craftsmanship giving away its age, but it looked to be in mint condition, as if it had hardly been worn.

"That diamond was mined in Australia," she said. "Almost three quarters of a century ago. It was cut and set in Paris."

He took the box from her hand and carefully set the ring back inside. Then he held the box up and looked underneath it.

Mrs. Hawthorne shook her head.

"Not everything has a price, young man. My sweetheart purchased it while he was overseas in the navy. He came home and surprised me with a proposal. He was a romantic boy. And he made me a great husband. He never would say how much he'd paid for it, but I know it set him back all his savings and likely half his inheritance, too."

"Are you sure you want to part with it?" Caleb asked.

"I remarried after he passed, and it just never seemed right to wear it after that. Plus, these old fingers of mine have shrunk up to near nothing but bone. I doubt if it would even fit on my thumb anymore."

"Don't you want to pass it on? Keep it in the family?"

"Ha!" She rocked back slightly in her chair. "I've outlived two of my kids, and the third is an ungrateful shit who's been using every trick he can dream up to spend my money before I'm even gone, including taking me to court as an incompetent. But he'll sure be surprised when he finds out I'm leaving all my property to the state."

Caleb eyed the ring in its case. It was absolutely perfect for her, and he knew somehow that she would love it: the detailed setting, the cut of the stone. But it was a large diamond, and he knew it must have been expensive, even all those years ago.

"I can't afford to pay you for it in cash, but I'll work it off if you'll let me."

"I'd offer to give it to you," she said, "but I know we're too much alike for you to allow me to. So I'll hold on to it for you, and you keep coming and working here when you can, and I'll turn it over as soon as I think you've earned it."

Then she took the case from his hand, snapped it closed, and slipped it back into her sweater pocket.

"You might be under the impression that I'm beginning to enjoy your visits. You wouldn't be wrong if you are. But I'd like you to know that I wouldn't allow the fact to tempt me into dragging out your payment. I'll hand over the ring when you've earned it. Not a day after. Now if you'll excuse me, I need to tend to some frailties of the sort you wouldn't yet understand and that I hope you never do."

She rose slowly from her chair and shuffled off, stopping at the entrance to the hall and turning back.

"I forgot to mention there's a leak beneath the kitchen sink, if you know anything about plumbing, and if you have time to take a look when you finish sorting boxes today. I know I won't be here forever, but I'd like to not have the floor rot out from beneath me before I'm gone."

IT HAD QUIT RAINING by the time Caleb finished his work at Mrs. Hawthorne's and mounted his bike to ride home.

He found the garage door open and Jane's car parked inside. He stowed the bike and went into the house, but the house was quiet, and both bedroom doors were closed. Mother and daughter were separated by more than just walls. He considered knocking on Jane's door, but then thought better of it, grabbed his gloves and headed out to work in the yard while there was still some light left. As soon as he stepped outside, the goat rose from where it lay and started nibbling at the ground, as if it had somehow been caught slacking on the job.

Neither Jane nor her mother appeared at all that night,

although Caleb could hear the murmur of Jane's bedroom TV through the closed door as he sat on the couch and scribbled with pencil on paper, sketching out the lyrics for a song he'd been working on. He made himself two peanut butter and jelly sandwiches for dinner and ate them alone at the kitchen table with a glass of milk. When he finally turned out the lights and stretched out on the couch for the night, he noticed for the first time how his body ached from all the work he had been doing. But it was a good kind of ache—the kind that let him know he was alive and kicking; the kind that made it okay to close his eyes and rest without guilt.

He lay awake for a long time, half in this world and half in the world of dreams, his mind wandering between memories of events already past and hopes of events yet to come. Jane was the subject of every willful thought. He saw her face and the way she always bit her lower lip just before she came. He saw the disbelief mixed with hope in her eyes whenever he told her that he loved her. It made him want to tell her all the time. It made him want to tell her forever. He tried to imagine her surprise when she saw the ring, when she heard his question.

But when, he wondered—

Not now, but maybe soon.

As he drifted off, he could smell her hair and feel her lips and taste her breath, and so real were the imaginings of his dreams that he stirred in his sleep, half believing that she had come to find him on the couch. Had anyone been in the room, they might have even heard him softly calling her name.

Chapter 16

HER MOTHER SHOOK HER HEAD.

"It's just a shame how you've let that beautiful rose go," she said, her tone shrill and accusing. "You need to prune it at least in the winter, I told you that when I gave to you."

Jane caught Caleb's eye and smiled at him knowingly, as if to say: I bet you wished you'd pulled it out now.

They picked their way across the backyard on small paver stones that Caleb had laid out to prevent them from trampling the new grass seed. Jane took up the rear, imagining to herself that they were leapfrogging above a deadly swamp and wishing she had the courage to push her mother off the stone ahead to be mired forever in the muck below.

Caleb stopped and pointed to the northern fence where he had marked off a rectangular patch of yard with railroad ties.

"That'll be your garden over there."

"Wouldn't it get more sunlight if you put it on the other end of the yard?" Jane's mother asked.

Caleb just shrugged.

"It's the perfect spot," Jane said. "Thank you, Caleb."

He smiled at Jane and carried on with the tour.

"I've got a place set here for an island flowerbed to break up the grass, and I buried low voltage lines in PVC so I can wire your fountain. I saw they had some at the hardware store if you want to pick one out."

"I hate the sound of running water," Jane's mother said.

"Well, Mother," Jane replied, "it's a good thing you won't be here to hear it then, isn't it?"

Caleb ignored their bickering and continued on.

"I've cleared all the blackberries and poisoned the ones that were trying to return. You can see the grass already coming up there on the creek bank. I even built a little enclosure there for your presidential goat, and he seems much happier now that he's free of that chain."

"I haven't heard him scream once all week," Jane said.

Her mother huffed.

"Seems foolish to waste good money feeding a pet that can't learn to even fetch a ball, but that's just my opinion."

Caleb cast an apologetic glance at Jane, then turned to her mother and addressed her directly for the first time.

"That goat earned his keep here, unlike some people."

It was Sunday morning, and her mother had been in her house for an entire week. Jane could see that her constant chiding was wearing Caleb's nearly unending patience thin. He had avoided her as best he could, but when she wasn't in the city making busywork over her son's upcoming trial, she was here making Jane and Caleb's lives miserable. Jane had noticed Caleb was spending more evenings over at Mrs. Hawthorne's place, and she couldn't help but think that it was largely to escape her mother that he went. But the worst part by far was the way they had to sneak around in her own home, pretending to hardly know one another during the day, and settling for covert rendezvous in her bedroom at night. She longed to go back to the time when they were stripping off one another's clothes and making love all over the house.

Caleb finished their tour and saw them back to the door, but instead of joining them inside, he claimed he wasn't hungry and that he had more work to do. Jane and her mother went to the kitchen alone, and Jane prepared them breakfast.

As she watched her mother pick at her eggs, and nibble at her toast, Jane wondered how it was she had any weight on her bones at all. After a long time her mother finally spoke.

"How long have you two been shagging?"

Jane froze, her fork loaded with eggs and suspended above her plate. She looked across the table at her mother.

"Excuse me?"

"Well, that's what we called it when I was young."

Jane set her fork down and folded her hands in her lap.

"I don't know what you're talking about."

"Of course, you do. You might think a lot of things about me, and some of them might even be true, but me being stupid isn't one of them."

Jane nodded.

"That's true."

"I see the way you look at him, and I see the way he looks

at you. I'm surprised you two can even manage to keep your clothes on and your hands off of each other until I go to my room at night. You'd think you could wait until I'm gone."

"Mother!"

"Mother is right. And we wouldn't have dared do anything of the sort when my mother was around, I'll tell you that. And don't you think he's too young anyway?"

"I don't think age has anything to do with it."

"Well, other people might."

"I don't care about what other people think."

"Maybe you should start caring. Have you ever considered that? Or have you always been so selfish?"

"I don't know, Mother. Was I selfish as a little girl? Or can you not even remember, you were so drunk all the time?"

"That has nothing to do with anything. He's too young, and it's too soon."

"What do you mean it's too soon?"

"I mean Melody's hardly even in the ground, and you've gone and painted over her room, and you're already sleeping with a boy her own age. It's shameful, Jane. It really is."

Jane sat staring across the table at her mother, her hands clenched into fists in her lap. Her mother stared back, a glint of enjoyment in her eyes, as if she were relishing her daughter's discomfort. Jane closed her eyes and counted slowly to ten, just like her sponsor had told her to whenever she felt rage coming on. Then she counted again, backwards. When she opened her eyes, she looked directly at her mother and spoke calmly.

"I want you gone by tomorrow morning."

Her mother's look of conquest changed to a look of fear.

"Your brother needs me here."

"Then stay at a hotel in the city. You can afford it."

"You wouldn't put your mother out like that."

"I would, and I will. I want you packed and ready to go by eight in the morning. I'll take you as far as the ferry."

Jane slid her chair out and stood, looking down on her mother where she sat. She looked to Jane like the face of evil, thinly erect in her kitchen throne.

"You've never been enough of a mother to me to earn the right to even mention Melody, or how I should or shouldn't feel about her. And if you ever so much as speak her name again in a way that's meant to hurt me, I'll write you off for good, and you'll never see me again. You got that?"

Then she turned on her heel and walked from the kitchen without bothering to wait for a response.

An hour later she was lying on her bed when she heard the cab pull up. The front door opened and shut; then she heard the thud of luggage hitting the trunk, the clap of the cab doors closing. She lay there looking at the ceiling in a trance, listening as the cab backed from the drive and pulled away, carrying her mother off with it.

Thirty minutes had passed, or maybe an hour, it was hard for Jane to know, when he tapped lightly on her door. Without taking her eyes from the ceiling, she called for him to come in. She heard the door open and then softly close, and she felt the mattress give as Caleb sat on the edge of the bed.

"Do you think that a person can go to hell just for wishing someone dead?"

There was a long pause before Caleb answered her.

"I think maybe a person's already in a kind of hell when they feel so hurt by someone that they'd wish them dead."

"You have to admit that you hate her, too."

"I'll admit she's impossible to be around. But mostly I just feel sorry for her."

Jane lifted her head and looked at him.

"You do?"

Caleb nodded.

"Why?"

"Because she has this amazing woman for a daughter, and she's so blinded by whatever demons she's fighting that she can't even let herself see it. And because at the end of the day, you've got to really hate yourself a lot to run around putting people down all the time."

Jane sighed.

"How'd you get so wise at only twenty-five?"

"Twenty-four," he corrected her. "I'll be twenty-five in July. And I think it comes from watching people."

"Do you watch people a lot?"

"Yeah. I find them interesting. I've spent a lot of time on the street playing music, or just sitting around writing songs, and for some reason when I'm there, most people just treat me like another brick in the wall. They go right on being who they really are."

Jane propped herself up on her elbow so that she could see him better. He'd ditched wearing that old hat, and she loved the way his thick hair curled around the back of his ears. His eyes seemed an even brighter green now that they weren't shaded with sadness all the time. It was still there, of course, the melancholy haunting his eyes, but it had somehow sunken to deeper depths, the way a lake might turn over in the spring.

"Do you like baseball?" she asked

"I don't follow it, if that's what you're asking."

"Do you like chili dogs?"

"I wouldn't be an American if I didn't."

Jane turned to read the time on her bedside clock.

"Well, the devil should be halfway across the Sound on her way to Hades by now. We'd be safe to catch the next ferry."

THEY PARKED AT THE TERMINAL—instead of driving onto the car deck this time—and boarded the ferry on foot.

It was a cold and windy day, but the sky was clear blue and the sun was glinting off the water. They grabbed hot cocoas from the cafeteria and went up and stood out of the wind, watching the passing scenery. There must have been a sailing derby of some sort, and boats crisscrossed in the distance, their colorful sails standing out bright against the white backdrop of Mount Rainier. They watched as a wedding party came out on deck and posed for pictures, the bridesmaids' hair flailing about wildly in the wind and getting tangled in their elaborate dresses, until they gave up and disappeared as a group into the ferry.

Jane stood on her tiptoes and kissed Caleb.

"What was that for?" he asked, smiling.

"Just because."

He pulled her to him and kissed her harder. He tasted like chocolate. Jane looked into his smiling eyes.

"And what was that for?" she asked.

"Just because.

"Just because what?"

"Just because I love you."

Jane smiled.

"I knew it."

The walk to the stadium from the ferry terminal took all of twenty minutes, and it brought them through Pioneer Square and right past the spot where Jane had found Caleb that day. She pointed it out to him, but he just nodded and smiled. They were following groups of fans dressed in home team blue, and Jane stopped to buy them each a Mariners hat from a street vendor so they could show their support, too.

"You've got a big head," Caleb said, as he sized her hat.

She snatched the hat away from him.

"I do not."

"Yes, you do. It's a beautiful head, but it's big."

She punched him playfully on the shoulder.

They bought bleacher seats from the ticket window and followed the other fans through security and into the stadium. They stopped on the way to their seats and loaded their arms with Red Vines, sodas, and chilidogs. When Jane added a giant bag of popped corn, Caleb laughed and shook his head.

"I still don't get why you're not three hundred pounds."

"Hey, now," she said, "you eat as much as I do."

"Yeah, maybe, but I'm out sweating my ass off in your backyard all day."

"Well, it's hard work for me, too. You have no idea how many calories I burn just sitting inside all hot and bothered and worked up over watching you."

They found their seats just in time to see first pitch. The open-roofed stadium was protected from the wind, but billowy clouds had blown in and were passing overhead, dappling the green field below with waves of shadow. From their high seats the players looked like toys, and they had to watch on the giant screens to see the batters swing at pitches.

"Seems kind of funny to come all the way down here just to watch the game on an enormous TV," Caleb said.

Jane held up her half-eaten chilidog.

"You come for these, silly. And the fresh air."

"And here I thought you were a fan."

Jane laughed.

"A fan of stadium food."

"Well, maybe we should have gotten you a giant chilidog hat instead. Assuming they had one that would fit."

"Smart ass," Jane said.

Caleb reached over and wiped sauce off her chin with his thumb. Then he leaned in and kissed her.

The arriving clouds soon blocked out the sun completely, and the stadium lights cast the green field in bright relief against the dark sky. The smells and sounds of baseball wafted softly by: popped corn and spilt beer; the occasional crack of a bat, followed by the cheering crowd. It was cold, but it did not rain. Jane pulled her jacket tight and leaned into Caleb. He put his arm around her. She couldn't remember a time when she had been happier. She finally felt comfortable in her own skin.

They cut out in the bottom of the eighth inning, deciding to beat the crowd to the gates.

"We're going to regret it if they make a comeback."

"From nine to one," Caleb said. "I don't think so."

With everyone in the stadium, the streets were empty and quiet as they walked back toward the ferry terminal on the pier.

"Were you ever into sports?" Jane asked.

"When I was young I spent quite a bit of time running from the local police, if you count that as a sport."

"Oh, yeah. Let's see if you can beat me to that corner."

With no further warning, Jane took off running.

She heard Caleb call after her:

"Hey, that's not fair!"

She was almost to the corner when he overtook her and caught her in his arms and spun her around. Her Mariners hat went flinging off her head. He bent her back like a ballroom dancer might and kissed her deeply. She felt her legs trembling from the exercise, she felt her heart racing from his touch. She couldn't wait to get him home and get him naked. When he stood her up, a young man handed her back her hat. Before she could thank him, he recognized Caleb, and said:

"Hey, Caleb. I thought that was you."

He was about Caleb's age, and Jane noticed his group of friends standing not far behind him—two other guys and one girl, all holding cased instruments in their hands. One guitar sat unattended on the sidewalk, and Jane assumed it belonged to the man speaking to them.

"Hey, Mitch," Caleb said, shaking his hand. "It seems like it's been forever. What's up?"

"You tell me, bro. Last anyone heard you were crashing at Spencer's place when he got the boot. Then you fell off the grid. Michelle said you were in Portland. John said you'd finally headed south for Austin with Jeremy."

"Jeremy's in Austin?"

"Shit, yeah, man. Says he's been getting tons of gigs, too. Making some good connections. I'll forward you his emails, if you want. You still got the same address?"

Caleb nodded.

"I haven't checked them in a long time, but I'll be sure to look for yours."

"Cool," he said, turning to smile at Jane. "So, who's this?"

"Oh, shit," Caleb said. "I got so excited I lost my manners. This is Jane."

Jane reached out her hand and shook his.

"Nice to meet you," she said.

"Equally," he replied.

Then he looked at Caleb and smiled slyly.

"No wonder you've been MIA. She's fucking gorgeous."

Caleb squeezed Jane's hand and smiled over at her.

"I know. And she's wicked smart, too."

One of his band mates standing behind him cleared his throat loudly. Mitch turned to look at them, then turned back.

"Fuck. I'd love to catch up more, bro, but we gotta run. We're playing at the Central tonight."

"Paid gig?" Caleb asked.

"Half the door. Hey, you wanna join us for a few songs? It's a long set."

"Nah. I don't have my guitar with me."

"I'll be happy to lend you one of ours."

Caleb glanced quickly at Jane, and then shook his head. Jane felt suddenly out of place among them, as if she were the outcast keeping Caleb from being with his friends.

"I don't mind," she said.

Caleb smiled at her.

"Thanks, babe. But I'm a little rusty right now anyway. I'll catch up with you guys some other time, Mitch."

"Suit yourself, brother," he said, jogging back to his friends and picking up his guitar. "I'll forward you those emails."

Caleb smiled reassuringly at Jane, squeezed her hand in his, and pulled her on toward the ferry. He looked back over his shoulder once at his departing friends.

"You could have gone," she said.

"I know it. I didn't want to."

"It seems like you did."

"Nah. I just miss music is all."

"Seems like maybe that's not all you miss."

"What's that supposed to mean?"

"It doesn't mean anything."

Caleb let go of her hand and stopped, turning to face her.

"You must have meant something by it. You said it."

She dropped her head and took a deep breath.

"I don't know why I said it. It just seems sometimes like maybe I roped you into this whole thing. With me, I mean. You sure didn't have much of a choice, did you? And, I don't know, maybe my mother was right—maybe I'm just too old for you."

"That's stupid, Jane."

"Is it? Your friends are heading out to play bars, to have a good time, and I'm dragging you home to boring old family-town Bainbridge Island. You even said yourself you missed the music. And here I've got you captive like some kind of kept man. Maybe I am taking advantage of you. I don't know. I just think we need to face the facts, Caleb. I'd rather do it now than have to do it later. Wouldn't you?"

When she had finished speaking, he stared at her. His eyes were filled with pain again, and maybe just a hint of rage, and she wished he'd just say something. Anything. Tell her that she was wrong. Tell her she was right. Or yell back at her even. A wind rose up and whipped at her hair, and she reached her hand up to hold her hat on her head. She felt like crying. A sandwich wrapper scuttled by; a beer can rolled after it.

"Aren't you going to say something?" she finally asked. "Anything at all?"

"You think you're taking advantage of me?"

"I don't know," she said. "Am I?"

He reached out and grabbed her shoulders. She thought for a moment he was going to shake her, but he pulled her close and crushed his mouth against hers. There was a new sense of possession in his kiss, as if he were claiming her right there on the windy sidewalk. And there was a kind of danger in the way he gripped her arms, something she hadn't felt from him before. It turned her on. When he pulled his mouth away, he looked directly into her eyes, and said:

"I'm going to take you home and rip these clothes off and fuck the self-doubt out of you. That's what I'm going to do."

She didn't say a word—she only nodded.

SHE WAS SO EXCITED that she left the car in the driveway rather than wait for the garage door to open, and the moment they walked into the house he made good on his promise.

He tossed her hat aside and spun her around in the hallway so that she was facing away from him. He peeled her jacket off. Then he pulled her shirt over her head, cupped her breasts, and kissed her neck. His hands were cold against her skin, and it made her tremble with anticipation. He continued kissing her as he walked her down the hall to the kitchen.

He stopped her at the table and reached out and swept the dishes aside. She reached behind to feel him, but he took her hands one at a time and planted them palm down on the table in front of her. Then he unzipped her pants and pulled them down, along with her panties. She kicked them off. He pressed a hand onto her naked back and forced her down to the table. She felt the cold tabletop against her cheek, against her breasts. His hands left her back for a moment and she heard his belt unbuckle, then his zipper. She heard his pants fall heavily to the floor. She felt exhilarated and aroused. She tried to turn her head to look at him, but before she could, he grabbed her hips and forced himself inside her. She pressed her cheek back to the table and moaned. He was so hard it almost hurt, and he held nothing back as he rammed himself deep, again and again.

She felt his hands grip her hips; she heard him panting. His thighs were slapping against her ass, and he began to moan, and the table began to slide an inch with every thrust. It felt good to be possessed—to be taken by a man. She arched her back and pressed herself into him, begging for more.

She called out his name—

"Caleb! Oh, God, Caleb. Fuck me, Caleb! Make me yours."

He thrust harder, faster, deeper.

She was teetering between ecstasy and pain. The silverware rattled on the tabletop. A cup fell. A plate crashed to the floor and shattered. She raised her eyes and saw his reflection in the glass of a framed picture—flexed quads, bare ass, strong arms, veiny hands gripping her naked thighs. He was thrusting and sweating and moaning like a wild man. His head was bent, and his hair hung down, covering his face. Her legs began to shake, her fingers curled into fists. She felt an orgasm coming and she didn't even try to stop it. She knew he felt it too, because he drove himself to join her with a violent burst of energy that made him scream out her name—

"Jane! Jane! Jane!"

When he came to rest inside her, she heard him whimper, almost as if he were crying. She lay still, bent over the table in a state of absolute relaxation that she guessed would beat any drug-induced high. He leaned down and kissed her neck. Then he whispered in her ear.

"You're amazing."

Her lips curled back into a smile.

"And you're an animal."

She opened her eyes and noticed that the table had moved several feet before coming to rest against the wall. The kitchen window was bare to the world, and had anyone walked by they would have seen right in. The thought made her feel naughty.

He pulled free, gently stood her up, and turned her around to face him. Then he kissed her tenderly.

"You okay?"

She nodded.

"Never felt better, actually."

"Good. Why don't you go take a shower and I'll clean up here. Be careful, there's broken glass."

She kissed him one more time. Then she left her clothes where they lay and tiptoed toward the hall. She stopped to look back at him, standing sweat-drenched and naked in the middle of her kitchen, catching his breath after rocking her world.

"You really don't think I'm too old for you?"

He shook his head.

"I don't ever think about it at all. And neither should you. You're perfect, Jane. And I love you."

She smiled.

"You had better put something on that hot body of yours before you give the neighbors a show. The goat won't get you out of this one if the cops show up again."

Chapter 17

BACK TO REALITY—that was her Wi-Fi password.

When Caleb asked for it the next day so he could check his messages, she paused for just a moment before giving it to him. She hated herself for being afraid, but she was

Fortunately, she had little time to worry.

The following weeks were busy ones for Jane. Now that she was back on her company's radar, they were sending her appointments back to back. There were a lot of new changes in the health insurance world, and she spent more time explaining them to people than she did actually selling them anything. But she enjoyed the distraction nonetheless, and what little money that she did earn would be a welcome change from the months of withdrawals she'd been making from her savings.

Every morning when she woke, the grass that Caleb had seeded was a little thicker than the day before. It started as just a hint of light green clinging to the dark soil, and quickly grew into sparse but unmistakable blades of Kentucky Bluegrass, chosen for her by Caleb because he said it reminded him of the color he saw when he heard her voice. She picked out a stone fountain from the hardware store, and Caleb installed it in the center of his island flowerbed, but they decided to wait until he finished the yard before officially testing it.

On a Saturday after her meeting, Jane came home to find her bicycle gone and Caleb gone with it. She assumed he was over at Mrs. Hawthorne's place. She walked the yard alone, inspecting his progress, her only company the silly old goat, idly chewing its hay and staring at her from its fenced enclosure.

She reached over the wire and scratched its head.

"Looks like he's almost finished, doesn't it, Bill?"

"Bbhhhaaa!"

She hadn't expected an answer.

"You think he'll leave?" she asked.

The goat cocked its narrow head and looked at her, its ears moving slightly, as if it were trying to understand her question.

"You think he's still going to Austin?"

It hung its head and chewed a mouthful of hay.

"I do believe you'd miss him as much as I would."

That night as she and Caleb lay in bed, Jane couldn't sleep. She tossed and turned and flipped her pillow to the cool side a dozen times before he rolled over in the dark beside her and asked her what was wrong.

"Nothing," she said. "Sorry if I'm keeping you up."

"It's no problem," he said. "What's on your mind, babe?"

"Nothing."

"You sure?"

"No."

"Then what is it?"

"I don't know," she said. "I guess I've been thinking about my brother for one thing."

"That's understandable," he said. "Think he's still in jail?"

"This was something like his fourth time driving drunk, so I doubt they're letting him off with a warning."

She heard Caleb sigh.

"I'm really sorry, Jane."

"There's nothing anyone can do, I guess."

"Maybe you should go visit him."

"In jail?"

"If he's still there."

"You think I should?"

"What matters is what you think, babe."

"Maybe I will then."

"You should if you want to."

They fell silent and several minutes passed.

Jane stared at the shadows cast by her alarm clock on the ceiling—they made interesting shapes if she wanted them to. She could hear Caleb's breathing beside her.

"Caleb?"

"Yeah?"

"You asleep?"

"Yes, babe," he joked, "I'm talking with you in my sleep."

"Does that mean I can say or do anything and you won't remember it tomorrow?"

He laughed.

"I can't imagine forgetting anything you said or did to me.

Ever. Is there something you need to talk about?"

"Maybe."

"What's bothering you, babe?"

"Do you still think about Austin?"

There was a long pause. She heard him sigh.

"Yeah. I think about it."

"Are you still planning to go?"

"Would you come with me if I did?"

"I can't move to Texas."

"Why not?"

"Because everything's here."

He pulled her to him, resting her in the nook of his arm. She put her ear to his chest and listened to his beating heart. He caressed her hair, and then kissed the top of her head.

"Let's talk about it later, okay?"

"Okay."

Jane felt as though they had walked up on the edge of a cliff together, and it was a relief to back away from it for now. It felt good to rest in his arms and just breathe. But no matter how she tried, she couldn't completely shut out thoughts of his someday leaving. She inhaled deeply and committed his smell to memory. Then she kissed his chest and closed her eyes.

"I love you," she heard him say.

She meant to say it back, but she fell asleep.

THE HORN BLEW, and the ferry pulled away from the dock. Their spring weather seemed to have fled, and it was once again raining. The ferry arrived at the Seattle pier. She drove to the courthouse, which was attached by a sky bridge to the jail, and parked in the garage. The elevator brought her to a check-in desk, and she gave a female deputy her brother's name.

"Are you related?" the deputy asked.

"I'm his sister."

She typed the name into her terminal.

"System takes a while."

While she waited, the deputy reached for a clear, plastic gallon of some horrendous-looking brown liquid and screwed off the top and drank. Strange spices and pulpy lemon wedges swirled in the upturned jug. Jane eyed her curiously.

"I'm doing a cyan pepper cleanse,' she said, screwing the cap back on. "It's good for your skin."

Jane just nodded.

The deputy looked back to her screen.

"Yep. He's here, all right."

She had Jane sign several forms and made a copy of her driver's license. She issued her a locker key and had her stow her cell phone and her purse. Then she directed her to stand on a line on the floor and look into a web camera while she took her picture. The printer behind the desk whirred and spit out a nametag sticker. She handed it to her.

"Put that on, and head through the door on the left."

The door opened to a sterile hall—gray tiled floors, gray painted walls. The hall was lit with runs of florescent lights that flickered dully overhead. There were no signs, and there was no one there to give her any instructions, so she walked the long sky bridge toward the door at its other end. The door was metal and painted orange, and there was no handle. She heard a series of clicks, and the door unlocked and opened. Another deputy stood on its other side. He walked her to a small sitting area comprised of yellow, plastic chairs and nothing else.

"Have a seat and wait here," he said. "We'll call your name and room number when it's ready. The rooms are just down the hall there, numbers overhead. You get twenty minutes."

Then he walked off and left her alone.

She sat down and folded her hands in her lap. It was eerily quiet and stark. With no phone and no purse to distract her, she had nothing to do but sit and stare at the floor and think. Think and remember.

Her brother was just over a year younger than she was, and she remembered always having had to retie his shoelaces for him when they had walked to the bus stop together. She could still see him, slogging along behind her with his laces whipping around his feet. "You're going to trip and hurt yourself," she had always said.

Her brother had never shown any motivation for anything except chasing excitement. Always the class clown, always the guy showing off and getting hurt. She remembered him setting up a launch ramp with plywood and coffee cans at the bottom of their hill and inviting the neighborhood kids to watch him ride his skateboard down and jump it. She remembered the ambulance and the beating she had gotten from her father because she hadn't stopped him. She remembered when they were older and her brother had grown big enough to fight their father back. The police had come several times. Her father had stopped hitting them then, but the verbal abuse had continued. She hated herself for feeling it, but she had been relieved when he died of a massive heart attack—alcohol-related, no doubt. Now her brother was walking down the same tragic path. She couldn't count how many times he'd been locked up for fights, or for driving under the influence, or for smacking around one of his girlfriends while he was drunk. Jane just hoped that he would hit bottom before it was too late.

"McKinney, room seven."

Jane looked up to see who had spoken.

She noticed an intercom speaker mounted on the wall, and she realized that the voice had come from there.

She stood and walked down the hall, past the windowless visiting-room doors. She stopped at number seven. She took a deep breath, grabbed the iron handle, pulled the heavy door open, and stepped into the small room.

Her brother sat on the other side of a scratched and faded Plexiglas partition, wearing jailhouse orange and a smirk. He looked disappointed to see her. She sat on the metal stool, picked up the heavy black receiver from its wall-cradle, and placed it to her ear. Her brother did the same.

"Hi there, Chili Pepper."

He called her by her childhood nickname.

"Hi, Jon."

"I go by Jonathan now," he announced. "It sounds more sophisticated in court."

Jane nodded.

"You don't look happy to see me," she said.

"It's not that. I just hate you seeing me in here like this, is all. I was sure when they called me out that it was Mom again."

"Has she been to see you a lot?"

"You know how she is."

"Yes," Jane said, "I know all too well how she is."

He shrugged, as if it couldn't be helped.

"Hey, how's the weather out there?"

"You don't have a window?" she asked.

"Not in this pod they've got me in now."

"Well, it's raining again."

"Shit!" he said, as if the weather outside somehow affected him. "You know what they say about the weather around here, though. If you don't like it, wait five minutes and it'll change."

Jane hadn't come to talk about the weather, so she sat looking at him and waiting for something real. There was an uncomfortable silence between them while her brother picked at a burn mark in the Plexiglas with his fingernail. His hair was long and greasy, and he needed to shave. He looked pale.

"What are they saying?" Jane finally asked.

"About my charge? They're trying to stick me with a felony DUI. Can you believe that, Sis? They say it was reckless endangerment too. I guess Mom probably told you I rear-ended a police car. But he was sitting at a green light. I swear it.

And he didn't have no lights on either. I'm gonna fight it all the way this time. No way am I going up for a felony."

Jane heard his denial and sighed.

"Well, what were you doing in Seattle, anyway?"

"Prince was playing at the Showbox."

"Prince? You don't even like Prince."

"No, but this chick I was diggin' does. Worst part is we got in a fight, and the bitch left with someone else. After I'd bought her ticket too. Can you believe that?"

"I can believe it. How drunk were you?"

"They said I blew a two-three at the station. But that's bullshit. You know they don't calibrate those machines. We can subpoena their records and prove that too. Plus, I had a rising blood alcohol. That's what my public defender says."

"So you're not to blame here at all?"

"What's that supposed to mean?"

"Nothing."

He scowled at her through the glass.

"Whose side are you on, anyway?"

"I only see one side, Jon."

"Jonathan."

"Whatever. Can we just change the subject?"

They sat looking at each other for a while.

"Are you doing okay?" he finally asked.

Jane was taken aback by his question. She wasn't used to him caring about anyone but himself.

"I mean, how are you holding up with everything?"

"With everything?" Jane asked.

"Well, with Melody, and the funeral, is what I mean."

Jane inhaled a deep breath and squeezed her eyes shut in an effort not to cry. The last time she had seen her brother was at Melody's funeral, and somehow his asking about her brought everything back in vivid color.

"I'm sorry. I know it's probably really hard to talk about."

She opened her eyes.

"It is hard. But I appreciate you asking. Things are getting better. On good days I forget for a few minutes. On bad days I can't think of anything else. I miss her a lot. But then I've been missing her for a long time."

He exhaled into the phone, a look of genuine sadness in his eyes. For a minute she saw her real brother in there.

"She was a real special girl, Jane. She really was."

Jane's attempt to hold it together failed. She began to cry.

"It's the same thing, Jon."

"What is?"

"You. Her. This."

He looked away and shook his head.

"You're not making any sense."

"I just hate all this drinking and these drugs, Jon. I hate it with all my soul. I wish you'd get better. I really do. I wish you'd just admit that you need help. Just let them help you, for God's sake, Jon. For my sake. For your own. It already killed Dad, it ruined Mom, and now Melody's gone too. Jon, please make this your bottom. It can be if you want it to be. Please. I know they've got programs they offer through the courts."

He was looking down now, his head bobbing slightly, and she thought he might be crying too, but she couldn't tell for sure. She waited for him to respond.

There was a series of clicks on the receiver, and a robotic voice came on and said: "One minute remaining."

He looked up and his eyes were desperate.

She forced an encouraging smile, hoping that something she had said had finally gotten through.

"Mom said you might help with my bail."

"Come on, Jon. I told you the last time that I wouldn't do it again. And I meant it."

He leaned closer to the glass, a pleading look on his face.

"I know I never paid you back, Sis. But I will this time, I promise. This time is different."

She shook her head.

"It isn't about the money, Jon. It's about you getting help. I might consider paying for treatment if they'll let you go."

He pulled the receiver away from his ear and held it up as if he intended to smash it against the wall. But then he thought better of it and hung it on its cradle. He glared at her through the glass, and mouthed the words:

"Fuck you."

Jane hung her phone up too.

But when she stood to leave, he snatched his phone off the wall again and slapped his hand to the Plexiglas, motioning desperately for her to pick up her phone.

She stayed standing and lifted it to her ear again.

"Could you at least put a little money in my commissary account? Please. They'll take it up front. Just give my name."

Jane hesitated and then nodded that she would.

His eyes welled up, and she thought that he said he loved her, but the phone had gone dead, and nothing came through.

A guard opened a door on his side of the glass and called for him to come out. Her brother looked once more at Jane and then disappeared through the door. The door slammed shut, and she was alone in the tiny room. She stood for a moment, looking through the glass at the vacated stool where he had sat. She hardly recognized him anymore. But then she wondered if she had really ever known him at all.

WHEN SHE PULLED INTO HER GARAGE, she was happy to see that her bicycle was there. She needed to be with Caleb now more than ever. She went inside and set down her purse and kicked off her shoes and walked into the kitchen. She found a candlelit table set for two, a vase of fresh flowers, champagne flutes, and a chilled bottle of sparkling cider. She heard quiet music turn on in the living room, and then Caleb stepped into the kitchen. He was wearing clean clothes, and his hair was styled with gel. He smiled at her and said:

"Welcome home."

She stepped to him and wrapped her arms around him. He kissed the top of her head, as he liked to do. When she finally pulled away from his chest, she looked up at him and smiled, trying to communicate silently just how much he meant to her. A shy smile rose on his face and he looked down, away from her eyes. She rose on her tiptoes and kissed him.

"Are you hungry?" he asked.

"Starving."

He stepped to the table and pulled out her chair.

"A girl could really get used to being spoiled like this."

"That's what I'm hoping," he said.

He opened the oven and pulled out a pan of lasagna. The smell of warm cheese and tomato sauce filled the small kitchen. He took her plate from the table and cut her a slice. He added a piece of garlic bread and a Caesar salad that he'd made. When they were both seated at the table, ready to eat, he poured their glasses with cider and proposed a toast.

"To love," he said, "because love is always enough."

They looked into one another's eyes until they had clinked glasses and had taken a sip of cider. Then Jane looked around again at the candles and the flowers.

"So what's all this for anyway?

He grinned at her and shrugged.

"It's just for you."

"We're celebrating me?"

"I can think of nothing more worthy of celebrating."

"That's sweet," she said.

"Plus, we can officially celebrate your yard being finished."

"You're finished?"

"Well, I planted the flowerbed for you today. The grass is

coming in fast. And the fountain's all ready to go. There isn't really anything much left, unless you still want me to dig that swimming pool."

Jane stared at her plate.

"So what now?"

"What do you mean what now?"

"Now that you're done."

"Well, I think we should have your friends over and show off your new yard. Don't you? Maybe the ladies you see every Saturday. I was thinking we'd do a barbeque."

"Oh, were you?"

"Unless you're ashamed of me or something."

"Hey, now. I could never be ashamed of you. You know better than even to suggest that. But a barbeque?"

"Well, why not? I grill a mean steak."

"You do?"

"Corn on the cob too."

It was impossible to not give in to his charm.

"I know you make pretty amazing lasagna, but who knew you were a man of so many talents?"

She thought she saw him blush, but it was hard to tell in the candlelight. He leaned closer and spoke in a whisper:

"I've got some other talents I might show you later."

Jane playfully brushed her lips against his.

"Is that so?" she asked.

He pulled her to him and kissed her. Then he said:

"I've got moves I've never used."

Chapter 18

THEY GATHERED IN JANE'S BACKYARD at noon on the following Sunday. It was a perfect day for it: blue skies and no wind. The flowers that Caleb had planted were bright against the backdrop of blue-green grass, and robins flitted between surrounding trees, calling to one another, and alighting on the new lawn to hunt worms. The creek rambled by, the hypnotic sound of water running softly over smooth stones.

Jane stood on the concrete patio and drank it all in—

Caleb turning steaks on the barbeque, surrounded by the other men. Her friends clustered in small groups, visiting. Some down on the bridge tossing pebbles into the creek. Others with their children at the goat pen, taking turns luring it to be petted with handfuls of grain. Grace sat in a patio chair, shaded by the umbrella and sipping iced tea. Her husband Bob sat next to her, wearing his pilot's uniform.

One of her lady friends from her Saturday meeting sidled up to Jane, eating vegetables and dip from a small paper plate.

"It really is a lovely backyard, Jane," she said.

"Oh, thanks, Rachel. It was all Caleb's doing."

"I'll bet it was," she said. "I'm just surprised you let him find any time to get the work done."

She bit into a carrot and winked.

Jane laughed.

"He is really cute, isn't he?"

"Cute? He's fucking gorgeous. What I want to know is, does he have a brother? Or even his father might do."

"I'm afraid you'll have to find your own," Jane said.

She excused herself and went to see how Grace was doing.

"You look a little flushed over here, Grace," she said, joining her and her husband at the table. "What are you really drinking in that iced tea glass?"

Grace smiled conspiratorially and sipped her tea.

"Are you enjoying yourself, Bob?" Jane asked.

Before he could answer, Grace said:

"He'd probably be enjoying himself more if there was rum in the tea. Wouldn't you, Bob?"

Bob ignored his wife's comment and answered Jane:

"It's a fine party, Jane. I love what you've done back here. And Caleb seems like a stand up fella, too. I had no idea he was from Spokane. Did you know I went to Gonzaga University?"

"I didn't know that," Jane said. "A Spokane boy, huh? I never would have guessed you were Catholic either."

"Well," he laughed, "I'm a recovering Catholic."

"Glad you're recovering from something," Grace said.

Bob went on, ignoring her again:

"Good people over there. That's a plus for Caleb. Anyway, I hate to dash, but I've got to be on a two-thirty to Pittsburgh."

He stood and kissed his wife on the head, smiled at Jane, and walked off.

"Don't text and fly," Grace called after him. Then she cocked an eyebrow at Jane and said: "You'd be surprised what they do up there when they should be flying."

"Things okay between you two?" Jane asked.

Grace rolled her eyes and sighed.

"This is your day to celebrate. Let's not spoil it with the boring details of an old married couple's petty grievances."

"Well, it was nice of him to come by."

"Yes, it was. Now tell me how things are going with Caleb. And give me details. You know all the ladies are talking about him. They think you're the luckiest woman on the island. Of course, I happen to think it's him who's the lucky one."

"That's very sweet of you to say. But I do feel lucky. And he's . . . well, he's just about as wonderful a man as I could have wished for. Last night he played his guitar and sang to me while I took a bubble bath. Does it get better than that?"

"Come on," Grace said, "that's not all he did."

Jane dropped her jaw, mocking exaggerated shock.

"You dirty, dirty woman, you."

"Just tell me—is he as good in bed as he is with that grill?"

Jane couldn't contain her grin.

"Even better."

Caleb walked over to the table, carrying a plate of steaming meat in one hand and a plate of grilled corn in the other. He set them on the table and leaned down and kissed Jane. Then he smiled at Grace and winked, as if he'd guessed what they had been talking about, and said:

"I hope you both like meat."

Grace blushed and fanned her face with her hand.

"Oh, aren't you just a tease. I like him, Jane. I think you should keep this one around for a while."

"What do you mean: this one?" Caleb asked, pouting.

"She's only kidding," Jane replied. "There haven't been

any other ones. I was a virgin before I met you."

Grace slapped Jane's knee playfully.

"You mean you're not a virgin? I knew you two were living in sin. Caleb, I guess you're going to have to make an honest woman out of her now."

"Oh, God, Grace," Jane said. "It's 2013, already."

Jane was happy when their playful banter was broken up by her guests flocking to the table in search of the food.

Caleb was a perfect host, making sure everyone had cutlery and napkins and something cool to drink. They'd brought out all the chairs from the kitchen to add to the patio furniture, and a few camping chairs from the garage. Those who couldn't find a seat ate their lunch sitting in the grass or with their feet swinging off the bridge. The kids had hardly eaten when they were up again and organizing a game of tag.

"This is really great, Jane," one of the husbands said.

"Thanks, Earl. I'm glad you and Judith could make it."

"Yeah, the last time we were here was . . ."

He smiled uncomfortably and clucked his tongue, as if to chastise himself for having misspoken.

"It's okay," Jane said. "It was Melody's thirteenth birthday party, if I recall. That was one of the good times, and I like to remember as many of those as I can."

Everyone nodded, and a kind of hush fell over the table.

"So," Earl said, turning to Caleb and changing the subject. "Jane tells me you might be willing to rent out your goat."

"You mean, old Bill Clinton?"

"Is that really his name?" another man at the table asked. "I thought the Democrats' symbol was a donkey."

"Maybe it ought to be a goat," someone said, "considering

all they do is eat and shit."

"Hey, now," Jane jumped in, "No politics and no religion."

"Well, what are we supposed to talk about?"

"The only thing any of us is qualified to talk about," Jane answered. "Ourselves."

Caleb set his corn down, wiped his mouth with a napkin, and glanced over at the goat.

"I'm not sure about renting him," he said, "but I might sell him to a good home. He did a lot of work around here and was a big help, but we don't have enough pasture for him."

"Why, hell," Earl said, "we've got two solid acres just over the bridge, west of Poulsbo. He'd be in goat heaven over there. And we welcome Democrats and Republicans just the same. As long as he isn't Mormon."

Everyone at the table laughed, except one woman.

"Hey, what do you have against Mormons?" she asked.

"Nothing," he said. "I was just playing with Jane is all."

"I'd sell him to you for three hundred bucks," Caleb said.

"Three hundred? Does he eat grass and shit gold?"

"You know," Caleb said, "I never thought to check."

"I'll give you one fifty."

"One fifty? I could scoop his shit and sell it for fertilizer and make that off him in a year. Not to mention he'll clear just about anything you set him on to eat for you. How about two-fifty, and you promise to treat him right?"

"Two hundred even, and we'll treat him like a member of the family."

"Sold," Caleb said, shaking his hand.

Earl turned to Jane.

"You've got yourself a real shrewd negotiator here, Jane. I think he might give my guys at the shop a run for their money."

"He's a musician, Earl. Not a tractor salesman."

Earl turned to Caleb.

"Is that right? I should have brought along my banjo and we could've had a go at entertaining everyone after we eat."

"You play a five or a four string?" Caleb asked.

"Five string, of course. You play?"

"I can pick a little."

"Jane, I really like this guy."

Jane smiled.

"Yeah, me too."

After everyone had eaten their fill, they gathered around the fountain. It had been Caleb's idea to dedicate it, and at his request Jane had asked everyone to bring a bottle of water filled from the tap in their house. He said it would bring good luck to have all her friends' energies mixed together. She thought it was a little quirky, but then that was one of the things she loved about him. Those who had remembered retrieved their bottles and poured their water, one at a time, into the fountain until it was full. Then everyone circled around it to watch. Jane stood near the house with her hand on the breaker switch.

"Ready when you are," Caleb called.

Jane threw the switch and nothing happened. She watched as Caleb stood there with a puzzled look on his face. Then a small sputter erupted from the fountain's spout, followed by a stream of water. Everyone clapped.

Shortly after dedicating the fountain, Grace came up to her and said she wasn't feeling well and needed some rest.

"You want me to drive you home?" Jane asked.

"No. You enjoy your guests. Liz is going to take me."

"Okay. Just don't take any of those Ambien. That one you gave me made me down an entire bag of Doritos."

Grace laughed.

"I guess I forgot to warn you about that."

As the afternoon wore on, the guests began to depart by ones and twos, each of them going out of their way to lavish thanks on Jane and Caleb for such a fun day. Several of them even remarked on how great it was to have something to do where there wasn't drinking involved.

Despite Bill Clinton's protestations, Caleb put his collar back on and led him to the street and helped Earl load him in the bed of his pickup truck. Jane stood in the driveway and watched as they tied him to cleats on either side so he couldn't jump out on the short trip across the bridge.

"Try not to keep him on a leash," Caleb said. "He can get a little loud about it."

Jane watched as Caleb scratched the goat's head one last time, even rising up on his tiptoes and leaning to quickly kiss it on the cheek. She knew he'd grown to love that silly goat.

Earl helped his wife up into the cab, then paid Caleb his money and shook his hand again. As the truck pulled away, Caleb stood in the street watching after it, and Jane stood in the driveway watching him. She loved how sensitive he could be.

"You're going to miss that goat, aren't you?" she asked, as he walked back up the drive and joined her.

"Are you kidding me?" he asked back. "That damn thing was gonna eat me out of all my pay."

Jane laughed.

"Well, at least you turned a profit on him."

They walked arm in arm toward the door.

"I might miss him just a little," Caleb said.

Jane gave him a squeeze.

"I knew it."

After they had seen the last of the guests off, and cleaned up most of the mess, Jane and Caleb sat alone in the backyard and listened to the fountain.

"It sure is beautiful," Jane said.

"Yeah, you picked out a good one."

"No, I meant the yard. You did a great job, Caleb. Better than I could have expected."

"If you give me a list of what you want in the garden, I'll pick up some seeds tomorrow at the hardware store."

"Is that going to cost me extra?"

Caleb looked over at her and smiled.

"I can think of a few ways you might work it off."

"You're a naughty man," she said. "And I like it. You were quite the hit with all the ladies today. Their husbands and boyfriends too, actually. It seems everyone loves you."

"I must have won them over with my cooking."

"Yeah," she said, "I'm sure that was it."

They were quiet for a long time, just sitting side by side and looking at the yard. Jane reached over and took his hand in hers. The sky eventually faded to blue, the air took on a chill.

"Should we go inside and get warm?"

"I like the sound of that," Caleb said.

He stood and took her by the hand and led her toward the house. He stopped short of the sliding door, bent and scooped her up in his arms and lifted her off the ground.

"Hey, what are you doing?" she asked.

"I'm carrying you inside."

"Did we have a wedding here today that I missed?"

"No," he laughed. "I'm just making sure you don't trip."

He carried her to her room and laid her gently on her bed. Then he lay down beside her and caressed her cheek. Evening had come, and blue light was spilling through the window. He looked at her for a long time, his eyes cast in shadow, and she wondered what it was he saw when he stared at her like that. He might have told her, but there were no words for it, not in this language or any other.

He kissed her—so tenderly that she felt like a China doll beneath his gentle lips, as though he were afraid he might break her. He carefully unbuttoned her blouse. She arched her back so he could unclasp her bra. He unzipped her pants and peeled them off her, his fingers grazing her inner thighs and sending a shudder up her spine.

"Are you cold?"

She shook her head.

He stood and undressed himself slowly, folding his clothes and setting them aside. When he had finished he was standing before her completely naked, and his normally tan skin shone white as alabaster in the dim blue evening light—he looked to Jane like a newborn god. He crawled on top of her, never once taking his eyes from hers. She opened for him like a flower. He was gentle, so gentle that she hardly knew when he had entered her, and he moved inside her like a man conjuring love from secrets hidden in the rhythms of his heart. And as he moved, she moved, and she watched his face in the blue shadows and he merged into an amalgamation of every lover that had ever come to visit her in dreams. She loved him more than she had thought it possible to love.

He brought his face closer to hers, and his hair fell forward and tickled her cheeks. Their lips were close but not touching. She could feel his breath, and she could smell his skin.

She whispered to him:

"I love you, Caleb."

Her words drew his lips to hers and they kissed.

She moaned and arched her back, pressing her breasts into his naked chest. He moved faster. She felt his heart beating in time with hers—two life forces conjoined. She had never felt so vulnerable and yet so safe. It was intoxicating. She let go a moan into his mouth and felt herself tighten against him—a spasm of pleasure so great it erased every thought from her mind. He let himself go with her, his lips never breaking away from hers, and in that moment she knew they were one.

When he finally fell beside her, he brought her head to his chest and wrapped his arm around her. His hand tickled her shoulder, and she thought he might be strumming a melody there the way his fingers moved.

"You know something, baby," he said, turning his head to look at her, even though it was now almost fully dark. "When I hear you say you love me, it almost makes me cry."

"Why?" she asked.

"Because it plays in my head in such beautiful colors. Like a rainbow in heaven or something."

Jane smiled and said:

"I love you. I love you. I love you."

She felt his chest drop beneath her head as he sighed.

"There aren't the right words to say it, Jane, but I need you to know just how much I love you."

"You promise?"

"With everything in me I swear it's true."

"Lucky me," she said.

"Lucky you? If I believed in luck, I'd have you beat hands down as the luckiest man that ever lived."

"Maybe we're both lucky," she said.

He smiled and kissed the top of her head.

Chapter 19

"ARE YOU SURE YOU WANT ME TAGGING ALONG?"

"Tagging along?" he asked. "Half the reason I said yes to this gig is so I could show off for you."

Jane smiled and opened her trunk for his guitar.

They stayed in the car and listened to classical music on the radio as the ferry carried them across the bay. Caleb said the colors cleared his mind. It was Friday night, and the other cars onboard were filled with mostly couples, some young, some old, but all of them done up for a night out in the city. Jane watched as six teens dressed for a dance spilled out of an SUV and escaped their chaperone chauffeur, if only for a few minutes until the ferry reached Seattle.

"Did you ever go to school dances?" Jane asked.

Caleb laughed.

"Me? No way. Did you?"

"I went to senior prom with Ralph Estes. He cut my lower lip with his braces and it wouldn't stop bleeding. Got all over my white dress, too."

"I don't like to think about you kissing another man."

"Oh, trust me, Ralph Estes was hardly a man."

"Maybe," he said. "But I still don't like it."

Jane smiled. She liked seeing him jealous.

The ferry docked. She drove them up Queen Anne Hill, past trendy neighborhood coffee shops, and boutique groceries where the meat market was still going strong, even though the butcher shop had closed for the night. As they crested the hill, Jane saw Seattle spread beneath them, the iconic Space Needle hovering above it and lit up like some space-age monument.

They drove past the Paradigm Pub, turned off the main drag, and found a spot on the street to park.

Jane popped the trunk and they got out.

"At least it isn't raining," she said.

Caleb stood over the open trunk and looked up at the sky.

"Sometimes it's busier when it rains."

"You worried there won't be enough people?"

"Nah," he said, grabbing his guitar and closing the trunk. "The Paradigm's always packed."

The doorman asked Caleb for ID, but let him pass when he held up his guitar. Jane paused to dig her license from her purse, but he didn't even bother looking at it as he waved her through. She tucked it back into her wallet with a frown.

The small restaurant bar was just making the transition from the after-work-dinner-and-drinks crowd to the serious partiers who wanted to get lost in shots and live music. Jane was bombarded with the sounds of excited chatter and clinking glasses, and the air smelled faintly of beer and marijuana. Most of the patrons appeared to be in their twenties, and as they passed an especially young girl, standing blurry-eyed and already drunk at the bar, Jane noticed a diamond stud in her nose. She couldn't help but think of her daughter, and she found herself wondering if Melody had ever been here before.

Caleb took her to a booth reserved for friends of the band

and introduced her as his girlfriend to the group of youths gathered there. They hardly looked old enough to drink. One pretty girl refused to make eye contact with Jane, pretending to recognize someone at the bar and excusing herself from the booth. Jane noticed Caleb watching her walk away.

"What's wrong with her?" she asked.

"Who? Michelle? Nothing. She's just like that sometimes. Don't worry about it. She'll warm up to you. Listen, I've gotta go set up with the guys."

"Sure, go ahead. I'll be fine."

"You want me to grab you a drink first?"

"No thanks. I'll get myself a diet Coke."

"Okay, but tell them you're with the band, and don't let them charge you."

Caleb carried his guitar away to the back room somewhere, and Jane sat in the booth and tried not to look uncomfortable as everyone talked around her. A server came by, balancing a tray of drinks. She set them in front of their owners, as if she knew their orders by heart. Then she smiled at Jane.

"Looks like you could use a pick-me-up, girl. Can I get you a Speedball, or maybe a Vod-Bom, or something?"

Jane looked around. Was she talking to her? Had she been out of the scene so long, she wondered, that cocktail servers now offered up drugs like they were the daily special?

"I'm sorry," Jane said, "but what did you ask me?"

"You look like you could use a Vod-Bomb."

Jane could hardly hear her over the noise.

"A what?"

"What can I get you to drink?"

"Do you have diet Coke?"

"Pepsi all right?"

"Even better."

It seemed like forever before she passed again with Jane's diet Pepsi. She wasn't even really thirsty, but she felt like she fit in better with a drink in her hand. Eventually, there was a lull in the talk at the table, and a young guy wearing eyeliner turned to Jane and made an attempt to include her in their conversation.

"So," he said, "Mitch told us that Caleb told him you live on Bainbridge Island."

Jane nodded.

"That's right."

"That's so adorable. My grandparents had a beach house out there when I was a kid."

"Well, I'm not on the beach or anything, but I like it."

"I remember it being pretty quiet," he said.

"It's still that way," Jane replied, raising her voice to shout above the almost deafening din. "Although I think there's over twenty thousand people living on it now."

One of the girls at the table looked confused and more than slightly drunk. She leaned forward and waved her finger at Jane, her eyes crossing and uncrossing as she spoke.

"But, like, don't you worry about the island, like, tipping with all those people on it? I mean, what happens if they all go to one end or something? I always wondered that. I wouldn't live on an island. And you shouldn't either."

The young man looked apologetically at Jane.

"She got an early start," he said.

Jane saw the band setting up onstage, and she sipped her soda and focused her attention on them. She recognized Mitch from their encounter in the street the other day, and a few of the others too, but the moment Caleb stepped into the stage lights, everyone else completely disappeared.

She'd never seen Caleb in this environment before, and it was clear that it was his natural habitat. He was tall and lean, with wide shoulders like a swimmer's, and his thigh muscles showed in his tight jeans. His hair hung carelessly in his face as he looked down and tuned a borrowed electric guitar. Every few seconds he'd toss his hair and look up, scanning the crowd with those haunting eyes.

Jane wasn't the only one looking either. She saw Michelle up near the stage, talking to some other guys, but with her eyes trained on Caleb. Jane had to admit that she was attractive. Very attractive. As if she had just walked off the pages of an urban fashion magazine to make Jane's life miserable. A perfect ass in perfect size zero jeans. Thick, brown hair, streaked with blonde highlights, and one pink extension hanging down. And her smile was a hundred watts of pure white, if a little fake.

Jane watched as she escaped the men she had been talking to and approached the stage. She looked up at Caleb and said something. Caleb smiled, as if he thought it was funny.

"Another diet Pepsi?"

Jane looked up to see the server standing next to her.

"Yes, please. Wait. No. Bring me one of those Vod-Bods, or whatever you call it."

"One Vodka Red Bull coming up."

By the time her drink arrived, the band had finished their warming up. Mitch took to the microphone and tapped on it to get the crowd's attention. A few people at tables kept talking, but most everyone else hushed and focused on the stage.

"Thank you," Mitch said, over a squeal of feedback from

the mic. "We're going to do our best to raise the roof on this place for you tonight. But first we'd like to thank you all for coming out to help us celebrate." He turned to his band. "What are we celebrating again? Shit. How about we just celebrate each other, and good beer, and Friday?"

Several people held up their glasses and cheered.

"We've got a very special treat for you all. Joining us up here this evening is the always popular, always amazing, guitar-shredding man of mystery, Caleb Cummings."

Caleb smiled and bowed slightly.

"So let's keep it fun, and keep it light. And don't forget your servers tonight. As they keep the booze flowing, don't forget to keep their tips growing. All right. Here we go."

He rehung the mic on its stand, and as if taking it for his cue, Caleb played the opening guitar riff to "Alive" by Pearl Jam. The bar and everyone in it seemed to fade until only Caleb remained, standing like a rock god in the spotlight of center stage. Fortunately, the music was too loud to talk over, so Jane had nothing to do but sip her vodka Red Bull and listen to them play, occasionally scanning the crowd for Michelle. The server reappeared with another drink for her, even though she didn't remember ordering one. She polished off the one in her hand and took it anyway.

When there was a brief break between songs, the young guy next to Jane leaned over to her and said:

"Caleb's pretty amazing, isn't he?"

"I never knew he could play like that."

"I know, right? He likes the singer-songwriter stuff, but I don't think there's anything he can't play. He used to . . ."

The band started up again and muted out what he was

saying. He threw up his hands and shrugged, and they turned their attention back to the stage.

After the song finished, Jane turned back to him.

"What were you saying?"

"About what?"

"About Caleb."

"Oh, yeah. Sorry. Hard to talk in here. Anyway, he used to have a standing gig on weekends at Lucre & Lush. They'd flock in to listen to him. He was doing pretty fucking good back then. But he found out they were stiffing the band on the door, and he quit over it. Said it wasn't fair. Guy's got balls."

"How did you two meet?"

"I was dating Lisa and she was friends with . . ."

The band began to play again. He laughed and turned away. Jane felt the vodka rising from her stomach to her head, bringing with it a welcome wave of relief. Relief from what, she couldn't say. Time slowed down. Voices grew distant. The walls of the small bar seemed to expand, enveloping an ever growing space. When the song ended, to wild cheers and huge applause, her conversation partner spoke again.

"Now, what was I saying?"

"You were telling me how you and Caleb met."

"That's right. I was dating Lisa, and she was best friends at the time with Michelle. We went on a couple of double dates."

"Michelle? The Michelle that's here tonight?"

"Yeah. Lisa turned out to be a bitch, and we broke up not long after. But Michelle's pretty cool."

"Caleb dated her?"

"Yeah, but that was like ancient history."

Ancient history? How could it be? The girl was practically

still a child. Jane felt her jaw clench and her cheeks flush. He must have noticed, because he laid a hand on her arm and said:

"Don't sweat it. He's obviously way into you now."

The band saved Jane from asking any more embarrassing questions, and she excused herself from the booth and went to find the restroom. It was a single bathroom, and there was a line outside the door—mostly girls talking loudly and texting at the same time. A guy walked past Jane and winked bigly.

"You can join me in the men's room, honey."

She meant to call him a pig, but she only shook her head.

When it was finally her turn, the girl behind tried to push inside with her, but Jane closed the door on her and locked it. She peed, then washed her hands, and checked her makeup in the mirror. The fluorescent power-saving bulbs made her skin look pale and lifeless. She re-applied her lipstick, pulled down a paper towel, and blotted it. She tossed the lipstick stained towel with the mound of others just like it in the trash.

The girl pounded on the door.

"Jesus," she said when Jane finally opened it. "You write a book while you were in there?"

"Believe it or not," Jane replied, stepping past her from the bathroom, "the world does not revolve around you."

The girl stuck her tongue out at her.

"You sound just like my mom."

Then she slammed the door.

When Jane returned, the band was on a break and Caleb was sitting in the booth, waiting for her. He pulled her down beside him and put his arm around her.

"What'd you think, babe?"

"It was really good."

"Well, good is okay, I guess. But we're still warming up, so we've got time yet to get great."

"No, I didn't mean it like that. You were really great. I had no idea you could play like that."

Michelle slid into the booth across from them, tossed her perfect hair, and smiled brightly. She said:

"He's always been able to out-shred anyone on a Stratty. Remember when you won first place in that riff contest at the Triple Door, Cal?"

Cal? Did she just call him Cal?

Jane thought she saw Caleb blush.

"I just got lucky that night," he said. "Tommy's guitar was on the fritz."

Jane pulled her drink to her and sucked it down through the double straws. Caleb seemed to sense that she was upset.

"Hey, babe. I'd like to play something special for you. You got any requests for the next set?"

"Can you play any Guns N' Roses?"

"Yeah," Michelle interjected, "I hear that the eighties are making a comeback."

Caleb ignored Michelle's comment and focused on Jane.

"You got a favorite?"

"How about 'Sweet Child o' Mine'?"

"One of the best guitar riffs ever," he said. "I'll bet the guys will let me sneak it in after the Buckcherry cover."

"Maybe you could play some Nirvana," Michelle said.

Caleb ignored her and turned to Jane.

"I better get back, babe."

Then he leaned in to kiss her. It was meant to be a quick kiss, but Jane buried her fingers in his hair and pulled him to her and kissed him deep, watching Michelle squirm out of the corner of her eye. When she let him go, he wore her lipstick.

"Fuck," he said. "That was hot. But I'm not sure I'd pass a breathalyzer after that kiss. What are you drinking anyway?"

"Vodka Red Bull."

"Careful," he warned. "Red Bull gets people into trouble."

"Sure it's not the vodka?" she asked.

"The vodka will make you pass out. The Red Bull will let you keep drinking vodka when you ought to be passed out."

"Well, maybe I'll switch to shots then."

He smiled and caressed her cheek.

"It's good to see you loosening up and having fun, babe. One special request heavy-metal power ballad coming up."

He slid from the booth and headed back toward the stage. Michelle wasted no time following him. Conniving little bitch, Jane thought, replaying her words in her head. "The eighties are making a comeback." Screw her. And if Caleb wanted to see her loosen up, she'd show him. She flagged the server down.

"Another Vodka Red Bull?" the server asked.

"No," Jane said, handing her a credit card. "Bring tequila shots for the whole table. And start me up a tab."

Everyone at the table nodded, excited for a free shot. The server slipped Jane's card in her pocket and counted them off, stopping at the drunken girl, who was leaning on a big guy next to her with her eyes shut.

"Is she okay?"

"Yeah," the big guy said. "She's just napping."

They had just pounded their third round of shots when she heard the opening guitar for "Sweet Child o' Mine."

She grabbed the hand of the eyeliner kid she'd been talking

to and dragged him onto the dance floor.

People crowded the small space, standing with drinks in their hands and singing along, but few of them were dancing. Those that were, were barely moving at all. As Jane danced, she caught glimpses of Caleb on stage in the spotlight, his eyes closed and his hair hanging in his face as his fingers worked the strings. She knew everyone was watching him.

She knew Michelle was somewhere watching too.

The music soon took hold of her inebriated mind, and she began to dance more wildly. The boy she was with disappeared, probably for the safety of their booth, but Jane didn't care— she'd show these kids how it was done. She balled up her shirt and tied it off, exposing her midriff, and she tossed her hair and shook her ass. She went pinballing through the crowd, dancing with strangers, male and female. She didn't care.

"Look at her go!" she heard a man shout.

"Someone's having a good time," a girl said.

Jane was encouraged by these remarks, and she danced all the harder. Someone handed her a drink and she downed it and handed back the glass. She felt liberated and free, as if she were back in her first year of college, before she'd gotten pregnant and been burdened with responsibility.

She remembered going to outdoor concerts at the Gorge, smoking pot and getting drunk and dancing until the sun came up. She remembered feeling alive and hopeful with her whole life still ahead of her. For one brief moment it was there again—the wistful hope that she had once felt. It hung in front of her like a sparkling disco ball, every mirrored facet reflecting another possible path, another exciting future, all waiting to be explored. It was a mysterious and private world no one could touch but her; a crystal moon orbiting forever in her mind. But it soon came crashing down, shattering into the broken shards of reality. The song had ended long ago, and she alone remained on the floor dancing. Blank faces stared at her as she whirled past them, spinning out of control. She stumbled and fell. She was briefly aware of pain in her knee.

Now up again.

Twirling faster, leaping higher.

She wouldn't let them stop her from dancing—

Until she careened hard off a shoulder and fell. She heard someone shout and glass shatter on the floor. Then she was wrapped in strong arms. A hand caressing her hair, a soft voice promising everything would be all right. Strange faces leered at her as she held onto his arm and staggered toward the door.

A whoosh of cold air.

An orange streetlamp.

The sidewalk sliding by.

She felt hands lowering her into a seat, a belt pulled across her chest. She saw passing headlights in a mirror. A nauseous feeling roiled up from her gut. She leaned over and puked onto the curb. He held her hair and spoke softly in her ear. What he said she'd never know. An eternity passed while the world spun around her, but at last, it steadied, and she felt the seat recline. She heard the thud of a shutting door.

She closed her eyes and imagined that she was in a coffin, being lowered into her grave. It wasn't so bad, she thought.

If only the pain would go away.

Chapter 20

HEAD POUNDING, dry mouth.

That's what Jane woke to the next morning.

Bright sunlight streamed through the bedroom window, and as she squinted into it, she began to recall the embarrassing events of the night before. She lay still for a long time, not daring to turn and face Caleb. But when she finally did roll over, he wasn't there. The covers were pulled up on his half of the bed and she couldn't tell if he had slept there or not. She would have been more concerned by his absence, however, if her immediate thoughts had not been consumed with how to stop the throbbing pain in her head.

She shimmied half out of bed, pausing when she noticed a glass of water on the bedside table with two Advil tablets next to it and a handwritten note that read:

Good morning, my little rock star. I'm out back working in the garden. Join me when you feel like it. I hope you slept okay. I love you!

When she finished reading she closed her eyes and let her head fall back onto her pillow. What was I thinking last night, she wondered. You weren't thinking, was her silent answer. If you'd been thinking, you wouldn't be in this mess.

"Ugh," she said. "I hate myself right now."

She sat up and took a sip of water, popped the Advil in her mouth, and swallowed them down. Then she drained the glass. She couldn't remember a time when she'd been so thirsty.

The floor seemed to move beneath her feet as she made her way into the bathroom. She turned the water on lukewarm and ran a bath, brushing her teeth while she waited for it to fill. She tried gargling with Scope, but the taste of alcohol made her nauseous, and she spit it out as soon as it hit her tongue. She stripped off her underwear, wondering where her clothes from the night before had gone, and lowered herself into the water.

She shaved her legs, nicking herself a few times because her vision was still blurry, and shampooed and conditioned her hair. When she had dried off from her bath, she found her favorite sundress and slipped it on and applied some light makeup in the mirror, trying her best to cover the dark circles beneath her eyes with concealer. But not too much—she didn't want to look all gussied up either, like some hung-over hussy making a walk of shame.

When she'd done the best she could, she plucked up her courage and went to find Caleb in the yard.

The sun was up over the roof of the house and shining on his bare back where he worked in the garden, digging rows for seed. He stopped to watch her walk toward him.

"Well, good morning, Sunshine."

"Good morning," she said, trying to sound chipper.

"Sleep okay?"

"Waking up was a little rough."

He laughed.

"I'm sure it was."

"Oh, God," she said. "Just tell me. How bad was I?"

"How much do you remember?"

"Not much."

"Well, that's probably best."

"That bad?"

"No," he chuckled. "I'm just screwing with you. You got a little sick is all."

"Did I get sick on you?"

"No, the sidewalk outside the Pub. You got your clothes pretty good though. I ran them in the wash this morning."

She hung her head, ashamed.

"I'm so sorry, Caleb. You must hate me."

"No way," he said. "I could never hate you, babe."

"Not even a little?"

"Nope. Not even a little. But I'll tell you, I never knew you could sing so well."

"Sing? I remember dancing, but please, for the love of God, don't tell me I was singing too."

"Oh, yeah, you were. You sang me all the Guns N' Roses hits on the ferry ride back."

He must have seen how embarrassed she was, because he stuck the hoe in the dirt, walked to the edge of the garden, stepped over the railroad tie, and hugged her.

When she looked up into his eyes, he was smiling.

"I warned you about that Red Bull."

She shook her head.

"I'm never drinking again."

"Well, now, it wouldn't be a proper hangover without a swearing off."

"I mean it, though."

"How about coffee?" he asked. "You drinking coffee?"

"I'd love some."

"Come on. I'll make you breakfast."

After a light breakfast and several cups of strong coffee, Jane began to feel like herself again. Her headache subsided to a manageable ache, and her initial fear of having upset Caleb last night dissipated as he doted on her in the kitchen.

"Shoot," she said, suddenly realizing that it was Saturday.

"What's wrong?" Caleb asked.

"I missed my Saturday morning meeting. First time in five years. Can you imagine missing an Al-Anon meeting because you're hung-over?"

He shrugged.

"Maybe you're in the wrong program."

"Ha-ha," she said. "Very funny."

He grinned at her smugly.

"Give yourself a break," he said. "Relax a little. You could help me in the garden."

"What are you planting out there?"

"Well, I got some lettuce and carrots down already. I plan on maybe some summer squash. Got arugula too. I wanted to plant you tomatoes, but Ralph at the hardware store said they needed to be sowed inside first. Might plant potatoes instead."

Jane was impressed.

"Wow! Is there anything you can't do?"

"Well, I've never told anyone this before, and it's a little embarrassing, but I can't kill spiders."

"You can't? How can you be afraid of spiders?"

"I'm not afraid of them. I just can't kill them. I can't kill any insect, really. But I'll transplant them outside."

"But you eat meat," she said.

"Of course."

"Well, that doesn't make any sense."

"Do you eat insects?" he asked.

"That's not even—" she stopped herself short and shook her head. "You're a strange man, Caleb Cummings."

He sipped his coffee and smiled at her across the table.

"What about a mosquito?" she asked.

"I guess I've killed one or two," he said. "But it was self-defense, I swear."

Caleb stood to fill his mug, but the pot was empty.

"You want me to brew more coffee?"

"Not unless you want it," she said. "I'm good. I could use a manicure, though. Why don't you come to town with me?"

He rolled his eyes.

"I think I'd rather work in the garden."

"The garden can wait."

"No way," he said, "I'm not getting roped into that again."

"Come on; you liked it the last time."

"I did not. And you really need to get a girlfriend to do this stuff with."

"But you're so much more fun."

He bent over and kissed her.

"The answer's no. But I'll make you a deal. I'm taking you to dinner tonight. Just the two of us. Somewhere nice."

"Dinner? Really? What for?"

"Because it's Saturday and I'd like to take you out. Does a man need more reason than that?"

"You said it was a deal. What do I have to do?"

"You have to promise to put out at the end of the night."

"I think I can do that."

"And you have to promise to stick with drinking water."

She laughed.

"Can it at least have bubbles?"

"It can have bubbles."

As JANE SAT IN THE PEDICURE CHAIR, flipping through a three-month old issue of *Cosmopolitan*, she saw a picture that reminded her of Michelle from the Pub last night. She hated the jealousy that it aroused in her. Plus, now that she thought about it, she was just a little upset that Caleb hadn't mentioned anything about having dated her.

"You want your usual French?" the pedicurist asked.

Jane shook her head.

"Let's do something different today. How about that black cherry polish over there? On the top shelf. I saw it last time."

After having her toes painted and her nails to match, she walked across the street to her hair salon.

The girl behind the counter smiled at her.

"Hi, Jane. Don't we usually see you during the week?"

"I don't have an appointment, but I hoped maybe Sharon could squeeze me in."

The girl frowned.

"Sorry. She's not working today. But Tyler could see you."

"Do you think Sharon would mind if I did? It's kind of an emergency appointment."

After reassuring Jane that her regular stylist wouldn't mind at all, the girl offered her a bottle of water and asked her to wait while Tyler finished with his current client. Jane sat in the small waiting area and looked out the window at people passing by. She avoided the fashion magazines. It wasn't long until she was seated in Tyler's chair and looking at herself in the mirror as he stood behind her, lifting her hair in his fingers and letting it fall.

"Oh, you'd look so cute with it short," he said.

What was it about male stylists, Jane wondered, that they always wanted to chop off her hair?

She shook her head.

"I'm thinking just a trim. But I'd like to add highlights."

He lifted a hand to his cheek theatrically.

"We can do that. We can definitely do that. Maybe foil in a

little natural highlight for you. Give you that just-home-from-Cabo look everyone loves."

"I was thinking more chunky. You know, dramatic."

"Okay, so a younger look. We can do that. But you sure you don't want me to bob it first? You'd look so cute."

"I'm sure. Just the highlights."

By the time he finished her hair, it was late afternoon and the salon was closing. She didn't have time to really get used to her new appearance before leaving, so she sat in her car and looked at herself in the mirror. He'd done what she had asked him to, and it was impossible to miss. She liked it. She did. She just wished she'd gone with something a little more subtle.

When she got home, the bike was gone from the garage. She assumed Caleb was over at Mrs. Hawthorne's place again. What exactly he did for that woman and why, she couldn't imagine. All she knew was that he had better be home in time for their date. She went inside to pick out a dress for dinner.

She was ready and watching through the kitchen window when she saw him ride up and stow the bike. He came through the garage door in a rush, and then froze mid-step in the entrance to the kitchen when he saw her.

"Wow," he said.

She spun around so he could see the dress.

"You like it?"

"No."

"You don't?"

"No. But I would like to grab you right now and show you

how much I love it. Except I'm covered in dust and dirt. You look amazing, Jane. Really amazing."

"Do you like my hair?"

"It looks different. What did you do?"

"Just some highlights. Too much you think?"

"No. I like it. I liked it the other way too. But this is nice."

Not exactly the response Jane had been hoping for.

"Let me just rinse off really quickly," he said. "I won't be a few minutes."

Oh, how wonderful it must be sometimes to be a man, she thought, when he stepped back into the kitchen less than ten minutes later, looking dapper in a pair of jeans and a button-up shirt that Jane hadn't seen before.

"Well," she said, admiring him, "I guess I'm not the only one with surprises in my closet. Where'd you get that shirt?"

"I picked it up in town the other day, before the barbeque. I wanted to have some options to look good for your friends."

He held out his hand for her.

"Shall we go, my lady?"

"Isn't this lovely? Are you going to lead me to your horse and carriage now, my sir?"

"Actually, I was hoping you'd hand over the car keys."

She laughed.

He drove her to the nicest restaurant in town, a quiet little steakhouse known for great service, even though its name was Slacker Jack's. She was impressed when Caleb told the captain that he'd made a reservation under his name. The captain led them to a private table lit with candles, and Caleb pulled her chair out for her before sitting himself. A perfect gentleman.

After their server had explained the specials, Caleb ordered a bacon-wrapped filet, and Jane went with the halibut cheeks. They asked for a bottle of sparkling water, and when the server brought it to the table and presented it to him, Caleb joked that he hoped it was a good year. They talked quietly during their meal, and the attention Caleb paid to her made her feel like a real lady. And it felt good.

They were looking over dessert menus when Jane opened her purse and slid an envelope across the table to Caleb.

"What's that?"

"The rest of your pay."

Caleb weighed the envelope in his hand, as if he wasn't quite sure whether to accept it or not. Then he tucked it away in his back pocket and smiled at her.

"And I'm picking up dinner tonight, too," Jane said.

He shook his head.

"Please," she said. "I'd like to make up for last night."

"You can make up for that when we got home. Do you have any idea how cheated I felt last night because I couldn't bring myself to take advantage of you while you were drunk?"

Jane almost spit her water.

"Yeah, right. Like you'd have wanted anything to do with me last night while I was puking all over myself."

"You were actually really hot on the dance floor. Before you kind of tipped over the line there."

"Was I as hot as Michelle?"

"Michelle?"

"Yeah. You know, Michelle from last night."

"What's that supposed to mean?"

"Come on, I saw you looking at her. And I can't blame you. She's very pretty. Plus, she's obviously still into you."

Jane looked down at her dessert menu, as if what she had just said meant nothing to her at all.

"Is that what this is about? The new hair and everything? You think you need to compete with Michelle?"

"Oh, I'm competing with her now, am I?"

"No. You're not competing with anyone. Why would you even think that?"

"You didn't tell me you two had dated."

"When would I have told you? I didn't even know she was going to be there last night. Zach invited her."

They were interrupted when the server came over to take their dessert orders. Caleb chose the carrot cake; Jane said she didn't want anything. When the server had left again, she said:

"Let's face it; I'm just too old for you."

Caleb leaned his head back and looked at the ceiling, as if imploring some god above for patience.

"I'm so tired of hearing about your age. Why is it that no one has a problem with it except you? You're the only one who even brings it up, Jane. Ever."

"Really? Like that bouncer at the pub last night who didn't even want to see my ID? They check everyone's ID there."

"Come on, Jane. He waved you through because you were obviously there with me."

"Whatever. What about Michelle then—making her rude comments about the eighties coming back?"

"Listen, Michelle's a bitch. Sorry. I hate to use that word, but she is. She is and she always has been. We dated for like a minute. You've got to get over it, Jane."

"You mean she's not the steady girl you said you dated for six months?"

"No. That girl moved to Boston for school."

"What about the girl you wrote the song about?"

"I told you. She's raising kids in Redmond. Jesus, Jane, get off this weird insecurity kick you're on. It's starting to be a buzz kill for real."

They were interrupted by the server delivering the carrot cake. He brought two forks, as any good server should. When he had retreated again, Jane sighed.

"I'm sorry, Caleb."

"You don't have to be sorry."

"But I am."

He reached over and took her hand.

"I love you, Jane. Just the way you are. Just the age you are. I know it might have been hard to know if I was here for the job or not before, but now the job's done, and the money's in my back pocket, and I'm still here. I'm here because I want to be here. All my life I thought there was nothing I could ever love like I love music. But then I met you."

Jane looked across the table at his face as he spoke. The candlelight reflected in his eyes, and she could see that he meant what he said. In fact she couldn't recall having ever heard one dishonest word cross his very kissable lips, except when he let her believe he knew Melody better than he did. Maybe all this insecurity of hers was born from silly fear—fear she'd conjured up herself because she didn't feel worthy of being happy.

"You really love me that much?" she asked.

"What can I do to prove it to you?"

She bit her lip cutely and smiled at him.

"How about sharing your carrot cake?"

HE TOOK HER HOME and made love to her twice.

The first time was filled with pent-up need and passion; the second time was tender and slow. She lay awake in his arms long after, not wanting to sleep, even though she was tired. She felt so good, and she was terrified the feeling might slip away while she slept. For the first time there was nothing between them. No work he needed to do, no money that she owed him. They were finally equals in everything, including love.

She kissed his chest and said:

"I hope you'll love me forever."

But she fell asleep before he could answer.

Chapter 21

JANE HAD JUST ENOUGH TIME between sales appointments to catch the noon ferry into the city to retrieve her credit card from the Paradigm Pub. She couldn't recall a more gorgeous spring day in Seattle. People seemed to be out everywhere—jogging the waterfront, riding bicycles, walking dogs. She even saw a group of tourists clumsily balancing on Segways as their guide led them along the pier. What ever happened to Segways, she wondered. Weren't they supposed to change the world?

The pub was cool, dark, and empty. The weather was too nice for anyone to lunch inside, with the exception of one poor guy who was already half drunk and picking idly at a bowl of bar peanuts.

Jane looked around for the bartender.

The man cracked a peanut on the bar with his fist.

"You know what the peanut said to the elephant?"

Jane turned toward him. He looked harmless enough.

"No," she said. "What did the peanut say to the elephant?"

"Nothing. Peanuts can't talk."

He slapped his knee and laughed outrageously, as if he'd just brought down the house. When he got a hold of himself, he cracked another peanut and popped it in his mouth.

"I'm serious," he said. "They can't talk. And I can prove it.

The bartender told me these were complimentary peanuts. But I've been sitting here two hours now, and not one of them has said anything nice to me at all."

He laughed and slapped his knee again.

Jane heard clinking glass and was saved from another bad joke by the bartender, carrying out a box of bottles from the back. He set them on the bar and addressed her:

"You looking for lunch or just drinks?"

"Actually," she said, "I'm here to pick up my credit card. I left without it the other night."

He nodded and turned to the register, flipping through several abandoned cards tucked inside a beer glass and wrapped in their matching receipts.

"You don't look like a Robert or a Daniel, so I'm guessing you must be Jane."

"That's me."

He slid her card across the bar to her, along with a charge slip and a pen. She looked at the total and shook her head.

"I can't believe I ordered this many shots."

"Don't be embarrassed," he said. "Happens all the time."

"Not to me it doesn't."

She added in a large tip and handed him back the signed slip. He looked her over for a second as if he recognized her.

"Hey, you were here Friday night with Caleb," he said.

Jane felt herself blush.

"I'm sorry if I made a fool of myself. I never really—"

He held up his hand to cut her short.

"Happens to the best of us." Then he leaned in closer and asked: "Do you know how to get a message to him?"

"Caleb? Sure. Actually, I'll see him when I get home."

"Could you tell him he needs to call Jeremy, or at least send him an email, and let him know if he's going to take that gig in Austin? He can't hold it open forever."

Had she heard him right? Was he talking about her Caleb? When she spoke it was all a stutter.

"You mean, Caleb?—Austin?—really?—a gig?"

"Yeah, he'll know what I mean. He told me the other night to tell Jeremy he'd get back to him, but Jeremy hasn't heard anything yet, and they won't wait much longer."

"Okay, sure," she said. "I'll deliver him the message."

"Thanks," he replied. "And we really need to get that kid a damn cell phone. He's living in the past."

Jane stood for a moment, leaning against the bar. She felt dizzy, almost drunk. The bartender grinned at her and turned back to his box of bottles and started restocking the shelves.

As Jane turned to go, the drunkard said:

"You know where peanuts fill up their cars?"

She walked past him toward the door.

"The shell station," he called after her.

His laughter followed her into the street.

Somehow the day had turned on her while she had been inside, and the sun that had felt so good now glared at her from an unforgiving sky. Everywhere around her people were still enjoying themselves, and she felt as if she were an actor in a tragic play who had walked onto the wrong set.

She drove by instinct to the ferry terminal and waited for the next boat in a trance. She had always known deep down that this would happen eventually, but she had been hoping it would be much later on down the road. She scolded herself for being so foolish. For having fallen for someone so young. He had his whole life ahead of him yet, and his future would take him down roads where she could never follow.

But she couldn't blame him either.

Who could blame anyone for something that just was?

She was sure he believed everything he had said to her. But how could he know? He didn't have the life experience to back up the words. He was such an old soul, such a kind heart, that it had been easy to forget that he wasn't even twenty-five yet. No, she thought, if there was any blame at all, it was all hers.

Once the ferry was underway, she pulled out her phone and scrolled to Grace's number. She had her finger on the call button, but she thought better of it and tossed the phone back in her purse. It seemed like she was always calling Grace with a problem, and it made her feel like a loser. She could deal with this on her own. She was a big girl now.

She had planned to head straight home, but as she pulled off the ferry she noticed a bumper sticker for Ivar's Fish Bar on the Subaru ahead of her that read: KEEP CLAM AND CARRY ON, a cute play on an old saying. She thought it was good advice in any situation, so she decided to keep her appointment. And she was glad she did, because her client was already waiting for her at Jumping Java, the island coffee shop.

She was a sweet woman who had been unemployed since being laid off from their local bank and her COBRA was more than she could afford. Jane felt for her, and she was glad to have a distraction, so she did her best to forget about Caleb as she got out her laptop and plugged the woman's information into her policy screen.

"Are you okay?" the woman asked her.

Jane realized she was staring out the window.

"Sorry. Yes. I'm fine. It should just be another minute. These remote office connections aren't always the best."

"Is it hard to get into?" the woman asked. "I mean, selling insurance like this?"

Jane shook her head.

"Not really. You have to take some courses to sell accident and health, and then you need to renew your ethics training every other year. I'm licensed to sell life insurance also, but you have to get your Series 6 for that. Why do you ask?"

The woman rolled her eyes.

"The market out there is terrible. I was thinking about real estate, but it seems like everyone I know has a license. Even my hairdresser sells on the side. And they're all so cutthroat, too."

Jane knew it could be tough re-entering the job market, especially for mature workers. She'd sat across from too many people who had lost their company health policies along with their jobs. It reminded her to be grateful for what she had.

"I think you should look into it," Jane said. "There are several good companies out there. I'm not sure if mine has any open territories, but I can give you their recruitment number."

"You sure you wouldn't mind? I know the last thing you probably need is to encourage more competition for yourself."

"Of course, I wouldn't mind. This isn't real estate."

After her appointment, Jane passed by her house and kept driving. She drove halfway around the island and then down to Fort Ward Park. She parked her car and got out and walked along the beach. The sound of waves lapping at the shore had always calmed her, as did scanning the sand for little treasures. She found a tiny pink shell, a piece of green glass. She sat on a shoreline bench and stared off into the blue horizon for a long time. She remembered sitting on this very bench and watching Melody turn over stones and carry back small crabs to show to her. Melody had always been a fearless little girl.

Eventually the water darkened, and the sky caught fire—a glorious sunset reflecting to her across the waves. How could something so beautiful exist on such a day? A seagull landed nearby, cocked its head, and looked at her, as if it might have something to say. But if it did have any message for her, it soon carried it off unspoken into the sunset.

She wondered if she really loved Caleb, or if he had only been a distraction of sorts—a way to take her mind off her daughter's death. She'd read about people avoiding certain kinds of grief until they were ready to face it. It was a kind of safety mechanism to prevent them from giving up. She had been nearly ready to give up, hadn't she? She had even considered suicide. But she felt ready to face it now. Alone, if necessary. She knew her daughter was gone, and she knew she was never coming back. The memories still shot through her like so many hot knives, but she'd gotten used to them. Hadn't she? Perhaps it was time for her to really move on now. Move on from her grieving and move on from Caleb, too. She knew one thing for sure: she loved him enough that she couldn't stand the thought of selfishly killing his dreams. She believed that he loved her, and she knew he'd stay if she let him. She also knew that he'd resent her for it in the end. How could he not? This had been his ambition from the start. There was just no way they could be together. He was too young and full of hope, and she was too tired and too scarred from a life of disappointment.

Almost as soon as the sun had fully set, a wind rose up off

the sound and whipped at her hair, carrying dark clouds and big drops of rain that stung against her cold cheeks. She tossed the shell and the glass back on the beach, stuffed her hands in her pockets, and walked back to her car.

She knew what she had to do.

SHE HEARD HIM FIRST, strumming his guitar and singing in the living room. The sound was so beautiful, she paused in the hall to wipe away a tear and regain her resolve.

Then she walked into the living room and stood in front of him where he sat playing. He had lit a fire log, and it was casting a warm glow onto his face. He finished playing and smiled up at her from his chair. She knew in that moment that this would be the hardest thing she'd ever have to do.

"Hi, babe. I was getting worried about you."

"Caleb, we need to talk."

She saw worry flicker in his eyes.

"Is everything okay?"

She shook her head.

He set his guitar aside and stood.

When he stepped toward her, she backed away. She wasn't sure she could go through with it if she let him touch her.

"Babe, what's wrong? Are you all right?

"Maybe we could just sit and talk," she suggested, taking the chair across from the one he had been sitting in.

"Okay. Sure."

He lowered himself back into his chair and leaned forward with his hands on his knees, a look of anxious expectation on his face, as if he were about to receive some punishment and was determined to take it in stride. Almost a minute passed, and she didn't say anything. She couldn't find the words.

"Are you pregnant?" he finally asked. "Because if you are you can tell me. I know the timing's weird and everything, but maybe it would be a blessing in disguise."

Jane almost laughed, but then she remembered what she had come to do and a sigh came out instead.

"No. I'm not pregnant."

"Then what is it, babe?"

"Why didn't you tell me about Austin?"

"What about Austin?"

"Come on. I went to the pub today to get my credit card, and the bartender told me all about it. You're supposed to call some guy named Jeremy about a gig he's holding open."

Caleb looked down and shook his head.

"Broken Coyotes."

"What?"

"That's the name of the band. Broken Coyotes. It's some folk-rock mixed group. They need a guitar player."

"And they want you?" she asked.

"Rumor has it they have a record label ready to sign them, but their other guy's in his third rehab and on an ankle bracelet for a year after that. Jeremy played them one of my tapes and showed them some video. They want to see me."

"It sounds like a great opportunity."

"It is. I could co-write songs with them, for now. And this would give me an in down there, you know. It's the real deal. No more playing on street corners and shit."

The ground seemed to shake beneath her feet, and Jane counted to ten. She inhaled deeply and let it out.

"Why didn't you tell me?"

"Because I didn't want you to know."

"Like I wasn't going to find out?"

"No," he said. "You weren't. Because I'm not going."

"What?"

"I'm not going."

"Now you're just being stupid, Caleb."

"No, I'm not. I gave it some thought, lots actually, and it is a great opportunity, but I'd rather be here with you."

"And that's it?"

"Yep. End of story."

"No. Not end of story. You can't just walk away from an opportunity like this."

"Yes, I can."

"For what, Caleb? To live on an island in Washington? To stay around here and be my gardener?"

"Is that what I am, your gardener?"

"No. I didn't mean it that way. You've done great work for me, and I got much more than I paid for, but now you have to go, Caleb. You can't turn this offer down."

He leaned forward in his chair, a mix of desperation and anger in his eyes.

"Is that what this is? You want me to leave?"

"No. I mean, yes. It's the right thing for you."

"What? You got your work out of me, and you had your fun, and now you're done with me? Is it that easy for you, Jane? Is it that simple to just move on?"

"That's not what I meant."

"Then what do you mean?"

Her throat constricted. She worried she might cry.

"It's ruined now, Caleb. Can't you see that?"

"What's ruined?"

"We are. Everything is. We were doomed before we even started. Something like this was guaranteed to happen sooner or later. It was baked into the thing. And it's probably better that it's happened so soon. It's probably saving us both from a lot of grief later on. You know it. And I know it."

He stood from his chair and paced in front of the fire.

"No," he mumbled. "This can't be the way it is."

Jane continued:

"You've got your whole life ahead of you. I've got half of mine behind me already. Even if you stayed, this would come back to haunt us now. The fuse is lit. You think you can turn down an opportunity like this—give up what you've dreamed about your entire life—just to stay here on Bainbridge Island with me? You think you won't regret that choice? You'll regret the hell out of it, Caleb. You'll grow to resent me for it, too."

He stopped pacing and turned to face her.

"Then come with me, Jane. Come with me to Austin."

She shook her head.

"I can't."

"You can do anything you want to. Come with me."

"I can't go back and take a different path," she said. "Not this late. Everything is here, Caleb. My house, my life, my job. I met with a woman today who is my age, and she can't even find work. She's me if I try to start over now."

"Then let me stay."

"No."

"So you won't come, and you won't let me stay. Where does that leave us, Jane?"

"We have to end this here, Caleb. I'm sorry."

"What are you saying?"

"I'm saying this is over."

"You don't mean that."

"I do. It's over."

He dropped to his knees in front of her, reached out and grabbed her shoulders, and looked into her eyes. He was crying.

"Don't say that, Jane. Don't say it's over."

She felt her own tears coming, and she knew that if she let even one go, the dam would break and the flood would come. She couldn't afford to cry now. Not here. Here she had to be strong enough for both of them. There would be plenty of time for her to cry later, when he was gone.

She shook her head and looked away.

"It's over, Caleb."

"You don't mean that, baby. You don't mean it. Just come with me to Austin. And if you won't come, let me stay here."

She shook her head.

"I love you, Jane," he said.

She sat rigid, ignoring his pleading eyes, shutting out his words. Because she loved him she had to pretend she didn't.

"Say you love me, Jane. Say it. I know you do."

"I thought I did," she said, "but now it's over."

She pushed his hands away from her shoulders and slid sideways from the chair and stood. He fell forward onto the empty cushion and buried his head in his arms and sobbed. She stood over him for one terrible moment, looking down. He was the most beautiful thing she'd ever seen: the absolute purity of his response, the absence of any false machismo, his willingness to display pure emotion. His hair was spread out on his arms, and his back was heaving as he sobbed.

She could hear his muffled words:

"Say you love me, Jane. Just say you love me."

She had never wanted to say three words more. Every cell in her body ached to hold him. Every instinct told her to take him in her arms and tell him that she loved him. She wanted to kiss him, to hold him, to lie in bed and watch his sleeping face. But she knew that if she really loved him, she'd walk away. She knew he'd thank her one day. She was doing it as much to save him as she was to save herself from a future heartbreak that might kill her. At least that's what she told herself. She heard her own voice, as if it were coming from somewhere far away:

"You should sleep in the other room tonight."

The short trip to her bedroom was the longest walk of her life, as if her feet were cast in lead. She gently closed the door behind her and stood there in the dark for a long time. She listened but she could no longer hear if he was crying.

When she finally moved away from the door, she went to the bathroom and washed her face in the dark. She couldn't stand to look at herself in the mirror. Then she undressed and crawled into bed. She wasn't sure when she started crying. It came at first like a small pang of regret that furrowed her brow as she lay on her side. Then her belly went weightless, like it might on a rollercoaster ride, and she clutched his pillow to her face and cried into it until it was soaked through. The tears aroused his smell from the cotton and made her cry all the more. She half expected him to come to her, she half hoped he might. But as the hours wheeled by in her desolate and self-imposed loneliness, she was left with nothing to console her except the tiny and fleeting feeling that she had somehow done what was right. For whom, though, she wasn't quite sure.

Part Three

Chapter 22

SOMETHING WOKE JANE—

Perhaps a sound, perhaps a dream.

She lay in her bed, washed in the gray light of early dawn, trying to remember what horror she had awoken from, only to realize that it was the horror she had awoken to. An image of Caleb's crying eyes rose in her mind, and she knew that she had made a mistake. A terrible one.

She jumped out of bed and burst from her room. She was halfway down the hall when she somehow knew. She opened his door slowly, wishing that she might be wrong, but the bed was neatly made up, and Caleb's things were gone. She walked into the living room and looked out the big window, lying to herself that he was just up early and working in the garden. But only the silhouette of the fountain stood out against the gray. The wall clock ticked loudly in the quiet shadows behind her, marking the irreversible march of time. She looked at the chair where she had last seen him crying. What she wouldn't give to take it all back—those words that had broken his heart.

She went to her room and pulled on sweats. She grabbed her purse and jacket. She rushed out to the car, backed from the garage, and sped away without bothering to hit the remote that closed the door. She passed a roadside LED sign, blinking an amber warning that clocked her speed at twice the limit, but she blazed past without slowing. When she pulled into the ferry line, she knew she was too late. The ferry was just pulling away, its lighted windows glowing brightly against the black water that spread before her like a chasm keeping her from her lover.

Workday commuters were lined up already in their cars, many of them with their seats reclined as they napped, and the woman at the ticket booth told her the next boat was due in thirty minutes but was already full—she'd need to pull ahead into the overflow lane and wait for the one after.

"It's an emergency," Jane said. "Can't you squeeze me on the next boat?"

The woman shook her head. She'd heard this before.

"You can always walk on," she said.

Jane turned around without paying the fare, drove up and parked her car in the lot. She walked down the passenger ramp and waited there for the next boat. She was surrounded by tired commuters, all of them dressed for work, their heads buried in cell phones, or newspapers, or anything to avoid making eye contact with those around them. It was strangely quiet for how many people there were on the platform.

Jane looked at them and she wanted to scream. She wanted to knock their cardboard coffee cups from their hands and stomp on their phones. How dare they act like this was just some other morning? Didn't they know that her heart had been torn from her chest? Didn't they know that she had chased away the only man she had ever truly loved?

Didn't they know? Didn't they know? Didn't they know?

Of course they didn't know, she thought. Because if they knew they'd all turn and laugh at her.

"You fool," they'd all say.

The ferry arrived, and two tired-looking passengers trudged off, probably coming home from a graveyard shift somewhere. Shortly after, when the announcement came for them to board, the silent commuters pushed their way onto the boat and quickly dispersed, on their way to the cafeteria, or to find some quiet corner in which to continue their solitary morning in peace. Jane went to the front of the ferry, stood near the door through which they would exit, and watched out the window as the lights of the city grew ahead out of the gray.

The crossing seemed to take forever and a day, although the sun had not yet risen when the ferry docked.

Jane was the first passenger off the boat, and she rushed down the terminal steps and onto the street, jogging toward the line of waiting cabs. The drivers leaned against their trunks, ready to help fares with their luggage. They all watched as Jane ran past them to the cab at the front of the line, calling breathlessly to its driver, saying:

"Airport! Airport! Airport!"

She must have looked like an asylum escapee, but she didn't care. She jumped into the backseat and pulled the door closed. As the driver got behind the wheel, she leaned forward and told him one more time, in case he hadn't heard her.

"Sea-Tac airport. I'm in a hurry."

"Yes, I can see that," he said, setting the meter and pulling away from the curb. "It's cheaper to go Airport Way, but the freeway is faster."

"Take the fastest route."

Jane settled into the backseat and watched the streetlights fly by out the window. When he merged onto the freeway, the lights disappeared, and the cab fell into shadow, the tail-lights of the traffic ahead glowing like a thousand pairs of tiny red eyes, staring at her from the gray. She could see the whites of the cab driver's eyes against his dark face as he glanced at her in the rearview mirror.

"Departures or arrivals?" he asked.

"Departures, please."

"What airline?"

"I'm not sure. Do you know which one flies to Austin?"

He shook his head.

"Maybe Alaska."

"Well, just drop me there then."

They drove for a while in silence.

The cabbie turned the radio on briefly to the local news and then seemed to think better of it and turned it off.

He glanced again at Jane in the mirror.

"You heading to Austin?"

"No, I'm trying to catch someone who is."

He nodded, as if she'd only confirmed what he'd already guessed. His eyes hit the mirror again.

"You sure they want to be caught?"

He asked it quietly, almost of himself, and then he looked ahead to the road as if he didn't expect any answer from her.

"I don't know," she sighed.

He nodded and drove.

"Love puts the eaglet out of its nest."

"What's that?" Jane asked.

"Oh, just an old saying from my home."

"What's it mean?"

"I'm not certain it even translates correctly. But it means

something similar to when people say: if you love someone you have to set them free."

"You mean: set them free and if they really love you, they'll come back?"

He nodded.

"Although I've heard it turned into a joke also. Something about if they don't come back, hunt them down and kill them."

They were quiet for the rest of the ride, and by the time they approached the airport, the sky had grown lighter. Jane watched a jumbo jet take off, angling up sharply into the pale sky before dipping left and flying into the sunrise. The cabbie exited onto the departures ramp, circled, and pulled over at the Alaska Airlines sign. He stopped the meter. It read: $44.35. Jane fished through her purse and handed him three twenties. He opened his change wallet, but she held up her hand.

"Keep it," she said.

Jane grabbed the door handle, but she didn't open it right away. Instead, she sat staring out the cab's window.

The ramp was packed with travelers hugging goodbye at open car trunks. She saw one couple kiss, and she watched the wife wheel her carry-on luggage toward the doors. The husband looked longingly after her before getting in his car and driving away. Still, Jane sat without getting out of the cab. She looked through the glass doors into the busy terminal. She saw lines of travelers waiting to check their bags. She scanned the faces, just in case. She sat watching for what seemed like a long time. The cabbie said nothing, as if the moment were too important to interrupt. Eventually Jane released the door handle and sunk back into the seat.

"Can you take me back?" she asked

The cabbie looked at her in the mirror and nodded.

"You sure?"

"I'm sure."

She thought she saw him frown as he pulled away from the curb, but she wasn't sure. He left the meter off this time, and as he exited the airport for the freeway, he quietly said:

"I go back anyway, so I'll take you for free."

BY THE TIME THE FERRY DOCKED at Bainbridge Island, the sun had fully risen on what looked to be a beautiful spring day. But there was no sun bright enough to chase Jane's clouds away. She got in her car and drove to Grace's condominium building and parked. Then she took her phone from her purse and sat with it in her lap for almost an hour. She lit a cigarette, but it burned out in her hand before she even took one drag as she sat staring through the windshield at a NO PARKING sign, puzzling over its meaning until the words bled together in a blur, and she forgot where she even was.

A rapping on the car window startled her, and Grace's husband stood outside with a concerned look on his face.

Jane rolled down her window.

"Jane, are you all right?"

"Hi, Bob," she said. "I'm okay."

"I was pulling out, and I saw you sitting here with your car running, so I thought I'd check. You sure you're all right?"

Jane nodded.

"I'll be fine."

"Okay. Well, Grace is upstairs if you want to go on up. She'd love to see you. I'm off to Denver. If the guest spots are all full, you can park in mine. Number fifty-three."

"Thanks, Bob."

He hesitated at her window a moment longer. It seemed like he wanted to tell her something, but then he appeared to think better of it. He turned and walked back to his car. Jane turned the key in her ignition, but her car was already running, and the starter gears ground loudly. Bob heard it and looked back, pausing at his door and squinting at her, as if checking one last time to be sure that she was really okay. She smiled and waved goodbye. He got in his car and pulled away.

Grace buzzed Jane up without a question, met her at the door, and let her in. Her eyes were rimmed with red, as if she'd been crying, and she looked tired to Jane.

"Are you okay?" Jane asked, momentarily forgetting her own grief.

"I'm fine," Grace said, "Just fine."

"You know what fine stands for, don't you?" Jane asked, trying to lighten the mood.

Grace laughed.

"Yes, I know it all too well. Fucked up, Insecure, Neurotic, and Emotional. And aren't we a couple fine, fine, ladies. Forget about me; I just have rough mornings sometimes. Come in and sit down. I've got hot coffee."

They sat in the living room, near the window overlooking the marina, and drank their coffee.

"So," Grace said, once they had settled, "tell me what's going on. You don't drop by this early just for my coffee."

Jane sighed.

"Caleb left."

Grace raised an eyebrow, waiting for more.

"Well, he didn't just leave. I sent him away. I found out he

had a job offer in Austin. A good one. Doing what he loves—
music. And I knew he wouldn't take it unless I made him go. I
didn't have a choice, really."

Grace sat back in her chair and looked at her, but she
didn't say anything. Jane hated the way she could do that—ask
a question without even speaking.

"Well, maybe I had a choice, but it was for his own good,
right? I mean, it was the selfless thing to do, wasn't it? Release
them with love. Isn't that what you always say?"

"I might have said that, dear, yes, but I was talking about
alcoholics who need to hit bottom. From what I know about
Caleb, that sure isn't him."

Jane started to say something, but she stopped herself and
sighed. She sipped her coffee and looked out the window. A
seagull flapped across the marina and landed on a dock pylon.

Jane looked back to Grace.

"Wouldn't he have stayed if he really did love me?"

"Were you testing him then?"

"No, I wasn't testing him."

"Then that's hardly fair, is it? To expect him to treat it like
a test of his love for you."

"I guess."

"What did you say to him?"

"I told him it would never work. That something like this
would always come between us. First he offered to stay. Then
he wanted me to come to Austin with him. Can you believe
that? Me moving to Texas? I told him . . . oh, God, Grace . . . I
told him I didn't love him."

Grace's face scrunched up as if it pained her to hear what
Jane had said. After several seconds of silence, she asked:

"Did you mean it?"

"No, I didn't mean it."

"When did all this happen?"

"Last night. And this morning. I've been chasing around like an idiot since dawn. I even went all the way to the damn airport, but I chickened out at the last minute. But then I'm not even sure he went there, anyway."

Jane paused to let out a long, involuntary breath, as if she'd been holding it all morning. She bit her lower lip until it hurt.

"What have I done, Grace?"

"Done is done," Grace said. "It doesn't matter."

"It doesn't matter?"

"No. What matters is what you do now."

"Then what should I do?"

"Do you want me to answer that question as your sponsor, or as your friend?"

"Well, what would you say as my sponsor?"

"I'd tell you to write an inventory on it."

Jane looked out the window again.

"And what would you tell me to do as a friend?"

There was a long pause before Grace spoke, as if she were considering the question, or possibly deciding whether or not to even answer it. Then she said:

"I'd tell you to go to Austin and never look back."

Chapter 23

THE DAYS GREW LONGER, and so did the grass.

Her house was empty and sad. Jane's thoughts seemed to echo there like so many cries, bouncing off the walls to join one another inside her head until the silence was maddening.

She took as many sales appointments as she could get in order to afford her some reason to escape, but even then she would sit across from her clients and think of her empty home, her empty life—a void left in both by Caleb's leaving. At the end of the day, she'd go home and eat dinner alone and sit and do Sudoku puzzles until her eyes hurt. Then she'd cry in bed with her nose buried in his pillow.

She was home early on Friday when the postman knocked on her door, because her box had filled. She sorted through the advertisements and bills and found Caleb's health insurance card. Seeing his name printed on the envelope conjured up fresh waves of pain, and she carried it to the backyard and sat with it in her hand as she stared at the fountain. The sun went down, the air got cold, and the fountain retreated into shadows until she could hear it running but no longer could see it.

The following morning she rose before her alarm, and her car drove her to her Saturday meeting as if on autopilot. Grace was not a gossip, and the other ladies had no idea that Caleb was gone. They all rushed to tell Jane what a wonderful time they had had at the barbeque two weekends prior, and how amazing they each thought Caleb was, and what a great couple they made. She smiled and nodded, knowing it would be easier to let them down as a group.

When it came her turn to share, she felt guilty before she even spoke. She knew this crisis was somehow of her making, and she felt as though she'd delivered enough bad news into their Saturday morning club. But she needed to get it off her chest nonetheless.

"Let me explain to you all how I'm an idiot," she began. "I chased away the only man I might have ever truly loved. You know, I just don't get myself sometimes. I don't know whether I'm afraid that nobody could ever really love me, so I sabotage it before they can prove me right, or whether I'm just a scared little girl hiding in the body of a forty-year-old woman. I don't know what to do and I'm sick over it. My sponsor suggested I do an inventory about it, but I can't get past typing his name. Then I delete it. Then I write it again. Maybe I need to write on paper. I don't know. Then she said I should just go to Austin and be with him. But everything I know is here. You guys. My job. My house. My memories of my daughter."

She felt tears coming on, so she paused to hold them back. She sipped her coffee to buy herself a moment.

"Anyway, I'm aware that I've been Debbie Downer enough around here. So thanks for listening to me all these tough years. I know I'll get through this; I know I'll get over him. I have to. What other choice do I have?"

After the meeting the women all hugged Jane, but none of them told her it would be okay, or that the sadness would pass, and she silently thanked them for that. Before she left Grace asked for a ride home. Jane knew it was her habit to stay and visit with the other ladies, so it was clear that she wanted to speak to her alone. But Grace didn't say a word as they walked to her car, and she just stared out the window as they drove.

When Jane pulled into Harbor Condominiums and parked, Grace stayed in her seat and didn't move.

"Are you mad at me for something?" Jane asked.

Grace sighed but didn't say anything.

"Did I say something wrong in the meeting? About you telling me to go after him to Austin? Because I know you gave me that advice as a friend, and if you didn't want me to share it in the meeting, then I'm sorry."

She received no response from Grace.

"Do you still think I should go after him? Grace?"

When Grace finally turned to her, she had tears in her eyes and a forlorn expression on her face.

"It isn't always about you, Jane."

Jane couldn't remember Grace ever having spoken to her like that, and it was clear that something was very wrong.

"Grace, I'm sorry. I didn't mean . . . what's wrong, Grace? Is something going on with you and Bob?"

"Bob? He's drinking again."

"He is?"

Grace nodded.

"Apparently he has been for over five years. He said he just doesn't want to hide it anymore. He says he's able to drink normally, whatever that means."

Jane didn't know quite what to say to comfort her friend. She knew how often Bob was away from home, but she never had imagined him keeping this kind of secret from Grace.

"What did you tell him?" she finally asked.

"I didn't tell him anything," Grace replied. "Truth is I hardly care what he does."

"You don't?"

Grace turned herself in her seat to face Jane fully.

"Jane, there's something I need to tell you."

"Okay. You can tell me anything, Grace. You know that."

"I know. But this is hard."

"I won't judge you," Jane said. "No matter what it is."

Grace looked into Jane's eyes, and Jane almost thought she saw an apology there, as if Grace had somehow let her down and needed to confess it. But as hard as her mind was working to puzzle out what it was that Grace needed to tell her, nothing prepared her for what came next.

"I'm dying, Jane."

The words had hardly pierced Jane's ears before a shockwave of disbelief hit her in the chest. Dying? Grace? There was no way. She couldn't be. Grace was her foundation, her baseline for living a balanced life. She had been a constant companion and the closest thing Jane had to a real family. Grace must have seen the denial on Jane's face because she nodded and said:

"It's called a glioblastoma multiforme. It even has its own little acronym: GBM. They said it's been growing in my brain for a very long time already."

Jane shook her head.

"You're not dying. There has to be a cure."

"There's no cure. I have a few months at best."

Jane felt her heart race in her chest and her forehead break out in a sweat. It felt suddenly hard to breathe.

"What about treatments? There must be treatments."

"All the available treatments only extend life. And even then not much. I'm not a good surgery candidate either because of the tumor's location. And I'll be damned if I'm going to spend my last days getting my brain zapped with radiation. I'm just going to die, Jane. And that's that."

Jane restarted the car.

"What are you doing?" Grace asked.

"I'm taking you to the cancer center in Seattle."

Grace reached over, turned the car off, and took the keys from the ignition.

"I know this is hard, Jane. It's hard for me to tell you."

"But they do great things over there," Jane said. "New things. Experimental things. Treatments."

"I've been there already."

Jane felt foggy and confused, like she might faint. A quiet minute passed as what she had heard began to sink in.

"How long have you known?"

"For a while now. But we didn't know how serious it was, how fast it was growing, until just recently."

"Grace. Oh, God, Grace. This can't be right."

"It's not right. But it's true, Jane. The reason I'm telling you now is because I want you to do me a favor."

"I can't believe this is happening."

"Jane, did you hear me? I need you to do me a favor."

"Anything. I'll do anything. Just say it."

"I want you to go to Paris with me."

"Paris?"

"Yes. Will you go?"

"Of course, I'll go. Of course. But why Paris?"

"I've always wanted to see it. Ever since I was a little girl."

"What about Bob?"

"We were planning to go together, but we've been fighting a lot lately, and with his drinking and everything I asked him not to come. But I don't want to go alone, Jane. I can't go alone."

"You don't have to go alone, Grace. I'm here. Whatever you need. We can leave right now if you want to."

Grace's eyes welled up, and she patted Jane's knee, turned away, and looked out the window again. Jane reached out and took her hand in hers and held it. Grace's hand was small and warm, the blue veins visible just beneath the surface of her paper-thin skin. Jane couldn't bring herself to imagine that this hand would be lifeless and cold someday soon.

She couldn't believe it. She wouldn't believe it—

But Grace had never lied to her about anything.

"You know," Grace said, breaking the silence, "it's funny, but I've been saving for retirement all these years, and here we are. I won't even need a penny of it. We're flying first class, and I'm paying for everything, and I don't want to hear a word about it. You got that? Not one word."

"Oh, Grace."

She didn't know what else to say.

Grace continued:

"And you made sure we had that life insurance policy years ago, and I've kept it up, so Bob will be just fine after I'm gone. Hell, he can throw a huge party and drink himself to death and join me right then if he wants to."

Jane felt a tear slide down her cheek. When it hit her lip,

she could taste the salt.

She squeezed Grace's hand in hers.

"Grace?"

"Yes, Jane."

"I know I've said it kind of lightly before, like we all do. But I want to really tell you so you know it."

"Tell me what, Jane?"

"I love you, Grace. I really love you."

Grace was smiling at her through tears. She looked like she wanted to tell Jane that she loved her too, but she wiped her cheek with her sleeve and said:

"Now don't go getting all gushy on me already. I'm not dead yet. And besides, you might just change your mind after you've shared a hotel room with me."

Chapter 24

GRACE SAID THAT THE RIVER SEINE looked more magical in person than it did in paintings she'd seen.

Jane had to agree with her.

They stayed at Hôtel Plaza Athénée, with its walls of ivy, and floors of polished marble, in a double room with a view of the Eiffel Tower. The first thing they did when they arrived was take pictures of each other jumping on the beds. Jane signed Grace up with an Instagram account and linked it to Facebook so they could share photos with the ladies from their Saturday meeting back home.

To the strangers who saw them in the streets, they must have seemed little more than two carefree friends on a lavish spring vacation in Paris. Sometimes Jane felt that way too, until a subtle tremor would cause Grace to spill her coffee, or a fainting spell would send her searching for a bench. These little incidents always called up the reality of why they had come, but despite their increasing frequency, she and Grace managed to spend long days exploring the city, seeing and experiencing everything while taking turns making one another laugh.

At a small café Jane asked the waiter why they didn't have French onion soup, and the look of genuine disgust on his face as he pointed out that it was simply called onion soup in France made them laugh until their sides ached. When they had finally recovered enough to order, Grace asked him if they didn't have any French fries. In the mornings, when Grace would call to check in with her husband, she'd tease that she and Jane had to run because their handsome French masseurs were knocking on the room door. When she finally made good on her threats and actually scheduled them massages with the hotel, her masseuse turned out to be an Austrian woman.

They were having so much fun, in fact, that Jane lost track of the days entirely, until she woke one morning and saw the date on their hotel newspaper and realized that it was Melody's birthday. She did the best she could to hide her sadness over breakfast, but Grace picked up on it anyway.

"What's wrong, Jane?"

"Nothing."

"Something's bothering you this morning. Wait. I know what it is. It's the fifteenth, isn't it? It's Melody's birthday."

Jane nodded.

"It's not fair for me to drag you down with me, though. Especially not now."

"Don't you dare say that," Grace said, looking genuinely offended. "You're not the only one who misses her."

They picked at their breakfast for a while.

"I've got an idea," Grace said. "Let's go and light a candle for her today."

Jane liked the idea of doing something, anything, to honor her daughter's memory on her birthday.

"Okay. Where?"

"Notre Dame, of course. It's not far, and it's on my list of things to see anyway."

The concierge called them a taxi.

They climbed in, and soon the towers of Notre Dame rose against the blue Parisian sky. The taxi dropped them out front, and they got in line behind a large group of Japanese tourists who were talking loudly and snapping photos of everything. Yet the lively chatter ceased as soon as they entered the church, as if the history of the place demanded respect even from those who didn't know it.

It was cool, dark, and mysterious. The worn stone floors were washed in a faint rainbow of color from stained glass above. A choir was performing somewhere, unseen, and their soft voices echoed beautifully in the high gothic ceilings, as if angels were circling overhead singing—and for all Jane knew, they were.

They passed sinners who bowed to saints, old believers seeking wisdom from the dead, and soon they came to a circular shrine of burning candles. Grace sat on a wooden pew. Jane paused there with her, but Grace waved her forward.

"You don't want to come up?"

"You go on ahead," Grace said. "I'd like to sit for a spell and just watch."

Jane approached the shrine alone.

She dropped a euro into the offering bucket and took a candle from the box. She held it to one already burning and lit it, then set it with the others. She looked at it, the solitary flame coming into focus, the others around it fading into a blur of soft light. She said a silent prayer. The flame flickered and then stood still again. A tiny light amidst many, the flame was not alone. It would burn forever in Jane's heart.

She tossed another euro in and took another candle out.

She lit this second offering from Melody's flame, and then set them side by side. She wiped away a tear and bowed her head.

When she returned to the bench, she noticed that Grace had been watching with a kind of distant smile in her eyes. They both knew who the second candle was for. Grace reached out and took Jane's hand in hers and squeezed it. Then they sat together for a long time, just watching the candles burn.

After they'd finished inside they paid to climb the towers. It was slow going for Grace up the steep spiral steps, and by the time they made it to the top, the group ahead had already descended. They stood alone with the gargoyles and gazed out over all of Paris, spreading beneath them. Grace clutched tight to Jane's arm, as if to keep herself from falling, although there was a wire fence protecting them.

"It's just so beautiful," she said. "Like a dream, really. It's everything I imagined."

"Are you glad you came?"

Grace closed her eyes and nodded.

Jane watched as she tilted her head back to feel the sun on her face, her lips curling along the well-worn path of her smile lines. How would she carry on without her Grace?

"Thank you, Jane. Thank you, thank you, thank you. You have no idea what this means to me."

Jane swallowed her grief and forced a smile.

When they had descended they decided it was a fine day to walk for a while before catching a cab back to the hotel. As they strolled the quiet streets, beneath the shade trees and past the river vendors selling old books and Paris snow globes, they encountered an old woman swaddled in tattered clothes and holding out a paper cup. Grace opened her purse and gave her a 20-euro note. The old woman's smile gave her the appearance of a wrinkled and toothless baby.

"*Te bénisse*," she said, bowing. "*Merci, mille fois.*"

Grace stopped at the next bank machine they passed and maxed out her daily withdrawal limit on two of her cards. For the rest of their walk, she gave a twenty to every beggar they passed, pausing just long enough to press the bill into their hands and say, "*Bonne journee*," the only French she knew.

She even stopped in old doorways to tuck bills into the hands of passed out drunks, their curled fingers still clutching empty bottles from the night before. She popped into a café and anonymously paid the check for two young honeymooners having a romantic lunch. She gave a hundred euros to a street-side ice cream vendor who hardly spoke any English, spending five minutes explaining to him that she wanted him to hand out as many scoops to passing children as it would buy. Jane had never seen Grace smile so much. Watching it all made her smile too, although she alone knew the sad news behind the good fortune of these strangers. She had no way to prove it, but she would have sworn that the spirit of Grace spread its golden light over the entire city that day, and somewhere in Paris someone might smile on occasion just to remember it.

The next morning Grace had a seizure. She was smiling at Jane as they made plans to visit the Louvre, when her face got slack and her eyes grew distant.

"Are you okay?" Jane asked.

She didn't respond or even appear to have heard her.

"Grace? What is it, Grace?"

She raised her arm from the table, as if she wanted to point to something on the wall, then she went stiff and fell off her chair onto the floor. Jane jumped to her side and held her.

"Grace? What's happening, Grace?"

Grace lay there, jerking and snorting on the floor. Jane ran for the phone and dialed the front desk.

"Help! Please. She's having a seizure. Call an ambulance. Yes, right now. In the room. That's why I'm calling. Help me!"

Security arrived first, and Jane let them into the room.

Grace was no longer shaking, and she looked at the man kneeling over her with a confused expression.

"*Avez-vous mal,*" the man said.

Grace looked over his shoulder to Jane.

"Is this man hitting on me? Because if he is, please tell him I'm flattered, but I'm married."

Jane smiled, happy to see that her friend was back.

Despite Jane's pleading Grace refused medical attention, telling hotel security that she had fainted but that everything was fine now. But it wasn't fine, and it never would be. When they were alone again in the room, Jane begged her to take the anti-seizure medication Grace's doctor had prescribed.

"It makes me feel weak and tired," Grace said. "I hate it."

"Please, Grace. Just take it for me."

"Okay fine," she said, relenting. "But you're the one who's going to be hauling my sorry ass all around the Louvre. And I'll warn you now, I intend to see everything."

Jane handed her the pill and a glass of water.

"Maybe we can go tomorrow," she said. "Today we stay in and rest."

It was two days before Grace had the energy to make it to the Louvre. Even then Jane had to check out a wheelchair from visitor services. When they got to the Mona Lisa, it was surrounded by a mob of people, and Grace couldn't even see it from her chair. Jane set the chair's brakes and helped her up. Grace leaned against her and looked at the famous painting.

"It looks like a postage stamp," she said. "I always thought it would be bigger."

As much as she was disappointed by the Mona Lisa, she was impressed by the sculptures, and she made Jane wheel her around to see every one until the museum closed. Then they returned to the hotel and sat on the room's terrace with a bottle of champagne, watching the Eiffel Tower sparkle against the darkening Paris skyline.

"It really is the city of lights, isn't it?"

"Yes," Grace said, nodding, "it really is."

"Are you warm enough?" Jane asked.

"This champagne has me feeling great. I don't know why I didn't drink it more often back home. Damn alcoholics ruin everything for everyone."

"Is Bob still drinking?"

"He was drunk when I called from the Louvre at five this afternoon. I could hardly understand a word he said. And it was only eight in the morning there."

"He's not flying like that, is he?"

"Lord, no," Grace said. "He took a leave of absence for this trip, so he's at home with nothing to do. I think half the reason we were fighting so much is because he didn't really want to come. He's not handling the news very well, Jane. I told him he could join us if he could manage not to drink."

"What did he say?"

"He told me that he missed me and to hurry home."

"What did you tell him?"

"I told him I won't come home to him being drunk. He gets it together, or I'll just stay in Paris and die. Hell, he can fly here and help you spread my ashes in the Seine."

They sat for a while, watching the city lights brighten as night came on. Birds called from the trees, and an occasional car sped by on the street below.

"I do love that old bastard, though," Grace added. "And I know it's hard for him to think about me dying."

"Is it hard for you?"

"Thinking about dying?"

"Yes."

"I'd be lying if I said it wasn't."

"Does it scare you?"

Grace didn't answer the question for several minutes, and Jane began to feel bad for having asked it.

"We don't have to talk about it."

"No," Grace said, "I want to. I was just thinking."

"Well, you don't have to answer it."

"The truth is it does scare me. But it's somehow helped me coming here. Not just having fun with you. And it's been a blast. It really has. But the history here. I look out over this city, and I think about all the people who have come and gone. Even at Notre Dame. Eight hundred years that thing has stood. Think of the generations of people who've said prayers there. The ones who laid the stones even. I don't know. Somehow knowing that all those people have gone to meet death ahead of me, that they're waiting, somehow it makes it all right."

"Do you pray?" Jane asked.

"I pray, but I don't know exactly what it is I'm praying to. I don't know what I really believe, Jane. And I don't know that it matters that I believe anything."

"I believe in love," Jane said.

"I guess I believe in love, too. And I believe in you."

Jane sat thinking about what Grace had said. She sipped her champagne, but she didn't really want to feel intoxicated. The terrace they sat on was ringed with beautiful red flowers, and a breeze brought their smell to Jane's nose. The scent reminded her of the flowers Caleb had planted for her around her fountain.

"You miss him, don't you?" Grace asked.

"I'm not sure what's happening in your brain," Jane said, "but apparently you now have mind-reading abilities."

Grace laughed.

"I sure as hell hope not. The voices I've already got rattling around in my head are quite enough. I just happen to know you well enough to see that look on your face. You miss him, and you should. He was one of the good ones, Jane."

"Yes," she said, sighing. "I miss him."

After another minute or two had passed, Grace said:

"I want you to make me a promise, Jane. You don't have to if you don't want to, but it would put this tired old mind of mine at ease if you would."

"Sure," Jane said. "Anything."

"Promise me you'll live the life I can't."

"What do you mean?"

"I mean that I don't have long now, Jane. And I'm making peace with that. But if this thing had turned out differently—if I'd had a second chance—I would have made damn sure that I lived every moment without fear. It's seems silly now that the one thing I was really afraid of is about to happen to me, and it isn't anything to fear at all."

"Death is nothing to fear?"

"Death is just the moment that your hourglass runs out of sand. That's it. It happens to everyone eventually. All any of us gets to decide is where the sand falls."

"What are you saying I should do?"

"Just do whatever you would do if you weren't afraid. Live the way I would have lived if I'd known. Live the life that I no longer can, Jane. A life without fear."

"But you never seemed afraid to me."

Grace shook her head and laughed.

"Did I ever tell you that I had an affair on Bob?"

"What? You did?"

"I did. And he's had his over the years too, but that's his business to share. Bob and I married young. Back then when he wasn't flying, all his free time was dedicated to booze, and I was left at home wondering. We were trying to have children then, before we learned I couldn't. Anyway, he was gone all the time, and I fell in love with this kid who raced motorcycles."

"Motorcycles?"

"And sprint cars too. Our house at the time was near the track, and I used to go down and bring him sandwiches and watch him race. I loved him. I really did. I loved him more than life itself. But I was afraid, Jane. Afraid of being judged. Afraid of giving up my security for an uncertain life with a young daredevil. And I stayed with Bob because of it. Bob's not a bad man, don't get me wrong. And I've even grown to love him in a way. But it wasn't fair to him for me to stay. It wasn't. And it sure wasn't fair to me."

Jane was stunned. She had always thought of Grace as the

wise and patient woman who had walked her through so much grief. She had never imagined her being young and having her own hopes and dreams; her own heartbreaks.

"What happened to him?"

"The boy?"

"Yeah."

"I was always curious about his whereabouts. I managed to keep up with his career for a while. About two years after we had called it off, I heard that he had died on the track. Broke his neck."

"But you still think you made the wrong choice?"

"I guess we make the choices we make. I'm not sure there is a wrong or a right to it. But I know now, looking back, that I'd have given up everything since then, every day, just to have had those two years with him. Or even one more day."

Their champagne had grown warm in their glasses, and the night air had grown cold around them. Grace stood, signaling that it was time for her to go back in. Jane remained seated and looked beyond the terrace at the Eiffel Tower, its lightshow now twinkling like the million thoughts flashing in her mind.

"I promise," she said.

"What's that?" Grace asked,

"I promise I'll live the life you can't."

Grace was standing next to her, and she reached a hand out and gently pulled Jane's head to rest against her bosom. Then she bent and kissed the top of her head, as if blessing her. It was the simplest yet most intimate gesture. A tear rolled down Jane's cheek. Somehow she knew it wouldn't be the last.

Chapter 25

GRACE HAD A TASTE FOR EVERYTHING, so they ordered the entire room service menu for breakfast—chocolate-filled croissants, fresh crepes, and baguettes with butter and jam. There were poached eggs, and little crystal dishes of yogurt and granola. There was a cheese sampler plate; a bowl of fresh fruit. Grace took tiny tastes of everything, but ate very little.

"You sure you're not pregnant?"

Jane immediately wished she hadn't asked the question, because Grace looked suddenly sick and got up and rushed to the bathroom. Through the door Jane could hear her vomiting. Grace's health was deteriorating by the day, and it was painful to watch—especially seeing how much it scared Grace.

After Jane had pushed the breakfast cart into the hall, she sat on the bed and thumbed through a glossy travel magazine while Grace sat in front of the mirror, applying her foundation. It took her more time each morning to cover up her increasingly pale complexion, but she told Jane that dying was no excuse not to look good, even if she felt like hell.

"Have you ever been to Venice?" Jane asked.

Grace looked at her in the mirror.

"No, but I've always wanted to ride in a gondola."

"Then let's go."

"Are you serious?"

"We're already all the way over here. Why not?"

Jane looked at Grace, hoping she'd say yes. She knew that their trip had to end eventually, but she wasn't ready for it to be over yet. Grace pulled her passport from her purse, flipped it open, and looked at it.

"I wouldn't mind having a stamp from Italy," she said. "You know, it's a shame I didn't use this thing more."

"So you'll go?"

Grace turned in her chair and smiled at her.

"Oh, hell, yes. Let's do it."

"I'm logging in and buying us tickets right now."

Grace opened her purse and tossed Jane a credit card.

"Use my card," she said. "You've got to be nearly in the poor house already as long as I've taken you away from work. And don't argue. I won't need it where I'm going."

THEY LANDED IN VENICE THAT NIGHT, and as they exited the airport gate, a short, uniformed woman wearing an official-looking hat glanced at their passports then handed them back.

"Aren't you going to stamp it?" Grace asked.

The woman shook her head and said something in Italian. All Jane understood was EU; she guessed that stood for European Union.

They got a cart for their luggage, and Grace leaned on it while they made the long walk from the airport to the water taxies. A stout, mustached man with a friendly smile took their fare and helped them on board with their luggage. They descended together into the boat. A light mist was falling, and the windows were beaded with water. There were several other passengers slumped in shadowed seats, but no one spoke.

Grace leaned her head on Jane's shoulder and closed her eyes. She fell asleep. Jane couldn't blame her—the hum of the boat's engines, combined with the guide lights sliding by in the dark water outside their window, lulled her into a near trance. She daydreamed that Caleb was here with her, and that it was his head on her shoulder. How nice to imagine a honeymoon rather than a wake.

They docked at San Marco Square, and Jane woke Grace. Together they made their way down the ramp, stepping carefully because of the way it heaved and slid against the dock. The same man helped them off; then the boat pulled away for its next stop, and they were alone with their luggage.

There was no cart here, and it was slowgoing wheeling the bags across the cobblestone walkways, past stone steps leading down into the still green waters of Venice's lagoon. The whole place had an otherworldly appearance, as if it were a middle-aged Atlantis descending to the seafloor an inch at a time.

A light rain began to fall.

There were no roads, no cars, and no people.

In the empty square, Jane noticed odd wooden walkways erected several feet above the square's perimeter, as if there had been a runway show for nimble-footed models. She looked about for their hotel, but saw nothing.

The rain came down harder.

"It must be this way," she said, leading the way.

They came upon numerous arched footbridges, spanning an endless maze of canals, and Grace paused on the steps to catch her breath several times as Jane made two trips on every bridge to carry their bags across. The rain fell harder, the stone walkways turned slick, and Jane began to worry.

She pulled Grace beneath an awning.

"You wait here with the bags," she said. "I'm going to get someone to help us."

She expected Grace to argue, but she only nodded and sat down on one of the bags. She didn't look well.

Jane ran ahead until she found a small restaurant tucked away in a narrow alley. She stepped through the door and was bombarded by a loud mix of Italian and Mandarin, something unintelligible from a fevered dream. The small tables were filled with Chinese, an energetic tour guide bouncing between them, translating their menus. A young Italian approached Jane.

"*Ciao*," he said, "*vieni e ottenere asciutta.*"

"I'm sorry. Do you speak English?"

He nodded.

"Yes, very well."

"My friend is outside in the rain. She's very sick, and we need help finding our hotel."

"Which hotel you stay?"

She looked at the confirmation email on her phone.

"Luna Hotel Baglioni."

"Very nice," he said, nodding. "But far away. I take you."

He snatched two umbrellas from behind the counter and led her back out into the rain. They found Grace where Jane had left her, sitting on one of the bags and leaning against the building. She looked half asleep. The young Italian handed Grace his umbrella and took a bag in each hand, nodding for them to follow. Grace was too weak to walk without help, so Jane closed the second umbrella, and they leaned together beneath hers and followed their guide. He led them back the way they had come, and Jane felt like an idiot—she should have printed a map. Puddles of rainwater were claiming San Marco Square, and they splashed through them. Soon Jane could see the sign for their hotel. She wondered how she had missed it.

The Italian paused to allow them to catch up.

"What are those for?" Jane asked, pointing to the catwalks.

"*Acqua alta*," he said.

"What's that?"

"Flooding. They say this one will be—how you say it?— unusually high for this season. Come now. We're almost there."

When they arrived at the hotel's entrance, a red-jacketed doorman quickly snatched their bags from the young Italian and ushered them inside to a warm and luxurious lobby. It was as if they'd entered some portal to another world, leaving the dark and rainy one behind. Jane handed the Italian his umbrellas. He was soaking wet, and a puddle was developing at his feet. She opened her purse and held out a hundred euro note. He held up his hands and shook his head, almost as if he were offended.

"*Nessuna necessità di pagare*," he said.

"But I want to repay you. You really saved us."

"Come eat at the restaurant," he said. "My family owns it, and you love the food, I promise."

"We'll do that," Jane said.

And they would, if she could find it again.

The young man smiled and retreated with a bow, pushing through the door and back out into the rain.

GRACE SLEPT that night and most of the next day.

She would occasionally have tremors in her sleep, and Jane

stayed by her bedside and monitored her constantly, worried that she might have another seizure. But she didn't. On the second morning Grace got up and took a shower, insisting that she was feeling fine after her rest.

"Let's go get some gelato," she said. "I've always wanted to have real Italian gelato in Italy."

"We can order it from room service," Jane suggested.

"It's not the same. Stop worrying so much. I'll be fine."

It was no longer raining, but the square was under nearly a foot of tidewater, and they crossed it on the raised platforms they had seen when they arrived. Jane walked behind and held onto Grace's arm, just in case. They passed a group of shirtless German tourists sitting in submerged metal chairs and posing for pictures with upheld cigars. Jane couldn't help but smile.

The flooded square gave way eventually to drier ground, and they walked the winding pathways lined with tourist trap restaurants promising authentic Italian cuisine on handwritten window signs. They passed tiny souvenir shops filled with blown-glass trinkets, until they found a walk-up gelato counter.

Grace had a scoop of chocolate; Jane had pistachio.

They traded halfway through.

Later Jane thought she recognized the alley where they had gotten lost, and they followed it to the restaurant and sat for an early lunch. The food was just okay, and the young Italian wasn't there, but Jane left a very large tip anyway.

On the walk back Grace stopped suddenly on a footbridge and looked around as if she didn't know where she was.

"Grace, are you okay?"

"What are you doing to me? Don't touch me."

"Grace? What's wrong?"

Jane held her shoulders and looked into her eyes, and she seemed to awaken from some daydream and recognize her.

"What happened, Grace?"

"I don't know. I'm fine now."

Whatever it was, Jane was happy that it had passed.

"Let's go for a gondola ride," Grace said.

"Are you sure you're up for it?"

"Well, I'm not planning on rowing myself, silly."

They found a group of gondoliers, lounging around their boats, laughing and smoking thin cigarettes. Their striped shirts made them look like prisoners on a break to Jane.

A tall one pounced on them as they approached.

"You speak English, no?"

"Yes," Jane said. "How much for a ride?"

He waved expansively toward his gondola.

"You come. Forty minutes, one hundred euro."

"We'll give you eighty."

He shook his head and crossed his arms. Jane leaned past him and waved the money at the other men behind him.

"Anyone willing to take us for eighty euros?"

"Fine," he said, "I take you."

He snatched the bills before his competition could accept. Grace looked at Jane and smiled, obviously impressed.

The gondolier took them through the canals, past cracked-plaster and yellow brick walls hung with bright flower baskets, and under arched-stone bridges, more than a few of which Jane recognized from their walk. He took them beneath the Bridge of Sighs, where he said passing lovers would be granted eternal bliss for the price of just a sunset kiss. When the gondolier told them this, Grace grinned at Jane and said:

"I'm not kissing you, so don't even try. You'll just have to come back sometime with a certain boy we both know."

Jane blushed.

Grace took on a pale and distant look before their forty minutes was up, and Jane paid the gondolier his other twenty and asked him to drop them at their hotel. He was kind enough to oblige the request, even helping them from the boat.

They returned to their room.

"I need some rest," Grace said. "Why don't you go out and explore. No reason to let me spoil another nice day."

"You know," Jane said, sinking into a chair, "I'm pretty tired too. I think I'll just sit here and read for a bit."

Jane awakened late that night to Grace screaming in the dark. She clicked on the lamp, rushed to Grace's side, and tried to rouse her from whatever nightmare she was having. But Grace was not sleeping. She sat upright in her bed with her hands balled into fists at her side and stared wildly at Jane.

"What have you done with my boy?"

"What's wrong, Grace?"

"You killed my boy, you bitch!"

"Do you want me to call a doctor?"

"Bring me my boy!"

"You don't have any children, Grace."

"You're lying."

Grace seemed possessed, and Jane didn't know what to do. She ran to the sink and poured a glass of water.

"Here, let's make sure you're hydrated."

Grace knocked the water glass from her hand.

Then she came to and looked at the glass on the floor, as if wondering how it had gotten there. She started crying.

"Oh, God. What's happening to me, Jane?"

Jane sat on the edge of the bed and held her.

"I don't know, Grace. I don't know."

She was sobbing, pleading with Jane through her tears.

"I want to go home, Jane. Please take me home. Please. I just want to go home now."

Jane rocked her gently, caressing her hair.

"Okay. We'll go home."

"I want my Bob. I need to be with Bob."

"I'll get us on the first flight, Grace. I promise. The first flight. It's okay. We're going home."

Jane held Grace's head close to her breast so she wouldn't see the tears streaming down her face, although she might have still felt them hitting the top of her head.

"I just want to be with Bob," Grace said again.

"It's okay, we're going home now."

"I'm scared, Jane."

"I know," Jane said. "Me, too."

BOB MET THEM AT THE AIRPORT, pushing a wheelchair.

She had called him from the hotel before they left, and at least it looked like he had managed to sober up.

It had been a long journey back to Seattle, flying through Paris, and Grace was extremely pale, shaky, and nervous, her eyes darting involuntarily in their sockets, as if she were being set upon by evil things on every side. She looked ten years older to Jane than when they had left.

"Thanks, Jane," Bob whispered, after helping his wife into the chair. "You have no idea how much this meant to her."

Jane knelt to speak with Grace in the chair, to thank her

for such a great trip, but Grace seemed to not recognize her at all. Jane's heart thudded in her breast; she couldn't swallow.

Don't cry, she told herself—not here, not now, not yet.

"Bob, why don't you two go on ahead? I'll stay and deal with customs about our bags, since they rushed us through on a medical emergency."

"Are you sure, Jane?"

"Yes. Go on. I'll have a car take me back, and I'll swing by and drop off her bag. It might be late."

"You're a saint," he said.

Then he smiled and wheeled his wife away.

Jane stood watching after them. She saw Bob lean down to hear something his wife was saying, and then he stopped and turned the wheelchair around so that she and Jane could see one another. They were still close enough that Jane could make out her face. Grace held up a shaking hand, as if to say farewell. Jane waved back. She was almost certain she saw Grace smile.

Then Bob turned her again, and they were gone.

Jane stood with her hand still upheld, and now she cried.

Chapter 26

THEY BURIED GRACE three weeks later on a Saturday.

The sun was out, the birds were singing, and Jane watched as a riding lawnmower passed like a toy on the hill high above the cemetery, the distant buzz of its blades audible over the muffled sobs of those in attendance.

She stood with the women from their Saturday morning meeting and listened as Grace's husband said a few words. He was slightly drunk, although no one there seemed to care, and he cried almost as much as he spoke. But it was clear that he had loved his wife, and that he would miss her greatly. Overall his eulogy was very nice. He had asked Jane if she wanted to speak, but she couldn't bring herself to do it. She didn't think she could honor Grace's memory without mentioning their trip together, and she felt that what they had shared in Paris should be private somehow. Besides, nobody present needed to be reminded just how amazing Grace had been. They all knew it in their own special ways.

With one loud squeak from a rusted pulley, but no other sound, as the mower had quit working and even the birds had stopped their singing now, Jane watched as the casket and its thick covering of flowers disappeared into the ground.

Goodbye, Grace. Goodbye.

Soon everyone drifted off toward the parking lot. Jane broke away and crossed the cemetery to her daughter's grave. She stood looking down at the marble stone, the green grass now fully regrown. She noticed a tiny yellow dandelion thriving in the protected corner where the headstone met the ground, and she was reminded of the candles she'd lit in Notre Dame.

She knelt and placed her hand on Melody's name.

The smooth marble felt cool against her warm palm, and she smelled the earth and the cut grass. She bowed her head.

"You're in good company now," she said. "You and Grace take care of each other, okay? Wherever you are. I love you so much, baby. I'll see you soon."

WHEN SHE RETURNED TO HER HOUSE, everything seemed different somehow, as if the formality of laying Grace to rest had opened her eyes and things would never be the same.

Her house was a mess. Unpaid bills were stacked on the kitchen table; laundry was overflowing in the hamper. She'd been surviving on little to eat except the Doritos in her pantry, and those too were nearly gone now. The fountain had run dry while she was in Europe, and when she'd finally filled it again, the motor was gummed up with slime and wouldn't pump. The grass was tall and headed with seed, and weeds had reclaimed the garden from Caleb's vegetables that lay rotting there in the dirt. There was even a patch of blackberry vines returning on the creek bank. And she was alone. So very alone. She would have given anything for even the company of that silly goat.

The sixth day after Grace's funeral, Jane decided to make an attempt at cleaning things up. She was changing the sheets in Melody's room when she found a note on the bed, weighted down by Melody's baby book. The note had been scrawled by a desperate hand and the ink was smeared with tears—

I know you don't mean what you said—I love you, and I know you love me. I'll come back for you when things are more equal between us. Until then, I'll be out there thinking of you and playing the guitar you got me.

Jane read the note again.

She wondered how it was she had missed it.

The sun was coming through the window, and she could see the pink showing faintly through the new paint where it was thinnest on the wall. She remembered Caleb helping her paint it, helping her grieve over what she had lost. She remembered just how sensitive and loving he had been, how gentle. She remembered making love to him on the floor, surrounded by brushes and buckets of paint, and she remembered feeling more complete than she had ever felt before, or was likely to ever feel again. She could still see his eyes and smell his skin.

She was startled from her thoughts sometime later by a knock on the front door. She rose to go see who it was. As she approached the door, a tiny sliver of hope rose in her breast, and she paused to close her eyes and make a silent wish. When she swung the door open, she was looking at Mrs. Hawthorne.

"Mrs. Hawthorne?"

"That's what they keep telling me, but I can't be sure."

She was supporting herself on an old cane, and a white van idled in the drive behind her.

"How did you know where I lived?"

"It's not a very big island, dear."

"I suppose that's true. Would you like to come in?"

The old lady rolled her eyes and nodded toward the van.

"He's in a hurry to dump me off at the raisin ranch."

"Where?" Jane asked.

"They've finally forced me into a home. I guess it's been a long time coming. However, I didn't drop by to complain to you about my sad situation, as tempting as it is."

"Well, what can I do for you?"

"Do you know how I can get in touch with that handsome boyfriend of yours? He up and ran off on me without a word."

Jane shook her head sadly.

"I'm pretty sure Caleb's in Austin, but I don't have any way of getting in touch with him."

The old woman sighed, casting a glance back toward the waiting van. Then she leaned closer to Jane, as if to include her in some grand conspiracy.

"Listen, dear. I can't be sure how long I'll be around. I do believe they intend to see me off as soon as they can, probably by poisoning my Jell-O. Do you think I could trust you to give Caleb something for me when you see him?"

"I wish I could say yes," Jane said, "but I'm not sure I will see him again."

The old lady smiled.

"Of course, you will, dear. Of course, you will."

She reached into her pocket and hauled out the box that contained the ring. She pressed it into Jane's palm and winked.

"He earned this working for me. I think he had some big plans for it, but those would be his plans to tell and not mine. He's a good man, our young Caleb is. And you can go ahead and tell him I said so. But don't you let on that I miss him too much. It's not fair to burden the young with too much guilt, especially over an old woman."

She grinned at Jane and then turned and walked to the van.
The young driver jumped out and opened the sliding door
for her, but she pushed his offered hand aside and climbed into
the seat herself.

"Keep your paws off me," she griped. "I might be old, but
I'm not crippled yet, you know."

Jane watched her through the tinted side-window glass as
the van backed from the drive and pulled away. She was sitting
proud and straight, and she did not turn to look back.

After the van had disappeared, Jane opened the case the
old lady had given her. Her mouth fell open when she saw the
yellow diamond engagement ring inside.

WHEN JANE WALKED IN, she found Ralph sitting behind
the hardware store counter eating frozen yogurt with a plastic
spoon. He licked the spoon and tossed it, along with the empty
container, into the trash and smiled at her with pink teeth.

"Howdy, Jane. Becca's been meaning to give you a call."

"Never mind about the insurance plan, Ralph. I don't even
want to sell you a policy any longer."

"You don't?"

"No. I'm here because I'd like to know if those Peters
brothers are still interested in my house."

"Well," he said, "you know the market's still in the dumps.
But I'm sure I could—"

"Don't hustle me," Jane said, cutting him off. "I plan to
list it anyway, so if they want a shot before it goes on the open
market, have them get in touch with me."

THEY CAME THE NEXT DAY—

Rodney and Richard; they were identical twins.

They wore matching Carhartt coveralls, but one of them was fat and the other thin, making it easy to tell them apart— although Jane quickly forgot which was which. She invited them in, and they stood in the foyer and looked around, their eyes eventually settling on Jane's friend.

"Is this your partner?" the thin one asked.

"This is Esmeralda. She's a realtor friend of mine."

He glanced at his brother and then looked back to Jane.

"Well, we were under the impression from Ralph that you were looking for a direct sale. We like to do our business under the radar, so to speak. You know, save on the commissions and all that. No offense, Es . . ."

"Esmeralda," Jane said. "And if you want to deal with me, she's part of the package. I'll pay her commission, of course."

"Suit yourself," the fat one said. "Let's have a look around. We've got three other properties to look at this afternoon, and I'm growing roots just standing here."

Jane walked them through the house.

They kept pointing at things and shaking their heads, as if they were disappointed by what they saw.

"Yep. Gonna need a new water heater for sure."

"And that window's fogged up too."

"Looks to be a broken seal."

When they stood for five minutes in the hallway, arguing over whether or not they thought the acoustic ceiling contained asbestos, Jane had had enough.

"What do you care anyway?" she asked. "You're just going to tear the place down and build new."

"Oh, she's a smart one," the thin brother said. "But here's the thing, Jane and Es . . ."

"Esmeralda."

"Esmeralda. We'll need to rent it out while we go through the plan and permit processes. Not to mention the market isn't right for building right now. Might not be for several years yet. So you see, we've got to be concerned about the house as well."

Before Jane could reply Esmeralda stepped in.

"Well, Jane's been living in it just fine, so I doubt you'll have any trouble. Plus, I could rent this place as is before you two could drive yourselves home, wherever that might be."

The brothers took the hint and moved on to the backyard. They stood in the high grass with their hands on their hips and surveyed the lot, their heads nodding and swiveling in unison like two dashboard bobble heads.

"That's a nice creek," one said.

"Cuts down on buildable feet," replied the other. "Might make the permit process tougher, too."

"Okay, boys," Jane finally said. "If you want to make an offer, we'll hear it now. Otherwise, we plan to put it live on the market tomorrow."

"Tomorrow?"

"That's right."

"Well, hell fire," the thin one said. "We usually need a few days to work out an offer."

Esmeralda shook her head.

"Stop putting us on. You knew what this property was worth to you before you even got here."

The twins glanced at one another, mind-reading perhaps. Then they turned back to Jane and spoke at the same time.

"Three fifty."

Jane laughed.

"If you want to come in here and rob me, you'd better have guns or something in those silly coveralls you're both wearing."

They looked at one another's outfits.

"I'll take five fifty," Jane said.

Now they laughed.

"Lady, unless you've got gold bars buried out here in the grass, we're not even in the same zip code."

Jane looked at Esmeralda.

"What can you get me for it on the market, Mel?"

"I thought you said her name was Esmeralda?"

"It is to you," Jane said. "Her friends call her Mel."

Esmeralda looked around, considering.

"I think I can get at least five and a quarter if we list it."

"Let's round down to five. Five hundred thousand less six points for commission makes—let's see—what's that make?"

"Four seventy," Esmeralda said.

Jane turned back to the brothers.

"Four seventy then. Deal or no deal?"

The brothers looked at each other and shook their heads.

"Four hundred even," the fat one said.

Jane stuck out her hand.

"Four fifty and you've got a deal."

"Four thirty-five."

"Nope. Four fifty or we list."

There was a long pause while Jane's hand hung there. Then the thin one stepped forward and shook it.

"We'll need thirty days to close."

"Fine," Jane said. "I'll have Mel here do the paperwork."

After they had made an appointment to sign the official offer with Esmeralda in her office the following Monday, the ladies saw the brothers out and watched from the door as they drove away in their enormous pickup.

"Went just like you said it would," Esmeralda said.

Jane laughed and shook her head.

"Men and their silly negotiating."

"YOU SURE YOU DON'T WANT THIS COAT?"

"No, take it," Jane said. "I won't need that heavy old thing where I'm going."

"What about these shoes?"

"They'll look better on you anyway."

It was one week after she'd made the deal with the Peters brothers to sell her house, and her friends from the meeting were going through her closet like starved retail junkies.

After they had taken all they wanted, they helped her haul everything else out onto the front lawn, even the furniture, and some went out to tack up posters and hang balloons, while others stayed to help with the yard sale customers. Jane priced everything to sell, and the things that wouldn't sell, she threw in for free with other purchases.

By the time the last car pulled away, and only Esmeralda remained, the sun was setting, and Jane had nothing left except the clothes she wore most regularly, a few of her favorite pairs of shoes, and a couple of boxes filled with personal possessions that she intended to keep. She had even sold the refrigerator.

"You want to stay at my place?" Esmeralda asked.

"No, thanks," Jane said. "I think I'm going to stay here."

"But what will you sleep on?"

"I'm so exhausted I could sleep right here on the ground. But I saved an old air mattress and a blanket that have a kind of special meaning to me."

"You sure? I've got a spare bed."

"I'm sure," Jane said. "I've got to say goodbye."

Esmeralda hugged her.

"I'm going to miss you. We all are."

Jane looked at her friend and smiled. She had expected to feel sad, but she didn't. She wasn't sure what she felt.

"I'll miss you, too."

Before Esmeralda got into her car, she called back:

"I'll be in touch with you anyway about the closing. And remember what Grace always told us: don't be a secret."

Jane nodded and waved.

After watching Esmeralda's tail-lights disappear into the dusk, she walked back into her empty house. It was strange to see the outlines where her furniture had been, the carpet bleached by years of sun. She stood in the living room and looked at the fireplace. She remembered Caleb sitting next to it and playing his guitar. She could almost hear the music, it was so quiet. She walked into the kitchen and paused to remember all the breakfasts they had shared there. She remembered Caleb on that first morning, with his burnt toast, his bruised face, and his cute smile beneath the brim of that silly hat he would always wear. She remembered the wild sex they had later on the table, after the baseball game. Next she went to her bedroom, and stood where her bed had been and closed her eyes and tried to remember what it felt like to be with him—to kiss his lips, to feel him inside her, to fall asleep with her head on his naked chest. She missed him terribly, and she only hoped that he could someday forgive her.

Finally she stood in the doorway to Melody's room for a long time. It looked just like it had before they moved in. She was aware of an immense grief when she thought about her daughter's death, but it no longer stabbed at her heart the way it had. She knew she would never be over it, that not a day would pass when she didn't think of Melody and wish that things had been different. But for the very first time since her daughter had left home, she felt a kind of peace about her—as if she were somehow finally okay. As if she no longer suffered. Perhaps not all spirits are meant for this world, but they pass through anyway and change for the better those which are.

Jane pulled the air mattress from the closet and plugged it in. The pump motor sputtered, then sprung to life and blew the mattress up. She unplugged it and capped the vent. Then she clicked off the light, wrapped Melody's favorite blanket around her shoulders, and lay down. The air mattress floated her back in time. She could almost feel her daughter's breath against her cheek in the dark. She could hear her voice.

"When will our stuff get here, Mommy?"

"Maybe tomorrow if it doesn't snow, doll."

"I hope it snows."

"Don't you want your things?"

"Yes. But I want snow more."

"Well, maybe it will snow then. I brought your boots along anyway, just in case."

Quiet then for a while.

Little toes squirming beneath the covers.

"Mommy?"

"Yes, dear."

"Do we get to stay here forever?"

"Well, forever's a long time, sweetie. But we bought it, so that means no one can make us move."

Eyes closed, almost asleep now.

Little fingers reaching out and touching her hand.

"Mommy?"

"It's time to sleep, Melody."

"Okay. But I wanted to tell you one thing."

"Yes, sweetheart."

"I love you, Mommy."

"I love you too, dear."

Chapter 27

SHE WAS LYING FLAT ON THE FLOOR when she woke.

The bedroom window was blue, the long night giving way to dawn. She got up and stretched, then looked down at the deflated air mattress and nudged it with her toe.

"So much for taking you with me."

She went to the kitchen and drank a glass of water, wishing that she hadn't sold her coffee maker yesterday. She found a granola bar in the pantry and ate it. Then she brushed her teeth and took a shower. She laughed when she realized she'd given away all her bath towels yesterday. Fortunately, she'd kept her blow dryer. When she had dried herself off and readied herself in the mirror to face the day, she packed up the last of her things and loaded them into her car.

Returning to the house for one last look, she stepped outside into the backyard. She could still make out the beauty of Caleb's hard work, even beneath the tall grass and morning shadows. The creek ran softly by. A songbird called from a tree. She noticed her mother's rosebush standing alone, amidst the returning weeds, its branches thick with pink blooms. Melody's favorite color. At least her mother had gotten that right.

She went around to her neighbor's door and knocked. She stood there waiting for a long time and had almost turned to leave when the door finally opened.

"Hi, Mrs. Parker."

Mrs. Parker eyed her suspiciously.

"It's early," she said.

"I know. I'm sorry. It's just that I'm moving—"

"I saw the yard sale and figured as much."

"Well, I came by to see if I could borrow a shovel."

"If you're burying something that you shouldn't be, I don't want any part of it."

Jane laughed.

"No. Nothing like that. I've got a rosebush that I need to take with me."

"It's awfully late in the season to be transplanting a rose."

"I don't have much choice."

She looked past Jane toward her house and her packed car waiting in the driveway. Her expression had a touch of regret.

"I meant to come by and deliver my condolences about your daughter."

"Thanks," Jane said. "That means a lot. She loved your willow tree."

"I know. I used to see her hanging in it all the time."

Jane looked away; she didn't want to cry today.

"The shed's beside the house there, and it isn't locked. Use anything you need. Just put it back when you're finished. And prune it good and take off all the leaves first."

"Take off the rose leaves?"

"Yes. Take off the flowers too. You need it to go dormant. Might give it a chance."

Jane thanked her and said goodbye. Then she went around to the shed and retrieved a shovel and pair of shears.

The slice of the shears cut the quiet morning, and the roses fell to the ground one by one with soft thuds. She trimmed the branches back and plucked off the leaves. When she had finished, the rosebush was half its former size, and it stood barren and naked, looking much like it had the first day she had planted it. She buried the shovel in the soil and dug around the root ball for several minutes, until the rosebush was free and leaning sideways in its pit. Then she went inside and got two trash bags from beneath the kitchen sink. She doubled them up and lifted the rosebush into the bags. She turned on the hose and moistened the roots, cinched the bag closed, and carried the rosebush to her car.

It was messy work, physically and emotionally.

She returned the shovel and the shears and washed up as best she could. Then she stepped out her front door one last time, locked it, and hid the key beneath a flowerbed rock where Esmeralda expected to find it. She paused at her car door and glanced back at the house. She felt nostalgic for it already, but she knew that it was time to leave. She got in and started her car and backed from the drive. As she pulled away, she honked twice, as if to say goodbye. But she wasn't sure to whom, or even why. The house shrunk in her rearview mirror, and the sun rose over the trees and shined on the road ahead.

She just made the 8:45 ferry.

It was Sunday, and the car deck wasn't even half full.

She left her car there and went up to the onboard café and bought herself a cup of coffee—two Splenda and one cream. Thank God for small miracles. She took her coffee outside to drink it on the deck, and she stood at the back of the ferry and watched the island recede into the blue sky, falling below the distant snowcapped Olympic Mountains. It finally became just a tiny tree-covered hump, rising from the water like a toy island in a miniature snow globe world. It had been her home for twenty years, but somehow it no longer seemed real.

SHE EXITED I-5 IN OLYMPIA and drove through vaguely familiar streets lined with gas stations and car dealerships until she turned up the hill and dropped down into the cul-de-sac where she'd grown up. The trees looked taller, and the houses seemed smaller, but otherwise little had changed. Jane guessed that maybe nothing ever would. It had been nearly ten years since she'd been back, and the feeling of angst in her gut as she pulled into her mother's driveway reminded her why.

She hauled the rosebush from the backseat and carried it to the front door and rang the bell. When nobody answered she knocked. She knew there was a key hidden in the porcelain frog beneath her mother's silver-beauty box-hedge, but the time when she might have felt comfortable using it had long since passed. At last she was a stranger here.

She was walking back to her car when a Cadillac pulled up to the curb and her mother got out, wearing her big church hat. The Cadillac pulled away, and her mother walked up the drive toward her.

"Hello, Mother."

"Hi, Jane. What a surprise."

She eyed the boxes in Jane's car, clearly trying to guess the meaning of her daughter's unannounced visit.

"Is everything all right?"

Jane nodded.

"I'm leaving, Mother."

"Really. I just got home from church. Can't you come in for coffee?"

"I mean I'm leaving town."

"You are?"

"Yes. I sold my house. I sold everything."

"What about your job, Jane?"

"I quit. I hadn't been working much anyway."

"And where are you going?"

"Texas."

"You're chasing that boy, aren't you?"

"I didn't come by to argue, Mother. I came by to drop off your rosebush. It's on the steps there."

Her mother looked past her to the rosebush at the door.

"Looks like a garbage bag full of sticks."

"Well, I pruned it back to give it a chance."

Jane reached to open her car door, but her mother laid her hand on top of hers.

"Why don't you come in for coffee?"

"I should get going."

"Just one cup."

Jane took a deep breath and let it out.

"Okay. But only one cup."

As her mother fished her keys from her purse, Jane picked up the rosebush.

"I guess I could plant the rosebush for you, too, if you've got a shovel and some place you'd like it to go."

"It was nice of you to bring it," her mother said.

"It just didn't seem right to leave it behind. They plan to tear the place down and build new."

"Well, I have a perfect spot for it."

While the coffee brewed, they carried the rosebush into the backyard and picked out a spot near the house where there was plenty of morning sun. Her mother brought out a shovel from the garage, and Jane started digging. She had been working for several minutes when her mother reappeared, dragging a sack of mulch, having changed out of her church clothes. Together they lifted the rosebush from its bag and set it in the hole. Then her mother held it steady while Jane repacked the soil around it with the shovel. Her mother opened the sack of mulch, and they took turns reaching in and tossing handfuls onto the ground around the rosebush—a mother and daughter working in the earth, just as they once had been, so long ago. Jane could almost feel Melody watching them, plying them with questions about flowers and dirt.

When they had finished and had thoroughly soaked the soil, they rinsed off their hands with the hose, and her mother went inside to fetch them coffee. They sat at the glass table on the patio, drank from their mugs, and admired their work.

"Think it'll make it?" Jane asked.

"Hard to say," her mother answered. "But roses are hearty plants. Probably have to wait for spring to find out. You know, I'm glad Marta insisted on the early service today. We usually go to the eleven, and I would have missed you."

"I'm glad too," Jane said.

And she meant it.

"Did you get the flowers I sent?" her mother asked.

"Yes, I did. Thank you."

"I was sorry when I read your email. I wanted to respond, but you know I'm no good with that silly computer. I know she was a great friend to you."

Jane just sipped her coffee and nodded. Grace had been a better friend than words could ever tell. She tilted her head back and looked up. There were high clouds obscuring the sun, but the light that filtered through felt good on her face.

"What's going on with Jonathan?" she asked.

Her mother sighed.

"I still can't get used to him wanting to be called that. It was always Jon, or Johnny. Only your father liked Jonathan."

"Well, that's reason enough not to like it," Jane said.

"He said you went to see him."

"I did. Is he still in there?"

Her mother nodded.

"He's agreed to a deal. One day shy of a full year. Keeps him out of the big prison, I guess. But it means he'll serve every day of it. He says he plans on getting sober this time. We'll see if it sticks. Should I tell him you were here?"

"Sure," Jane said. "And tell him I'd love to hear from him if he gets a year clean. I can't be around him otherwise, though. I've had too much heartbreak to be around active alcoholics."

They sat for a while without talking.

Jane watched a big red-breasted robin land in the yard and peck at the grass, hopping over to inspect the rosebush as if it were surprised to find it there.

Eventually her mother reached out and took her hand.

"Jane, I made a lot of mistakes. And I know it's too late to change them. I know that. I do. And I know we never really got along. I'm not sure why. I guess the truth is I never understood you. But I never had to worry about you either. Not like Jon. And I just want you to know that of all the things I did wrong, of all the mistakes, the one thing I know I got right, the one thing I've always been proud of, is you."

Tears welled in the corners of Jane's eyes, and her throat ached. She was afraid she might cry for real if she spoke, so she simply squeezed her mother's hand and smiled. In that moment Jane realized that she and her mother had never hugged. Not as adults anyway. She briefly wondered what it might feel like, but her mother released her hand and picked up her coffee mug.

They both knew it was time for her to go.

"I should hit the road," Jane said.

Her mother nodded and rose from the table.

She followed Jane to the door, and they stood together for an uncomfortable moment, neither knowing what to say.

"Will you promise me you'll stay in touch?" her mother asked. "At least occasionally?"

It occurred to Jane that her mother hadn't asked where in Texas she was going or even how long she planned to stay.

"Sure," Jane said. "And I'll have the same cell number if you want to call me. At least for a while."

Her mother nodded but said nothing more.

The screen door banged shut behind her, and Jane climbed into her car, started it, backed from the drive, and pulled away. She could see her mother's shadow just on the other side of the screen, watching her leave.

Neither of them waved.

BEFORE SHE HIT THE FREEWAY, Jane pulled over at a Shell station and filled her tank with gas. She went inside and bought water and snacks for the road and paid for a carwash.

As the mechanical brushes wiped away the months' worth of grime, Jane sat in her soap-covered car and thought about all she had been through since leaving home so many years ago. The excitement of moving north to Seattle, and then eventually being accepted into the university. Getting pregnant, moving to Bainbridge Island, having Melody. There had been some really great years that had followed, years that she would always treasure. But then the long nightmare had begun when Melody discovered booze and drugs. Sitting there now, Jane felt as though she were starting over again—leaving home once more at forty, but this time heading south instead of north. And this time she had a plan. This time she knew what she wanted. She laughed at herself to think it had taken her so many years to figure it out.

The overhead dryers whirred to life, the car jerked forward on the tracks, and the carwash spit Jane out into the light. She swept the last of the rinse water away with a pass of her wipers, pulled out, and merged onto the freeway.

The Sunday afternoon traffic was light, and she got into the fast lane and rolled down her window, letting the wind tease her hair. She turned on the car radio—"Alive and Kicking" by Simple Minds was playing. She couldn't imagine a better song to start her journey.

Except maybe one sung by Caleb.

She smiled at the road ahead and wondered how long it would be until she picked up the first Texas radio station.

Chapter 28

WHEN SHE HIT PORTLAND she turned east onto Interstate 84 and crossed the Blue Mountains, driving past scenic vistas of evergreen trees and distant valleys filled with wildflowers. She drove for nine hours, pulling over at rest stops to stretch her legs and freshen up, until she reached Boise, Idaho, where she rented a room at a Best Western and fell fast asleep.

She was on the road again before dawn. She drove through a dark thunderstorm that was clinging to the tops of mountains she crossed, turning on her headlights and leaning forward to see through the windshield even with her wipers on high. She made it to Salt Lake City by lunch, and she ate alone in a café. Then she filled up with gas, loaded up with bottles of water, and got back on the road, determined to make Albuquerque by nightfall. The scenery was stark and mostly boring, and she drove for long stretches without even seeing another car, with only the radio to keep her company. Reception was spotty, although she was always able to find at least one gospel and one Latino station—she preferred the soothing sound of Spanish.

Nightfall caught her crossing the southernmost corner of Colorado on the 491, and she drove on into the darkness— black as nowhere, the world shrunken to just the reach of her headlights, beyond the windshield a black canvas painted with stars. She was startled by a deer that leapt in front of her car, its eyes flashing red in the wash of her headlights before it shot off into the night, just as she shot through where it had stood. She had been certain she was going to hit it, and she pulled over to steady her nerves and consult her map.

She drove on, but she was tired. She traveled south on 550, looking for any place safe to pull over again and rest her eyes. By and by, Albuquerque appeared out of the night, spreading across the dark and deserted plains like a sprawling oasis of light. She stopped at the first hotel she came to and rented a room. She flopped on the bed and fell asleep in her clothes.

She crossed into Texas by eleven the next morning, pulling over in a south plains town called Littlefield. She ordered lunch at a diner filled with Waylon Jennings memorabilia and workers on break from a local denim factory. She topped off her tank and hit the road again. It was dry, dusty, and dull. She ran her AC on high with the vent pointed at her face just to keep her tired eyes open. The closer she got to Austin, the more tired she got, and the more doubt began to creep into her mind. What if he didn't want to see her? What if he was dating someone else already? Where would she go? What would she do? She blinked the thoughts away and focused on the road.

As twilight approached she passed a drive-in movie theatre running an old black and white on its enormous and dilapidated screen, a throwback to a bygone era. She thought she recognized the film, but it passed too fast for her to be sure. Several hours later she arrived in Austin.

She had priced downtown hotels before she left, and she followed her printed directions to the Hampton Inn where she rented their cheapest available room.

She dreamt that night that Caleb was in her bed—a dream so real that she half woke with his taste on her lips and called his name out in the dark. He had whispered something to her in that dream that she meant to always remember, but it slipped away as soon as she rose the next morning.

She opened the curtains and looked out on a sunny Texas day. She went down to her car and retrieved her bags. She'd been too weary to carry them in the night before. She was relieved to have nowhere to drive today. She took a shower and blew her hair dry and did her makeup in the mirror. Then she slipped on a sundress and went out on foot with just her purse.

She walked to old town and stopped at the famous Driskill Hotel and spoiled herself with lunch on the covered patio. The weather was warm, the people friendly, and she was beginning to think that she might just like Texas.

When her server came to refill her iced tea, she asked him where she could find live music in town.

"Where can't you find live music is an easier question to answer," he said. "What kind of music are you looking for?"

"Have you heard of a band called Broken Coyotes?"

He shook his head.

"You might try 6th Street, though."

She paid her bill and walked down 6th Street, reading the posters in the club windows. She saw nothing advertising Broken Coyotes. It was still too early for live music, so she walked up the hill to the State Capitol building, took her shoes off, and walked on the soft grass with her bare feet, admiring the bronzed heroes of the Alamo and the architecture of the stone dome.

She found a café with Wi-Fi and got online with her phone

and searched for Broken Coyotes. She found some old music festival listings for past gigs in the area but nothing new.

That night she walked the streets alone, popping into clubs and searching for him. Several places charged her a cover just to go inside and look, and she was beginning to worry about money, since her house sale had yet to close. As the night wore on, the music got louder, and eventually it poured from the clubs, along with the drunks, into the streets where rickshaws rode wildly through the crowds and young men stumbled after staggering girls carrying their heels in their hands. A beer bottle crashed at Jane's feet as she passed police officers breaking up a fight. She decided it was time to call it a night.

The next day she searched again. She went into bars and asked about Broken Coyotes, but most people she spoke with knew nothing about them. It seemed there were endless bands in the area, forming and breaking up, coming and going, all fighting to be heard above the almost constant cacophony of live music played nightly. Jane began to worry.

What if Caleb wasn't even here?

What if the band had moved somewhere else?

She was walking down Colorado Street when she saw the sign. She had almost passed it by, but the word "Coyote" leapt out at her, and she turned back. It was posted in the window of a club called Rosa's Place, and it read:

BROKEN COYOTES

LIVE TONIGHT AT 9:00 PM

She committed the address to memory and walked back toward her hotel with a smile on her face.

She tried to nap, but she was too excited to sleep. She ate a PowerBar for dinner and washed it down with an orange juice from the hotel vending machine. She took a shower and shaved her legs, then washed and conditioned her hair. When she was freshened up and feeling good, she put on her cutest dress, went back to Rosa's Place, paid the cover, and went inside. She was an hour early, and the bar was just beginning to fill up, so she ordered herself an iced tea and snagged a seat at a table near the stage. An hour had never passed so slowly before.

Her heart leapt when some of the band members appeared on stage. They fussed with their equipment and performed a sound check. The place was already packed, and strangers had crowded around the tiny table with Jane, but she didn't mind. Not tonight. The lights finally dimmed, the crowd settled down, and the band filed onto the stage—the short lead singer with hair to his waist, followed by a blond drummer, and a tall kid on the electric base. Then the guitar player stepped onstage and everyone clapped. Except it wasn't Caleb.

Her disappointment must have been written all over her face, because when they had finished their first song, the man beside her got her attention and said:

"You look a little out of it. Can I buy you a drink?"

"No, thanks," she said. "I'll be fine."

When the band stopped for a break an hour later, telling the crowd they'd be back on in ten minutes, Jane got up and approached the stage. The lead singer was marking up his set list with a pencil when he looked up at Jane.

"I'll have a vodka rocks," he said.

"I'm sorry," she replied, "but I don't work here."

He stuck the pencil in his mouth and chewed on it, raking

over her with his eyes. Jane recognized the look.

"Well, if you want to party with me in the backroom after the show, you gotta bring some friends for the band."

"I just wanted to ask you about Caleb."

"Caleb?"

"Yes, Caleb Cummings."

"Never heard of him."

He turned back to his set list.

"He was supposed to join your band."

"Oh," he said, nodding, "the kid from Seattle. That guy's got some talent. But we went with Vincent instead. No room for two songwriters in a band, if you know what I mean."

"Do you know where I can find him?"

"No clue. But he's a lucky guy if he gets found by you."

That night Jane tossed and turned and hardly slept at all. In the morning she went out again and asked for Caleb by name in every bar and club she could find. She walked until her feet hurt, and a sole broke free from one of her shoes. She ate when she was hungry, just to maintain her energy, but she didn't taste the food. The hot Texas sun burnt her neck and her nose, despite the sunscreen she'd picked up in a corner market. Still she walked on. She entered a hundred dusky bars reeking of last night's spilt beer, and she was met with a hundred tired faces with blank stares and bad news.

"Nope, haven't heard of him."

"Never played here."

"Maybe try Red River."

"No, Market district."

"South Lamar."

It was Friday evening, and she was alone in a strange town

in a strange state with all of her remaining worldly possessions spread between two suitcases and the trunk of her car. She began to think she'd made a mistake even coming. Her mind wandered to what she might do if she never found him. She knew she wouldn't return to Seattle, but where would she go?

She found herself just after sunset that evening surrounded by tourists on the Congress Avenue Bridge. They were leaning against the rail and looking over. She wondered if someone had jumped, so she stopped and looked too. There were dozens of tour boats in the silver water below, cameras flashing on their crowded decks. Then a woman below shouted, and a child next to her pointed. Jane saw a few shadows dart out like scouts, and then a wild fluttering stirred up an earthen smell. A million Mexican free-tailed bats flew out from beneath the bridge and funneled up into the crimson sky. They twisted and turned in skyward shadows that looked almost like black contrails in the windless sunset sky, spreading over the city and dispersing on their blind and hungry hunt. Oh, Lord, Jane thought. If she could only separate into a million selves and ride upon their backs, she might have a chance.

But a strange peace fell over her then. It was as if the night had whispered in her ear that all would be well, whether she ever found him or not. She suddenly realized that this journey had always been about her finding the courage to move on.

She thought about her daughter and the good times they had shared. The memories made her smile. She knew she had been blessed to have had her, even for the little time that she did. She thought about Grace and how lucky she had been to know her, to love her, to call her a friend. She remembered the promise she had made to Grace on that hotel balcony in Paris.

She had promised to live the life that Grace couldn't live, a life free from fear. She knew that Grace would always be with her, and Melody too. She knew that, while she might be by herself now, she would never really be alone.

The sound of a lonely guitar pulled her from her thoughts. She stopped and looked around. She wasn't sure how long she had been walking, and she was in an unfamiliar part of town. The music rose again, carried to her on a gentle breeze, and she followed it down the street and around a corner.

Several people sat on the steps of an old warehouse turned bar, drinking beer and smoking cigarettes. He stood at the base of the steps, his head bent, his hair hanging, playing his guitar and singing a song. She stood and listened.

Served up on a silver tray
Love is a bill too high to pay
As high as any hope can soar
Fear descends as a tax collector at your door
And if you've shed your skin too soon
It opens a hole in you that the wind blows through

I just wish our love had not been in vain
That she'd felt it too, that we'd meet again
Through my dark days, through this constant night
I sing out her name – Jane, Jane, Jane
It's a name I'll remember for the rest of my life

Most mornings I forget to pray
Oh, how I begged the angels she'd let me stay
Begged until their sweet mercy poured

A gift of light from a forgiving lord
It rose until it filled my room
And from the light a new hope grew

What if our love was not in vain
That she felt it too, and we'd meet again
Through my dark days, through this constant night
I sing out her name – Jane, Jane, Jane
And I wonder what would've been if I'd stayed to fight

They say love's a game that losers play
Oh well, I say, I never won anything anyway
So I've learned to live with an open sore
A gash in my heart that love once tore
I was just too young, blinded by youth
But as I sing this now I know the truth

I know our love was not in vain
That she felt it too, that we'll meet again
Through my dark days, through this constant night
I sing out her name – Jane, Jane, Jane
And when I find her again, I'll make her my wife

While he had been singing, the street and the steps and the people had all faded away until all Jane could see there was him, standing alone beneath the amber streetlight.

She reached into her purse and closed her hand on the silver dollar he had left on Melody's grave, so long ago it now seemed. She tossed it into the open guitar case at his feet. She saw him watch it land, but he stared at it for several seconds, as if he might be saying a prayer before looking up. Then he raised his head and looked into her eyes, and she knew in that moment that she would love him for the rest of her life.

LATER THAT NIGHT, as they lay naked in his bed together, washed in the red neon light coming through his window from a bar sign across the street, Jane rested her head on his shoulder and laid her open hand on his bare chest, watching it gently rise and fall with his breath.

She had never been happier.

"I was in such a hurry to get you into bed," she said, "that I forgot to mention I brought something for you."

He caressed her naked back with his fingers.

"Oh, you did? What did you bring me?"

She reached over and turned on the lamp. Then she pulled her purse onto the bed and pawed through it.

"Here," she said.

He took it from her hand, looked at it, and laughed.

"Don't tell me you drove two thousand miles to deliver my health insurance card," he said. "I don't know whether to be impressed or heartbroken."

Jane smiled.

"I'm just playing. That isn't really it. Here."

She held out the blue felt box in her palm.

His eyes lit up, and he took it, propped himself against the headboard, and looked at it. He was grinning from ear to ear.

"Where'd you get this?"

"Mrs. Hawthorne brought it by."

He opened the box and looked at the yellow diamond ring.

"And just so you know," Jane said, "I expect you to get

down on one knee when you give it to me."

"Oh, you think this is for you, do you?"

Jane leaned in and brushed her lips against his, teasing him.

"I sure hope so. However, in the interest of full disclosure, I should warn you first that I'm homeless and unemployed."

"That's okay," he replied. "I've got a day job that pays the rent here. Plus, my little balcony there could use some plants to liven it up. Maybe I'll put you to work for me this time."

"Hmm," Jane said. "It's a tempting offer, but only if you still make us breakfast every morning."

Caleb smiled.

"You're turning into quite the negotiator."

"Deal or no deal?" she asked.

She stared into his beautiful eyes, waiting for his response. She saw none of the sadness that had always been there before. Instead, all she saw was happiness and love.

"Deal," he said.

He started to rise, but she took the ring box from his hand and snapped it closed and set it on the bedside table. Then she rolled over on top of him and straddled his chest.

"Whoa there," he said, grinning up at her. "I thought you wanted me to get down on one knee."

"That can wait," she replied. "This can't."

She planted her hands on his naked chest, leaned down, brought her lips to his, and they kissed.

THE END

About the Author

Ryan Winfield is a novelist, poet, and screenwriter.

When he's not climbing mountains or traveling in search of new stories, he's writing in his downtown Seattle home.

Jane's Melody is his fourth published novel.

For more information go to:
www.RyanWinfield.com

CPSIA information can be obtained at www.ICGtesting.com
Printed in the USA
LVOW01s1132310813

350424LV00015BA/556/P